DIRE
CONSEQUENCES

SUE JAMES

Your story deserves a place in the world.

It's time you started writing it.

Chapter One
HENRY

I was on the verge of emptying my stomach again, although to be honest, there would be nothing there. An electricity coursed through my body that I had never experienced before. From the second Siana held that vial to her lips, my heart hadn't stopped pounding a terrifying beat beneath the cage in my chest. The atrocities she rained down in the lab and courthouse would forever stay burned into my mind. An unsettling horror story that would never fade.

I had often overheard Siana reading to Josie or Nira. Books with pages full of adventures, and heroes who defeated monsters. I had seen the look on Ethan Rightley's face just hours ago as she stared him down right before snapping his neck. The Rightley monster destroyed by Coranta's hero. An unwelcome thought sent a chill up my spine and burrowed its way into my brain. I never thought to ask what happened after the villain died. Did the hero get to live happily ever after every time? This didn't feel like happily ever after to me. Or was there always another villain, watching? Waiting. My eyes pulled across the cramped back seat to Siana. Her gaze was empty as she stared right through me.

I clutched the vial she had given me tighter and tried to push visions of what she did at the lab away. The thought made my stomach turn again.

My head was still a mess of coiled fog as the sounds of screaming made their way to the surface. I had found Josie on one of the ever descending floors of RightCorp lab. My heart ached as I realized that my partner, my best friend, was pumped full of Soterapine. Rhett had to have known it was happening. He was the so-called leader of this entire operation. How could he have just left her there to be used by them? After all his claiming to be for the good of the people, he hadn't done a great job of protecting the ones that deserved it the most. Josie sat, unmoving in the seat across from me, another victim of the Rightleys.

The car gave a slight jostle to each of the people inside as it kept a steady speed away from the city of Coranta. Never in my life had I given a second thought to anything past the city walls. And yet, there I was, facing a world of emotion that was foreign to me, about to cross an ocean to a land just as foreign. The latch on the car door seemed far away as I stared at it through glassy eyes. A bead of sweat traced its way down my jaw in time with my outstretched arm. If I jumped while the car was moving, would it kill me? Could I grab Josie on the way out? Would she be able to run in the state she was in? Could I leave Siana behind? At that thought, my heart stopped clambering in my chest for the first time in hours.

This wasn't Siana. Not anymore. Whatever she had taken in that courthouse had taken over, but the death and destruction that followed her was not of her own doing. It couldn't be. My head was spinning again as I struggled through what it meant. No, I had never felt anything compared to what she had, but there was no way anyone could hold that much hatred in them and still be human. Right?

I was just some cop for Coranta. I was supposed to be watching my neighborhood with Josie and dragging Siana home to her sister and aunt when she caused too much of a stir. Not this. My insides warred at the thought of a simpler time.

Josie stared out the window at the line of metal pods that popped up at intervals on the distant horizon. This must have been the barrier Willulf had talked about. RightCorp had been busy.

Robinson, the man from Hartlem, the land across the vast ocean we would soon cross, finally spoke up again. He had begun the drive from the courthouse on edge, speaking of the Director and plans to meet with him. This was the first he had spoken since the lab. "How would you like us to proceed?" His voice was compliant, but the edge of what I assumed was fear lingered.

"Do you already have your people posted?" Siana's voice no longer held the fighting spirit I loved.

"Yes. They're all in place and ready for the shift. However, seeing as how you…incapacitated the one person who knew how to operate all of this, I can only hope that everything it set up correctly." He stared just over her shoulder instead of into her eyes as he spoke.

"I didn't incapacitate Dr. Hawthorne, Robinson. I killed him. Speak bluntly in the future. I don't have time for flowery words."

I thought of the many books she had read. The kingdoms and characters overflowing with 'flowery words'. My heart broke for her all over again as I realized this person would rather burn their pages than appreciate their beauty.

Instead, she stared out at the horrendous metal pods that cut out across the land and marred the once beautiful scene. She regarded each one with the same amount of thoughtfulness that she had once held for her books. The look was different, harder. The usually soft lines that traced her mouth and eyes when she focused on something were gone.

How could the serum she took do that to her? How could it trap her so far in her shell that even something as small as a smile line was buried? My heart continued to sink in my chest as I stared at Josie. Our best friend. She would keep her safe. It didn't matter what the serum had done to her. She would always keep Josie safe.

"Do you know how long they'll remain functional? Will bodies need to be replaced?" She was speaking of humans as if they were mere batteries. Not a trace of emotion or regret hid behind the brown eyes I had once found myself lost in.

"From what we were told, each pod can sustain life for up to a year with the amplifier." Robinson said as he gestured toward Josie.

"Hartlem will need to work fast." Her gaze shifted back to me. "Henry, stay with Josie. I will be right back. Do not move."

I nodded my head as she slid out of the car and shut the door.

Josie had barely spoken a word since we had left the lab. "Josie. Jo. Please, I need you to snap out of it." I shook her as gently as my electrified nerves would allow. "Josie, please. We need to get you out of here."

A twitch in the corner of her right eye was her only reaction until she finally spoke. "Henry. There's no need for this display. This has been the logical step to protecting Coranta. Siana knows this as well as Hartlem. I need to let them know you aren't planning on being compliant." She shifted forward in her seat and stretched her hand to the door.

"No." I pulled her hand back as she stared at me. The vast emptiness of her eyes hollowed out the pit that had been sitting in my stomach. The yellow vial that I was still clinging to had gone warm and its contents had gone from a thick sludge to a sloshing toxic goop from the heat. When Siana had handed it to me in the Courthouse, she had said to give her this when it was all over. This would bring her back. But if she did what I knew, she was about to do to Josie. She couldn't come back from that.

What this person that looked like Siana could do was terrifying. But I could risk my life if it meant I could save Josie and, in doing so, Siana's as well.

The dark windows were my only hope as I slid my way over the partition and into the driver's seat. Josie did little, but continued to stare blankly. Siana and Robinson had made their way to one pod and begun appraising it. He had finished whatever he had been telling her and was reaching to unhook a door.

My insides squeezed as my heart shot up my chest, a coiled snake that was trying to strike its way out. There, inside the first pod, was the body of a man, and on his chest was the same cage like suit I had once woken to find myself in. The beeping sound that had accompanied it was playing in my head.

My foot found the gas petal before my brain registered. It was time to take Josie and run. The spinning tires left a dusty cloud as we sped down the path that had led us to this horrific place. Maybe her shift wouldn't reach us if I could get far enough away. Maybe she would be in there somewhere and let us go. Maybe she still knew how to show mercy.

My chest tightened as I struggled to breathe. The adrenaline shooting through my veins was wrecking havoc on my body, so much so that a strange haze began to take over my vision. I gave a panicked glance in the rear-view mirror. The group from Hartlem was running toward us, splitting the cloud of dust that we had left. Spots popped into my vision as the overload of emotions and panic continued to rise.

The dizziness gave way to pain as I realized what was happening

Siana was going to kill me. The brakes squealed as my foot slammed down of its own volition. The distance between us and the barrier was at least enough to where I could no longer see it, but the sounds of shouting and pounding feet made their way to us before I could fully recover.

We weren't going to get away. I knew that. But if we were going back, we weren't going to help with their plan. Josie didn't say a word as I pulled her over the seat to sit beside me. My breath was still ragged from Siana's control as I pulled the stopper on the yellow vial. It gave a satisfying pop as tiny droplets of the yellow liquid spilled out.

"You'll find another way to help her come back. I know you will." Not sure who I was really talking to, I poured the vial into Josie's mouth and held my hand there to stop her from spitting it back out at me, which she was violently trying to do. As she choked on the substance, I pleaded to the void to let it be the thing to help her. My hand was coated in the yellow goop as I pulled it back from her face, recoiling at the possibility of what I may have just done to my best friend.

She gasped out as the coughing died down. A light returned to her eyes. "Henry!"

"You have to get out of here. Whatever that thing is, it's not Siana anymore and it will kill you."

"Henry, it is Siana."

"No. No, it's not. But we'll bring her back. She can fix everything. The real her can fix everything. We just have to help her find a way back first." The door swung wide as I pulled Josie out of the car with me. "Let's go. We just have to make it to the rehab facility. If we stay hidden, I think we can make it."

Tears filled her eyes as she sat back down in the driver's seat.

"What are you doing?" the panic returned in a suffocating wave.

"We need to help Siana with the barrier."

The serum hadn't worked. Was she still being dampened by the Soterapine?

Before I could do anything else, Hartlem's guards were on us. Josie, finally out of her catatonic state, was screaming at the men who held tight to her arms to let her go. It had worked. She was free. Or, at least, her mind was.

Radio static scratched at my ears as a man behind me spoke.

"Sir, we have them, but something isn't right. The amplifier is active."

Robinson's voice came over the other end. "How so?"

"She's lucid and fighting back."

As if on cue, a pained yelp came from her direction. But it wasn't Josie that had made it. A vicious bite mark now marred the skin of the man that still gripped her. Before another word was spoken, she was being flung back into the car.

"Henry." The voice that came over the radio line was hollow and sent a chill chasing every nerve in my now pummeled body. "Henry, did you give the yellow vial to Josie?" Silence was all that answered her as I balled the hand still coated in the yellow liquid into a tight fist.

"Leave her there. She can't be used now."

A metallic click came from the vehicle. Josie was trapped again. "Make your way back with Officer Eklund." Every word she spoke was another crack in my heart.

I yearned for the days when she called me RoboCop as Hartlem's guards marched me back down the path toward her. The sounds of screaming and Josie's small fists pounding on glass followed me all the way back down the gravel path.

"It looks like you'll need to speed up production. This barrier won't hold for a year. Not without a proper amplifier." Siana stared me down as her words struck Robinson.

He crossed the distance between us in a fraction of a second. A jolt of pain rocked my entire body as his fist collided with my face. Over and over again. A guttural sob pulled its way up my throat as the pain split my head open. The anger radiating out of him was terrifying. He was going to kill me. This was where I was going to die. Through glassy eyes obstructed by blood and dirt, I tried to plead with the woman who had once held every part of me.

"Siana, please."

She placed her hand up to Robinson, who shrank away as fast as his feet would allow. His face contorted with a hatred that was focused directly on Siana. She didn't show any reaction on her stony face as she bent down to where I had been forced to the hard earth. The gravel crunched under her feet and punctuated her movement.

"Henry. Everything I do is for the people we left behind those city walls. What you did was selfish. Not everyone will survive to see this new Coranta. Some have to make sacrifices for it."

"Please don't say that. Please." My hand still felt sticky as I reached for her face. "I know you can't think that. I have to hope." The dirt, blood, and serum made a disgusting concoction that smeared across her cheek as I held her face.

"Hope is all you have ever had, Henry." She brushed her hand over her cheek. It did little to clear the filth. Instead, it smeared down her face and to the corner of her mouth. She licked her dry lips. A slight look of disgust pulled at her face before she wiped at the smear of filth again. "And now you don't even have that."

The uneven dirt and rock ground at my back as a bloody cough ripped through my chest, leaving a spray of bright red spots across the front of her shirt. My blood, now spreading out to mix with Nira's. Her sister's blood hadn't had time to fully dry yet.

"I'm sorry Nira." My chest buckled as I whispered into the rapidly cooling air.

A flash of confusion swept across her brow before her emotionless mask fell back into place.

"It's time to move to the other side, Robinson. I'm ready to activate the barrier."

"And what about your friends?" He kicked at the dust, but I didn't move. Too close to falling into unconsciousness, my body ached from his assault.

"He's of use to Coranta still. Anymore harm to him is not necessary. Leave the other one, though. We don't need her."

The hairs on my neck stood on end as I could feel both of their icy stares piercing through me. Robinson spoke first. "He may not survive the trip to Hartlem."

I waited. Siana's voice was icy. "I don't need him to."

All hope I had to bring her back was gone. She was gone, and from the sound of it, I would be too. And soon.

9

Chapter Two
SIANA

The sloshing of the waves rasped at my ears as the ship pulled farther away from the sandy bank that lined the Continent. A cloud of exhaustion had been wrapping itself tighter around me since I had performed the shift to create the barrier. The strange golden haze that had been coating my line of sight was showing cracks. The gleam that it had cast giving way to small fractures.

"He may not survive the transition." Robinson's voice was an unwelcome intrusion.

My eyes trailed behind him. "Who?"

"Your friend. He may not—"

"Let me stop you right there. I do not want nor care for your opinions. That will not change. Now that the barrier is up, you will take me to the Director of Hartlem so I can discuss with him what will happen next. The only thing that has changed is that you no longer have to deal with Mr. Rightley."

My neck felt stiff as I slowly turned it toward where Robinson stood. I could sense the repulsion skittering through his veins as he stared down at my feet.

"I'm so glad that we understand each other." My body didn't hesitate as I removed myself from the railing and made my way inside the spacious vessel. The large boat was equipped with everything someone may need to make the journey across to Hartlem. This time tomorrow, I would be catching a glimpse of my new home. There was no telling what sort of war-torn existence was awaiting me. The weight of sleep was pulling at my eyelids, carrying with it a dark cloud.

My feet clacked against the metal of the stairs as I made my way farther down into the ship's center. My knowledge of traveling by boat or any other means was limited. The most I had been in a car was with Henry when we traveled to Port Hartlem. My stomach clenched as the ship rocked to one side. The Golden sheen quivered on the edge of my sight as I thought of Henry. It was a strange sensation that pushed the exhaustion that was seeping in my bones ever deeper. The final few steps to the room that would house me until we made our way across the vast sea were unsteady. A grimy layer of filth made my shoes squelch, making an uneasy sound as it combined with the creaking of the boat that strained to hold back the waves. The door to the sleeping quarters was heavy and refused to budge past half way open. As I pushed my body through the cold and wet entryway, something nicked my face. A small piece of rusted frame that had curled away from its place on the door now held a single drop of my blood. The dark red faded into the brown russet color of the jagged metal.

The others making the journey to Hartlem were nowhere in sight. The small space had beds for at least three others to rest, but I doubted anyone would join me anytime soon. The warm line trailing down my face had me turning toward an aged metal mirror. A flash of a memory burned in my mind.

The sterile chrome and polished surfaces of Dr. Hawthorn's lab circled me as I stared at the reflection that had once shown on those same surfaces. Not the same reflection, though. Corrosion obscured this one. An oil slick like trail marred the face that stared back at me. The small trickle of blood was already beginning to dry on my cheek, showing only the faintest change of hue where it had mingled with another substance smeared across the corner of my now dry mouth.

A dull pain pulsed inside my chest as I thought of how it had gotten there. The sugary taste still lingered as I struggled to build the saliva that would wash it away. Henry would heal. Those were the last words that escaped my lips as I drifted off on the damp bed, the sway of the boat lulling me to sleep.

A sharp whistle was bouncing its way through the ship when I finally opened my eyes again. A bustle of hurried footsteps accompanied the shrill sound in through the door that was still holding firmly where I had forced it open. The sleep that had coated my eyes melted away slowly as I followed the sounds up and out of the teetering vessel. The sun had seemed to retreat on its path across the sky. It had felt like I had fallen asleep only moments ago, but as I approached the front deck, the long brown line along the horizon told a different story. Far behind me lay the Continent, protected by a barrier I had created for it. And ahead of me stood Hartlem. And I would do whatever it took to protect them as well, if it meant that Coranta and all that remained behind would be safe.

A restless sea pounded the side of the boat. The salt spray washed over the railing, leaving a tacky film everywhere I touched. Time passed slowly, all the while the surrounding group shuffled in preparation for our arrival to Hartlem. Each, though focused on a different task, kept a wary eye in my direction. Their heart beats blinked in and out of my mind. The flow of strange tastes and smells flooded my senses. I let them all mingle together as the shoreline inched closer.

Two large islands guarded the entrance to the waters surrounding Hartlem. One was a flat expanse of land covered in what looked like centuries' worth of garbage and debris, something like you might expect from years of war and turmoil. The island to my right was very much the opposite. A towering mountain clawed at the sky, almost as if it were trying to escape the waves that slashed at its base. Both islands seemed equally uninhabitable. A flicker of pain laced in fear left a sour taste trickling down my throat as we finally passed between the two land masses. My eyes wandered around the deck, trying to find the source. Salt coursed its way through my nostrils as I inhaled deeply, trying to pinpoint the senses and where they were coming from. Someone on board was less than happy about our arrival in Harlem.

Robinson approached from the back of the ship and made his way forward. The senses I felt trailed behind him. The Gold haze was now just a blur that blended in with the fog rolling off of the waters engulfing Hartlem's coast.

He kept his distance as he approached. "I've thought about how we should relay the change of plans to the Director. It would be best if the explanation of what happened came from me, and I'm sure you will want to get settled into your new lodging right away."

"What you mean to say is that there's a hierarchy in Hartlem that you would like to keep well intact. And should I be the one to relay events, it will put your leadership and, therefore, usefulness into question."

"I'm not sure that…"

"No." A golden pulse split the fog around the boat as I spoke. "That wasn't a question. I have no need for your politics."

"If you're suggesting this is some kind of power struggle, Ms. Viteri…"

"No. This is not a power struggle. For that, we would need to be at least somewhat equally matched. And you're well aware that we are not." My fingers felt sticky as I rolled the grim stuck to them into tiny bits that flaked off and drifted away in the ocean mist. "Let me make one thing very clear for you, Robinson. I have no intention of going anywhere. As long as your boss protects the Continent, once and for all, I will stay and fight. I will use every bit of my power to help win your war because that is what was promised. If you want to spin your story, that's fine with me. Just remember, I get what I want in the end." Flashes of Ethan Rightley popped in and out of my mind as the sickening sound of his neck snapping played on the wind that brushed over the slippery deck. Robinson took a single step back. His momentary retreat causing his face to fall into a grimace as the slightest crooked smile pulled at my lips. He was an animal scared and backed into a corner with no other recourse but to retreat or react.

"Do you think your friend, the cop, will make it?" His voice didn't waver as he stared straight into my eyes. I guess this was his way of reacting. He really was a stupid animal. "Aren't you worried about what will happen to him? He has no powers to help him."

The threat that he was hinting at was just another way to gauge my emotions.

A strange fluttering pulled at my stomach as I tilted my chin down. The smallest of lights seemed to glow in his eyes as he registered my expression. "He made his choice. That is something all of Coranta will now have. At least the consequences of their decisions will be of their own making."

The ship buckled and sloshed against the strange waves that seemed to pull at it from all sides. Almost as if invisible hands tugged at each rail, trying their best to pull the vessel toward a different island. Neither seemed to be welcoming us with open arms but instead wanted to plunge us into the murky depths.

Another flicker of something shot to my stomach before it subsided and the boat continued on. As we finally escaped the looming shadow of the island to the right, the shore of Hartlem became clear. Tall buildings peppered the landscape in front of me. The massive city on the shoreline stretched out to cover the entire expanse of coast from each side and, from the looks of it, kept going back inland for quite a distance, as well. It was massive. Far bigger that Coranta. Staring at the vast city from this distance, it was difficult to see any signs of a war-torn district. The island behind us was the only sign of war I would see until the ship drew closer to the dock. Here, the pain and devastation of war was plain on every person. They gazed at the docking ship in pure amazement. Cheers erupted as ropes were tied around large metal poles on the concrete dock. I looked out at the sizable crowd that was gathered. The people of Hartlem that stood before me were dirty and covered in soot and grime. Clothes torn but smiles wide on tired faces. Each looked up at the ship with what I could only describe as hope. My hand left another trail of grime across my face as I reached up to wipe a bead of sweat that inched down my hairline. "What is this?"

"You will soon learn how valued the Sense Guard is here in Hartlem." Robinson stepped toward the railing. A look of reverence passed over his face as he stared at the people below. A single pull at his mind left a warm, smoky sensation in my chest. He cleared his throat before lifting his palm from the railing to give a small wave to the crowd below.

My vision began to pop with bright colors. An aurora of lighthearted waves rushed over me as the cheering from the shore became thunderous. A slight ache radiated out from the base of my skull and coated my spine with razor-blades. A poem I had read in my work at the library sprang to mind as another wave of emotion that was not my own threatened to capsize me. "While follow eyes, the steady keel." Thousands of eyes were on me now; but was I the Captain or the Prize?

My insides buckled as I grasped thousands of tiny threads and pulled them to me. "Enough." The shoreline that had been deafening in its roar became silent. Each head that had been full of wonder now sat hollow, each feeling the calm before the storm.

The sea of people was ghostly still, and made my way down and through the enormous crowd — the only sounds were the hushed waves brushing against ship and shore.

The large gateway that separated the docks from the city was coated in a thin layer of rust. My eyes floated in a gray haze as they wandered around the sight of the city branching out from the gate's open mouth. My scalp tingled as a small thread tried to wrap its way around my mind. My eyes trailed along the city with slow precision as I turned my head to see the person trying to sense me. A group of women and men stood outside a large black vehicle unlike anything that I had seen in Coranta. It seemed to be made of heavy metals and its dingy dark gray color made the group standing around it stick out in comparison. Ten of them, all in the same pitch black uniform, stared back at me as I shot a jolt of electricity down the line that was tethering me to the one on the end. He doubled over, gripping at his upper thigh, trying to stop the onslaught of pain.

"Siana." A cheerful man's voice came from behind me. "That was impressive! We are so pleased to have you here. We are so grateful to you for your work on the Continent."

The man approached me, a wide smile on his face as he grasped both of my hands in his. "Robinson tells me that you have some requests about the barrier, and I want to make sure that we take care of that right away. But first," He gave a small shrug and inhaled through his teeth, "Would you do me a huge favor and drop that very impressive sense shift you've got going on down there? I know it can get a bit overwhelming, but everyone is just here to celebrate your arrival."

He smiled again and gestured to the crowd behind me, still silent and waiting while the man who had prodded at me still jerked on the ground in pain.

With a nod, I dropped all the threads that had trailed behind me. "Take me to Mr. Hartlem."

"Mr. Hartlem? That is adorable. The Director is going to love that one." A high-pitched trill of a laugh followed as he motioned toward another dark gray vehicle. "Right this way, Siana."

The sound of muffled chatter crescendoed to roaring cheers as the people on the docks realized what had happened. As I took my place in the vehicle, my hand instinctively brushed against the soft fabric of the pristinely cleaned seats. It sat in stark contrast to the outside of both the car and the world around it. A red smoke blossomed its way around my vision as the man who had tried to sense me glared in my direction. The sharp red of his anger matched the red trim that lined the shiny black material of his uniform. Another of them leaned to whisper something in his ear and the red smoke was gone with a snap. His head tilted up as the mass of people from the beach made their way toward us. They disappeared into the smiling and cheering mob just before we drove away.

The man smiled. "Thank you. For what it's worth, I know you gave up so much to be here."

"Who are you and what was that back there?"

"Ah, yes." He patted my knee before continuing, "I'm Cole Turney, I take care of." He paused and let out a small breathy laugh, "Mr. Hartlem's public affairs. And you, my friend, are a public affair."

My hand trailed back and forth over the soft fabric as he went on and on. "And that back there was your welcome party, so to speak. All of Hartlem has been waiting for your arrival.

The Sense Guard will be unstoppable with you leading them now."

"Sense Guard?"

"Yes. The brave warriors that come from the continent to help us battle the foe at our front door. Each of them has control of at least one of the senses.

Some have more, but you, my new fast friend, you have all five." It wasn't a question as he stared at me with a sickening appreciation. His eyes shifted up and down my body as if he could see the abilities that were lodged within.

"We, of coarse were happy to work with Ethan. However, hearing of your — redirect, I have to say, the Director was quite thrilled." He smiled, "There is much good that you can do here, Siana. For both Coranta and Hartlem. The Overseers of the Continent would never have made the choice that you did. And everyone will be the better for it."

I remained silent as the car continued to creep steadily through unfamiliar neighborhoods.

"You are going to be a very popular person here." He gave my shoulder a slight nudge. "Well, as long as you play nice with the rest of the Guard."

The streets were bare of people. It truly looked like everyone had been waiting at the waterline for my arrival. Buildings lined the streets. Each looked dirty and overcrowded, but with one crucial difference: electricity. Lamps peeked through worn glass windows while street lights stood tall and intact on each corner.

Lines crossed his forehead as he followed my gaze. "I know. It's a sad sight. However, with any hope, you and the rest of the Sense Guard will restore Hartlem Proper to its former glory."

My body remained stilled as we moved forward. A strange swirling lined my vision as we continued on through the empty streets and further away from the crowd. The buildings outside the glass window were a blur as my head began to drop. An invisible, heavy hand pushed at my chest as my heart began to fight against the weight of it.

"You must be tired from traveling. We won't hold you up from resting for too long. In fact," His excitement bubbled as he reached his hand out to point toward a large building out of the front window. "We are almost here."

The towering structure was bigger than anything I could have ever fathomed seeing in Coranta. There were multi-story buildings back home, but this. This was a giant amongst the rest of the city that bowed at its feet. "A quick trip to the top, a discussion with the Director about your assignments, some blood samples from the doctor and then it's off to your lodgings to meet with your partner and then take a much needed rest." The smile he gave was genuine. The soft golden hue he gave off was full of hope as the air in the car became lithe and airy with the smell of sunlight and grass. A memory of a happy time and childlike wonder. He really did believe something amazing was coming and that I would be its herald. The swirling glow pulsed in around my vision again as the vehicle came to a stop.

He truly thought that I was going to be another one of Hartlem's dutiful soldiers. I was here to do what was needed for the Continent and Coranta, but I would do it however I saw fit. My senses snapped out at him, bursting his golden hued bubble and pushing him to a dark cloud of pain and anguish. The whites of his eyes expanded as emotions flooded his mind and the taste of blood curled around my tongue. "There will be no blood samples."

My feet landed gently on the dark concrete as I moved forward into the metal and glass building. Cole's footsteps came more slowly than before as he forced himself to catch up.

"There is a restroom just over here if you would like to splash some clean water on your face before we head up."

"That's not necessary." The elevator doors were set back into the far wall of the large lobby. Cole sputtered something as he kept my pace. The doors were quick to open, and we both stepped inside. He stared at me.

The gentle glow from before was gone. In its stead, apprehension rested on his face. The view of the lobby shrank as the metal doors raked their way across the track in the floor. I didn't have to pull a thread to know his heart was slamming in his chest. A vein pulsed at his neck as his breathing quickened. The smile on his face was forced as he quietly cleared his throat.

The planes of my face laid flat and unfeeling as I continued to stare him down in the closed elevator. "Which one?"

"I'm sorry, I don't—" He took the slightest step backward but found the wall of the elevator already at his back.

This was tiring. "Which floor?" I said.

A short, airy breath escaped his chest as he began to laugh. "Oh. Of course." He reached for the large keypad and pressed one button below the top floor. The small metal enclosure gave a lurch as we started our accent. Cole continued to shift on his feet. A small animal trapped in a cage with something it had just realized it should fear.

The room had been emptied, probably to be sure that I wouldn't do anything. Even with the serum fresh in my veins, I couldn't have used my shifts against them if I wanted to. Something had felt off since my interaction with Henry. Killing Ethan and Dr. Hawthorne had taken little thought.

The power had been eager to obey. Activating the barrier, though, had taken more energy than I had expected. The feeling as if I had left something, some part of my new power behind, was still clawing at me.

The amount of I had expended at the docks was no less taxing and by the time I had made my way to the top floor of the sky high building at the edge of Hartlem, I was thoroughly drained.

"Director." Cole gave a smiling introduction and rushed forward toward the large desk. It was clear to see he was comfortable enough in this space to intrude into it at full speed. Or it could have been that he was trying to get as much distance between us as possible. The room was a large, open space. Two walls were completely full of windows. The windows to the right looked out on Hartlem. A broken city that I would soon learn to be full of filth and fighting. The windows to the left a beautiful array of blues. Filled with sea and sky. Somewhere out there was the Continent, the barrier wall, and Coranta.

Cole made his way to stand behind the man seated at a large wooden desk. "I would like to introduce you to Ms. Viteri. I have already been able to witness the feats that she can accomplish and might I add that they are truly awe-inspiring." A twitch began to show on his face when his gaze was on me for too long.

"Thank you, Mr. Turney. You may leave us." The Director's voice wasn't as harsh as I had thought it might be.

"Thank you." The words escaped him in one breath and he was back in the elevator in the next. A single ping and the arrow flashed up.

"It's truly a pleasure to meet you, Ms. Viteri." He gave a stern look toward the window, looking out toward the vast waters that led to the Continent. "Although, I must say, I didn't think I would have the pleasure of working with another Viteri."

My attention caught on his words. Of course he had worked with my father before. Did he really think I hadn't pieced that together already? Or was he trying to gauge whether I could be pushed? So the Director dealt in emotional warfare as well. Good to know.

"I've been anticipating your arrival for a very long time." The Director gestured toward a wooden chair opposite him and I made my way across the room to sit. "You and your sister. It disappointed me to hear of her passing. Our records and accounts showed great potential for both of you.

Some of our own doctors on Recreor have been eagerly awaiting both of your arrivals to Hartlem, but I'm sure, with the changes happening, they will be very interested in your..." he paused momentarily as he flipped though pages on his massive desk, " altered abilities."

If he wasn't aware that Nira was alive, I didn't see any reason to inform him. A sharp grip settled over my heart, pulsing for one painful moment before subsiding again. He didn't seem to notice as he continued on. "Tell me, where did you find the serum that resulted in your take down of Ethan Rightley as well as the incapacitation of the Dires in Coranta?"

"There's no more." He had known about the box with my father's things. Chances were, he had already guessed that's where it came from.

"When you leave here, one of my doctors will collect a blood sample to analyze—"

"No. My blood will remain right where it's at. I'm more than capable of fixing your problem on my own." If they found a way to create more with my blood, I would lose my upper hand. That wasn't happening. If I was going to live here for the rest of my life, I needed to make sure I remained irreplaceable.

He gave a sharp nod and cleared his throat. His demeanor changed. A stiffness ran across his neck and jaw as he gave me a piercing eyed stare.

"How would you like to proceed? Am I expected to bring any of the people causing trouble in, or do you want me to take care of the problem on site?"

"You will follow any orders Robinson gives you. They will change based on each mission." His focus turned toward the window, looking out across Hartlem. My eyes followed his gaze along the city skyline.

"Since you are so eager to get started, you can begin today." He looked back at me. "Robinson and your partner will escort you to a problem area we have been facing just outside the outskirts of the city. Eliminate all threats that you make contact with. Robinson will report back to me with your progress."

"Fine, but if I'm jumping right in, you will too. Your people need to start on the wall immediately." He controlled his temper much better that Ethan had, but the lines around his eyes and the tense in his jaw gave him away. He didn't like being questioned. He was obviously used to giving orders and from the looks of it, it had probably been a long while since someone had made a demand of him. "Look, I know that this didn't all go according to your plan. I'm also aware of the deals that you had with Ethan Rightley. I'm not asking that you change your plans. In fact, I'm here to guarantee that you don't."

He leaned back, hands folded in his lap. A slight tilt to the head made him have to look down his nose at me. It wasn't the first time someone had looked down at me. For the Director's sake, it would be best if it was the last time he did. "As long as you fall in line as Ethan assured us you would, I don't see any reason to—"

"Build a permanent wall- one that is stone and steel instead of flesh and blood, and leave the Continent alone. The barrier will be built so that Hartlem and all others allow the people there to live in peace. You will activate no other Sense Shifters on any side and I will work with your Sense Guard using my considerable power to stop your war in Hartlem."

He leaned forward slowly. "Considerable power? We were supposed to have both you and your sister. Two full Sense Shifters. Two soldiers able to do the work of many. If I'm to keep my side of the bargain, I need to know that you can make up the rest first."

"Without an amplifier at the barrier, it will not last. You need to have your workers move fast to finish on time."

"Have you ever been in a negotiation before, Ms. Viteri?"

"This is not a negotiation." He looked to at ease speaking down to me. It was time to change that. "There is a reason Mr. Turney couldn't stay in the room and it had nothing to do with your power. There is a reason why a substantial amount of guards are present on the floors right above and below us, and it has nothing to do with your power. There is, however, an alertness in the air as present and obvious as the tension in your jaw, and it has everything to do with mine."

He remained still for several steady heartbeats. Much steadier than the ones I could sense all around us. They must have been listening very closely.

My eyes wandered to the black box on his desk as a red light began to flash on it. The size and shape like that of the ones assigned by RightCorp. This one, however, was clearly made for communication, as it had a small square attached to a cord on it.

"Impressive." He stood. "We've already sent shipments out. You most likely saw them as you made your way here. The barrier will be constructed and the Continent will be left to its own devices." The small red light continued to flash on the box.

"Good." I made my way back to the elevator.

His voice trailed behind me. "Mr. Turney will help you find your way to the medical floor so your vitals can be checked before your first mission."

"Tell Mr. Turney I will meet him in the lobby. I have no desire to be poked and prodded this or any other day. I'm here. You don't need to know what's in my blood to know I can help you."

"Ms. Viteri, we are at war, but we aren't your enemies. If you get hurt, we need to be sure that we have the necessary resources to help you. That includes knowing your blood type."

"No. You want to see if you can extract any of the serum that let me snap Ethan's neck without laying a finger on him." The elevator button glowed as it came down from the top floor.

"I won't lie and tell you that I'm not at all interested in that. With that knowledge, we could create something that could save everyone here."

"I've heard that speech before." I looked at the black box that still lit up on his desk. "You had better get that."

He turned and pushed the flashing light as another voice floated into the room, this one a female voice. The static that accompanied it made it difficult to decipher what was being said. The voice was cut off as the doors rasped their way closed and I began my descent down to the city. My new Coranta.

Ethan Rightley was right about one thing. I had been made with a purpose. I could see that as soon as my father's serum had been introduced to my system, and it made the most sense to continue on with that mission.

Chapter Three

A blast rattled the windows of the vehicle that held me, Robinson, and my new partner. Smoke billowed a distance outside of the city of Hartlem proper, the gray tones matching the peppered streaks in the older mans hair. My new partner, Thakkar, stared forward with glazed eyes, the explosion sending a surge of anger through him and our driver. Robinson sat, unaffected by the blast that was just in sight far ahead of us.

The red trim on Thakkar's black leather uniform matched the color brimming my vision. "One of these days, we will be there quick enough to stop their destruction."

He looked back at me. "I'm sorry that you must fight on your first day in Hartlem. It's a shame that it should begin like this.

"I prefer it this way. What are they focusing their attacks on?"

"We aren't sure. We think it may be that they are targeting places where some of the poorer citizens have taken over for shelter. Old warehouses, more uninhabitable places along the outskirts of the city, places where the people were trying to make a home despite the chaos. These outliers find them and take everything from them."

"It sounds like you should provide better for your people." Robinson had been keeping himself out of our conversation, but this question was all for him. "It seems like the most likely answer would be to help your people find better ways of living inside of Hartlem Proper."

"There isn't enough livable space inside the city."

"What about the buildings like Hartlem Tower? From the looks of it, it could house a small town."

He avoided, "Until the deal with Ethan and then you, we provided for our people well. Now that we no longer have access to the Continent, we will have to find new ways to be useful." Robinson's stare was pointed. He blamed me.

"What does the Continent have to do with you providing for your people?"

"The Gifts." Thakkar had been silently watching our back and forth but now chimed in. "The Gifts were the Continents way of contributing. The Dires and the rest of the people gave some of their resources to us, and in return, we kept the fighting here."

"Now, we're giving our resources to your wall and losing a valuable tool to sustain our citizens." The car slowed as we approached the source of the dark smoke. A fire still billowed around wooden beams of an animal holding house. There didn't look to be any animals in sight, though, or people.

My new shoes felt too tight as they hit the hard packed dirt. It would be hours if not days before the fire blazing in front of me died. Thakkar placed a hand on my shoulder as he stared out around us. The lines of his face deepened as he reached out with his senses.

"What are you looking for?"

He kept his eyes closed as he spoke. "I'm trying to see or hear anyone who may be inside or hiding nearby."

A deafening crash split through the area as the back wall that was holding the building up collapsed in on itself, sending a spray of charred and splintered wood into the air. I pulled on the tethers of life surrounding me. I could feel Thakkar's anger pulsing out around him, just barely tamped down by his need to focus. A dark shadow fell over Robinson's face as I pulled at his senses. As soon as I did, I could feel his heart pick up speed as he struggled to control his breathing. His reaction had nothing to do with the fire still blazing behind us.

"Viteri," he spoke through clenched teeth, "focus on the mission."

I pushed out my senses several hundred feet past the flames and wreckage, past the field of grass that was yet to be touched by the fire, to a place hidden behind curtains of green foliage where the bright afternoon light couldn't reach. There, crouched in the dark, were two people — watching and waiting. The subtle taste of spiced meats mixed with the yellow glow of excitement coated the pull. "Found you." I placed the words in their heads just seconds before their vision turned black, hearts beating uncontrollably and feet marching steadily toward where we stood in front of the blaze they had started.

Panic coated the tether between us as I continued to force them forward. They were still too far to make out any features as they continued their involuntary march toward us.

A strange honey taste made my mouth water for only a moment as footsteps crunched beside me. Robinson walked toward them with a hurried purpose to his step and a rage pouring off of him like a toxic river. They were still moving toward me when he pulled a gun from his side, and without slowing, aimed it in quick succession. My hand flew to my head as a bullet pierced each one. Each line giving an excruciatingly painful stabbing sensation before sharply snapping.

A sea of emotions crashed through me as a flood door opened in my head. I stared at the familiar sight of bodies laying in the grass. A vise tightened in my chest as the smell of the fire seemed to close in around me all at once. A memory barreled through me as I thought of Nira, laying unmoving in the grass. Henry kneeling down beside her. A deep crimson red tunnel threatened to suffocate all of my senses.

There was a pull on my shoulder as my name was called, the voice seeming far away. "Viteri!" The voice sounded again. I reached in, willing the black toxin that allowed me not to feel to rise to the surface again as I fought to make the person touching me retract their hand.

It didn't move. Instead, the soft, worried voice echoed again. I took a slow breath and forced myself up on my feet. It took more effort than it had to will the now dead rebels. My eyes snapped open as a dark veil shifted over me again. The hand still placed on my shoulder shot back as I focused my attention on it and pushed its owner further away from me. Thakkar looked on with stunned amazement. "How did you do that?"

"In the future, refrain from touching me." I didn't look at him and instead looked for Robinson. Had he seen me?

A bead of sweat rolled down my neck and between my shoulder blades as I thought of the ramifications of what had just happened.

Robinson was still in the distance, but his eyes were fixed on me. Thakkar gave a visible shake before starting toward him. Robinson's hand went up, waving him off and crossing some of the distance toward us. "Good job, Viteri. This could have taken us hours." Though his words held praise, his emotions were giving off a sickly muddled green. A repulsion flowed from him and coated the surrounding air. His eyes flicked upward as he glanced back at the bodies a ways off. "Thakkar, call me a clean-up crew and take Viteri to her lodging."

"Yes, sir."

The tinted windows left the inside of the car feeling dark as the tree line I had pulled the two now dead rebels from. "Why didn't they hide further in the forest? Even if they hadn't thought I would be here, wouldn't someone from the Sense Guard still feel them there?"

Thakkar's hand dropped from where he had been propping up his chin on the door. His voice held a tone of exhaustion mixed with a sense of awe as he spoke. "Everyone knows not to venture deep into the Grey Forest. The horrors waiting there are far worse for them than anything the Sense Guard could do."

"Far worse than what you just witnessed?"

We both sat in silence as we drove back toward the heart of Hartlem.

Chapter Four
SIANA

Hartlem was a maze of trash and crumbling buildings. They were wasteful beyond measure. Coranta may have been void of feeling, but at least it was well kept. Not Hartlem. This is where all our gifts had gone and they wasted them, just like they had wasted their city. No wonder the Rightleys wanted to block us off from them. I smiled again as I thought of Ethan.

The trash that littered the ground crunched under the boots I had been issued. The uniform of the Sense Guard was clearly meant to intimidate. Not that it mattered. The things the Guard could do would strike fear even if they wore brightly colored jumpsuits. Cords of red and gray trim accented the black pants and jacket, while tightly woven intricate patterns spread along its back and sleeves. The many pockets on the pants served little purpose for me. The other Sense Guards filled them with all sorts of weapons, and first aid. I needed neither—for now, at least. A small kernel of doubt had burrowed itself in my mind after what had happened on my first day in Hartlem. Something had felt off ever since.

Like I had been pushed through a shadowed veil that wavered back and forth. I caught glimpses of emotions on either side. Whatever had happened, it was dangerous. The serum that had boosted my abilities seemed to waver the more I felt. It was vital that I blocked as much as I could. Unfortunately, the more I tried to block, the more I thought of them. All of them.

My fingers smoothed and picked at the red lining on my sleeve as I thought about the rebels again. It bothered me they would hide in a forest that they feared so much instead of running away. They would have had more than enough time to run away. My thoughts swirled instinctively back to another night full of fear and a dark wooded escape. We should have run.

A sharp breath hissed past my lips and clawed at my lungs as my nails dug into the palms of my hands. In the days since I had been in the Guard, I had trained myself to stay unfeeling. The more I felt, the less power I had access to. I pushed at my own senses, burying whatever I could below the haze before continuing on toward today's mission.

The command base for Hartlem was in what used to be a busy district. Now, it was desolate. The only building used was headquarters. Unlike Coranta, thanks to a hydro-power plant, electricity flowed through all parts of Hartlem. The strain on what they called the electrical grid was intense and often resulted in lights that flickered as the power pulsed through it like a slowing heart beat. And it gave off a sickly glow. A parasite sucking the life out of the rest of the surrounding city.

A warm sensation flitted against my neck as we neared the building. My hand felt nothing but damp skin as I reached to shoo away whatever pest was resting there. Not this shit again. The only pest I would find was walking in step beside me.

"Thakkar, if you try to sense me again, I'll break your nose."

My new partner was more company than I would like, but the Director had insisted. The first week with him had been an unbearable barrage of questions and unwanted information about his entire life story. At the first meeting with the rest of the Sense Guard, I made it very clear that I wasn't here for any of them. I was here for one purpose. When prodded about it, I prodded back by forcing them all into silence for the rest of the meeting. None of them had tried or even wanted to speak to me since. None of them but Thakkar.

The warmth was gone in an instant as he shuffled away from me. "I don't mean anything by it. I just think that, if you tried to understand, you would feel better about what were doing. Everyone else, even the entire Guard is scared of you. I'm not sure what happened to you, but you're here for a reason. We can help the entire Continent by helping Hartlem. It's been twenty-three years since I left and I miss Coranta every day, but--"

"I don't miss Coranta."

"How could you not miss Coranta?"

"Thakkar." There was a familiar resentment in my tone, a warning that he had heard at least a dozen times since our first meeting.

"I'm sorry. I won't ask anymore."

"Somehow, I don't believe you." A small coiling sensation ran through my chest..

The smell inside the concrete and steel building was acrid—like a mixture of dirt and old oil. Thakkar moved behind me to take the stairs toward the 8th floor. My boots squeaked as I halted just inside the stairway door.

"Take the elevator." It wasn't a suggestion.

Thakkar's footsteps gave a heavy thud throughout the lobby as he turned and made his way to the scratched elevator doors opposite me.

As the heavy metal scraped across their overused tracks, I pulled on Thakkar's senses. The sorrow that feathered off of him would have been heartbreaking if I allowed it. Everyone here had lost something very dear to them. It was the reason their powers were unlocked in the first place. The only difference was I reminded him of her. I saw her in his memories when we had first met. Her long, dark hair curling at the ends as she played. Her laughter rang through his memories. She would have been my age. If she hadn't been killed, she might very well be standing here instead of him. Another casualty of Coranta and Hartlem no matter what.

Besides that, my extra shadow had given me some useful information. Like how rightfully fearful both Robinson and Turney had been when they presented me to The Director. Not his actual name. His name was Ashfort, but insisted on being called The Director. He had given me the complete rundown of the workings of the Sense Guard and their role here in Hartlem. And most importantly, he detailed out Hartlem's enemy. They refused to give them any true title. Where in Coranta, there was the Sector, here they labeled anyone who fought to destroy the city as a rebel. Nothing more. Thakkar said that it was because giving them a name would give them a term to rally behind. It also meant that anyone could be labeled as a rebel, no matter who they were aligned with. Clever. I wondered if the Director had come up with that idea himself.

The door to the 8th floor mission center always stuck. As I shouldered my way to the entry, I could sense at least twenty of them congregating in the space beyond. The room gave off an array of emotions, most of which stemmed from successful late night patrols around Hartlem and its outskirts.

The door whined as I opened and closed it, the room going silent as I made my way to the front.

The yellow glow transitioned to a muddy green as I read them. Most mixed with some amount of resentment, jealousy, or aw, but all some level of fear. They had seen firsthand what I was capable of.

I took my seat at the front and waited for the whispers to circulate again while Robinson busied himself with a stack of red folders, each one holding reports and information about various missions for the day.

"What's the progress on the barrier?" I could feel the eyes of the room on me as my voice overpowered the quiet gray space.

"As expected. It's going to take some time." The same answer as always. As long as it was happening, that's all I cared about. He took his place in front and focused his attention on a paper he was holding. "Today may be a rough one, team. We've gotten word that the rebels are sending any children they can find out into the Grey forest." A combination of hushed and hurried whispers circulated. The heavy uncomfortable scratching of heavy benches on concrete floors punctuated the gravity of what Robinson said as several Sense Guards stood. The shock and anger that flowed from them left the room in a bright red glow.

"Why does that matter to us?" Asking sent a wave of nausea through me, but it needed to be asked.

The whispers continued. "Cold-hearted", "Monster", "Bitch". I didn't need to tap in to my power to shut them all up. All it took was a slow turn of the head.

"Continue."

Robinson didn't hold back. "It matters to us because some of those children have the gift. Meaning that they have the same genetic marker that makes each person in this room a Sense Shifter."

"Which no longer matters since, after this war is over, I have been assured that there will be no more Sense Shifters. Which begs the question, yet again, why does it matter to us?"

The red haze swirled around, although. His face was guarded, but the hatred he felt for me was palpable. Every part of my being itched to push him into a sense shift. To bring him back to the Courthouse and remind him why he needed to fear me. The rest of the Sense Guard kept their shifts to themselves when not in the field. They considered it an ultimate offense to shift someone without their permission. The irony in that couldn't have been lost on them. As much as my body ached to pull Robinson's threads, I needed to be smart about the situation. So instead, my unblinking stare stayed fixed in place. Apparently, that was all it took to set him off.

"I get it. You don't give two shits about what happens here or what these people have gone through. You just want to get your hands a little bloody, earn your wall, and retire to Recreor. Well, Siana, the Grey Forest is without a doubt the most dangerous place on this or any continent. It is pitch black and full of the most horrendous ways to die imaginable. Even you, with your lab created indifference, would piss your pants when standing at its edge." He tossed the pages on his desk. "And these disgusting waste of space piles of shit are sending their children off to a fate worse than death rather than have them join us."

The room was silent for a long time as the red hue faded from the room, as well as Robinson's face and neck. "Now that Viteri is caught up, let's get down to assignments for the day." He went over mission reports from the night patrols and prattled out names and section of the city for everyone else. Thakkar scribbled down hasty notes as he went on. My mind wandered while he continued on. My chatty partner would fill me in on anything I chose to miss.

Thakkar gave me a slight nudge as Robinson finished with assignments. "That means any child that you find, you are to collect and bring to the safety center next to Hartlem Tower. Those are orders straight from the Director."

The early morning street lights had gone off by the time we made it back down and out of the building and Thakkar had already come up with a plan of action by the time we made it to the sidewalk. "If we cover the factory lines first, it should make the trip back easier should we have to detain anyone."

"You mean if we have to rip someone's child from them? Words are important, Akshat, so let's use them correctly." A feeling tugged at my chest again, but I quickly pushed it aside.

I stared at the gray hairs that crept over his closely trimmed beard. I couldn't help but wonder if his hair had all been the same shade of deep black before he had joined the Sense Guard or if years of this work had aged him faster. He had done this since before I was born but, although his body still seemed fit for the job, I could feel his mind was tired beyond its years.

"We are helping them, Siana. You'll see that. And when the fighting is over, they will all go home."

"I know you truly believe that. Hope is what I sense the most from you." The glow that surrounded my vision accompanied by the sweet smell on the air bolstered, "But let me ask you this. What monsters must we be to them to prefer sending their children to the unknown?" His hope flickered.

"Why are you doing this?" The small voice that came from the shadows trembled as I inched closer to the darkness.

"Where are they?" I said as I looked around the rotting metal skeleton that was once upon a time some type of factory.

Its decrepit frame was plunged into dark nothingness while, for hours, I had waited outside. The red folder I had looked over at least a dozen times while waiting on my perch atop an adjacent building was back in Akshat's hands as he waiting impatiently outside. Our mission had been to find the people who were running the newest charge against Hartlem. The information gathered had led me here, standing in front of a small child with a look of pure terror in her eyes.

"I'm alone." She said.

A satisfying crunch went out as I walked across the grime and grit coated floor. All day I had seen people come in and out of this building, but now, the only visible trace of them were the tracks left behind.

"I can feel them, sweetheart. So please, feel free to try again."

"You're one of them." The shadows shifted as the little girl's panic began to rise. I could feel the adrenaline as it went from a pulse to a rush through her tiny veins. She couldn't have been more than eight or nine. The old me would have pitied her. Would have mourned for the childhood that was taken from her. My own heart lay still in my chest as I stared down at the child.

"My name is Siana. Tell them to expect me again. And if I find another child waiting for me to cover up their tracks," I closed my eyes and took a deep breath. The tendrils of fear that were curling out from the space beneath her feet were a map to the people hiding below the hatch she stood on. I honed in on one. A sickly yellow pulse grew as I closed in around the owner's heart.

A guttural moan echoed from the space. "I will not be so lenient next time."

The shuffling of feet was barely audible as the people hiding under the floor fought to re-start the man's heart. The man who had closed the hatch above him when I set off their silent alarms. The man who had rushed every one into the shelter but one.

The man who had left this little girl to die at the hands of his enemy. Their efforts would not be fruitful. His story ended here. A smile tugged at the corner of my lips as I sent my power out and squeezed. His fear and anguish fueling me. He would have left her here to meet this same end without remorse. I may have made myself a monster, but even as I pushed all emotion away, one thing never changed — one truth persisted. Children should not be made to face the evils of this world on their own. They shouldn't be made to face me.

A hollow snap came from his hiding spot as I gave him his final end. A muffled scream echoed from below and I slowly breathed it in. As I opened my eyes, the little girl stared at me. A glimmer surrounded her as the mixture of sour fear and warm light left a pungent taste in my mouth.

The hollow feeling in my chest closed in again as I turned, leaving the group behind. When I emerged from the factory, night had fallen around the broken city.

"Did you find anything?" Thakkar made his way toward me, emerging from a dark alley just on the other side of the building I had exited.

"Just a scared little girl." I replied, continuing to walk further away from my find. He followed.

"We should go back and take her in."

I stopped. "We leave her there. Do you understand me? She stays."

"Yes, but in the briefing this morning, Robinson said to bring kids if they were alone."

"And I said that we leave her there. Alone."

We continued back to the mission center and, for the first time in weeks, he didn't say a word.

A bitter ripple of tension went through me as I marked another day on the board outside the cafeteria kitchen. What had started out as a triumphant goal board had slowly become a torturous reminder of how long the barrier had been up; how long Melissa and Nira had been asleep; how long Siana had been gone? 68 days. Another wave of sadness pulled like a curtain over my thoughts as I made my way to the kitchens.

"Rhett. We need more flour. We're having trouble keeping up with demand now that everyone is awake." Josie popped her head out of the window that led to the kitchen for only a second before dipping back in. "Once everyone starts moving out to the rest of the fractions, it shouldn't be too bad, though." Josie's voice was even though concern had shown through her eyes.

She had been vital in the transition of the dires. She had stayed busy throughout the entire process, focusing on helping the people when she couldn't go help Henry and Siana. Instead of taking her with them, Siana had taken her to start the barrier and left her there. How she had done it was still a mystery to us. Now she was in Hartlem, trapped on the other side. Leaving us no way of knowing her state of mind or how to save her or Henry.

"I'll leave for Renbrough tonight and bring back what I can. I've been wanting to check on my mom, anyway." I glanced sideways at her as I picked up a knife and began peeling vegetables alongside her. "I appreciate the work you are doing with us, Josie. I don't think we would have had as much success transitioning everyone without you. But, you know you don't have to keep going like this every day. This isn't Coranta." I looked down at her hands.

The nicks on them made it clear she still wasn't at ease in the kitchen as she was with people, but now with everyone awake, there was little else to do. "You can take a break without punishment here."

She took in a slow breath. "What they did to me isn't my fault. I know that. What they did to Siana and Henry, and all of Coranta, wasn't any of our faults. I know that too. But I hesitated, and that is my fault. I had a chance to stop her, Rhett. I had a chance to bring her and Henry back, and I didn't. That's on me. And when I'm really ready to deal with that, I will take a break and sit with it. But right now, I don't have the time to spare for my pity party. So thank you, but no. I'll keep helping where I can."

I simply nodded. I understood that hurt more than I cared to share. My mind went to that night in the woods every day. How things would have changed if she and I had just ran. I understood the need to keep running to work, even if it was only to keep the thoughts from catching up.

The steel counter that opened up the side of the kitchen to the cafeteria was lined with people. The last of the dires that had been woken up and moved. It had taken longer that any of us had anticipated and hadn't gone exactly to plan. We started off by moving out Source members, then we went borough by borough at first. We quickly realized that we were taking too long and people were dying.

We couldn't move fast enough to keep everyone under and sustained. The result was a broken Coranta. Everyone there was in charge of their own emotions, and they had let them overrun them. The Dires had taken the city and now it was on fire. The ones sitting in front of us now were the last of the group moved out with Nira and Melissa. These dires had the chance to slowly wake up with help from the ones who had done it before them. Thomas rested his arm on the counter, giving his usual air of confidence. One of our original Source members from Renbrough.

He worked closely with Prue now that she could no longer be Captain Sheridan. Everyone lost something in the Wake.

"Hey. The shipment from Wilullf just got here. They said you didn't want it released to anyone but you."

"Thanks, Tom. I'm on my way."

Josie took her turn to give me a sideways look. "What are you up to?"

I wiped the carrot juice off my hands and rolled the sleeves of my shirt back down. "Research."

"You can't bring the barrier down yet. We both know that. And you can't do it at all without killing them." The pain in Josie's voice stung. The feeling of ice in her stomach amplified my own as I moved to push her senses away from me. I faked a smile. "Which is why I research, for now."

"I know you're going to bring them back. I just don't want you to have to do what she did to do it."

"I don't think anyone could sacrifice as much as she did. She saved us and everyone here knows that."

She looked out at the people still filling into the cafeteria. "The people here know that. But the ones still in the city despise her. I'm afraid she might be safer where she is."

If it helped her to believe that, I wouldn't kill her hope. "She's safe for now."

My hand still felt coated in ice as I gave her a gentle but quick tap on the shoulder. The chill it left behind didn't leave her as quickly.

I could hear her whisper into the air as I went to follow Thomas. "And so is Henry."

Life echoed through every hall of the enormous building that was finally being used for its named purpose. To rehabilitate Coranta. The Rehab Center also served as a way station. A place for the dires who had transitioned before they decided where to go next. Willulf and Renbrough fractions were full of people now. Communities working to start a better life. Fuller fraction was doing as much as it could to help while trying to keep to themselves on the far west side of the Continent. I couldn't blame them. For decades, they were able to maintain a stable community of people who worked and lived off of the land. As long as we sent the Gifts, they were allowed to live. Not only a simple but Soterapine free life. The research I had gleaned since the fall of Ethan had been immense. Even as an Overseeing family, the Willulfs had been kept in the dark like everyone else.

One thing was blissfully certain. Those who came to the rehab facility from Coranta didn't return, but now for different reasons.

Sheridan was waiting as I made my way to the loading dock doors. She had been gone for over a week now, gathering information from Willulf Fraction and any reconnaissance from our plants in Coranta.

"Any news from Kindolf?"

"Not yet, but we did receive something from inside the walls." Sheridan handed me a piece of cardboard, the words, SENSE SHIFTERS KILLED ON SIGHT, scrawled in what looked like charcoal across its front.

"Lovely." I said. "What about the files from Wilullf? Tell me you found those."

"I found those, and I did you one better." She pulled up on the folding door to reveal a truck full of supplies. Among the items in the back of the transport truck were boxes full of medical equipment.

"I could kiss you, Sheridan."

"A drink would be just fine. You can save the kiss for Siana when you figure out a way past that barrier."

My heart contracted at the thought. "Fair enough. Help me move this stuff and someone will get you that drink."

"You're not gonna join me? I thought you would want to celebrate. This is a big step toward finding an answer." Sheridan dropped one of the large boxes with a thud. How could stacks of paper be so heavy?

"I have to make a trip to Renbrough tonight. We need more food to hold us over." The satisfying rip of tape on cardboard echoed through the truck as I took a peek inside.

"I can come with you. Hobbs and I can be ready by the time you leave."

The boxes took longer to move than I had expected as we shuffled them into the empty space I was using as my room. The dark stone walls had once been a storeroom. Now, void of all its contents, it looked like an old dungeon. The small bed and table pushed to one corner were barley used as of late.

I spent most of my nights working through pages of notes taken from RightCorp labs. I had searched for anything that might help us break through the barrier that Siana had constructed. Even now, the thought of it made my insides crawl.

The loud thud of boxes and lab equipment being dropped on the hard stone floor made my teeth hurt. I needed sleep more than I had let on. The sun had barely come up and already my eyes were heavy.

"Did you hear anything I just said?" Sheridan was standing just a few feet away with a white box in her hands.

"What? What's that?"

"I don't know, but it has tubes in it and this one has your name on it."

She held a dirty-looking glass vial to the window. Whatever had once been inside was shriveled and brown. I was careful not to drop them as I raised each tube eye level to inspect them. Six tubes in all, and all with a name written on the label and each with a unique form of dried material inside. Among the six names were Rhett Willulf, Nira Viteri and Siana Viteri.

"Is that what you've been looking for?"

"I'm not sure." I searched the other boxes for some sort of clue as to what the vials meant. Each of the boxes was overflowing with paperwork. A puff of air escaped me as my legs hit the edge of my unused bed. Sheridan let out a quick chuckle as she patted my shoulder.

"Hobbs and I will make the run to Renbrough. Looks like you'll be busy with some light reading today." She made her way to the door.

"Say hi to my mom for me?"

"Can do. And hey, try to use that bed. You look like shit." Sheridan smiled and threw me a wink before closing the door behind her.

The day inched by as I made my way through the pile of paperwork. Years of data collected by RightCorp. Names flashed through my vision over and over again. Hawthorne, Viteri, Willulf. Nausea rolled through me as my memory surged through each experiment that matched the pages I was burning through. Every test took up more than its fair share of space in my memory. I was envious of Siana for not remembering. Even Nira had forgotten so much. Nira had asked to be shown more, but there were some things that I couldn't show her.

It was for the best that they didn't remember, and there had to be a reason that they didn't. Maybe that would be the key to figuring out why their powers were so different from other shifters.

My eyes blurred as I reread the page in my hand for the hundredth time. I threw it down on the pile before moving to the next. Reading through the files was dizzying. Each page was a strange combination of botany and human biology. Familiar plants flipped by from the pages.

A soft glow lit the room. A heat was settling behind my eyes as I stared out the window at the rising moon. All the information in these boxes and I was no closer to bringing her home.

"You missed lunch." Josie's voice was harsh on my ears after hours of only rustling papers. "And dinner."

"Something here is going to help her. I know it." My eyes were sore where I rubbed them. I'm going to bring her back."

"All of them. I love her too, but she's not the only one that needs saving." Her eyes glared into mine.

"And you won't save anyone if you don't take care of yourself."

"You're right."

"I know I am." The already messy floor gained a few more papers as she moved a box from the table and looked inside. "So, what are we skipping meals for today?"

"Take a look at this." I held the report in my hand out to her. "The gardens around Rightley Manor were used to research and test different plants brought over from Hartlem. I already knew that, but the extent of the experiments, the properties they held…It's more than I realized." My finger traced the words I had already read at least a dozen times.

"This seems to suggest that all the powers, the ability to sense shift, all of it comes from the plants."

"So what does that mean for taking down the barrier?" A glint shone in her eyes as her gaze immediately went to the moonlight filled window. The nearest pod was an hour's walk away, but I knew that was where her mind was drawn.

"All records I could find said that samples of everything were kept in the main RightCorp lab. With any hope, they would still be there. If we knew what each plant did, what effect it had, we may be able to harness it to help. I'm hoping that if I can find out what they used on Siana and Nira, maybe we can use it to overpower the barrier."

A bouncy curl fell forward as Josie tilted her head to search in the box she had just moved. "It seems a bit strange that these aren't typed out. Usually, if it's an official RightCorp document—"

"Let me see it." Josie slid the box my way. It was full of hand-written notes and letters. She was right.

Every other box had been full of official documents. This was different. Most of the reports had been neatly organized and typed. Hundreds of scrawled notes rested in the box at my feet.

My eyes regained focus as the adrenaline of discovery surged through me again. My gut told me this was something that I could use. My hands shook as I hurried to pick up the box. A fan of fluttering white fell from the bottom as the cardboard split open. Each paper taking on a life of its own as it floated and slid away from my grasp.

"Damn it." My heart was pounding too fast to stop and pick each one up. Josie moved quickly to help. The pages mingled with the already discarded reports that laid strewn about the room.

A tiny doodle of what I guessed was a dog poked out from the corner of a handwritten page caught my eye. The sharp letters and small print were easy to spot as Dr. Viteris'. His handwriting was unmistakable.

Despite the push back I've received, I'm certain that it will be vital to continue work on the wash solution. Please, no matter what you may believe, our girls still have a chance to live a normal life. Or, if nothing else, RightCorp should want some form of fail-safe. Just in case they get too out of hand. What if they hurt someone? Will RightCorp or worse Hartlem be so forgiving knowing they could never control them? Let me continue my work. Tell the Rightleys it's needed in case of emergency. I'm close. The seeds that Hartlem sent could be the key to canceling out the mutation in their blood. If you would just give me one of them.

Please, Lilly. Our girls deserve a way out. All the children do.

A large red stamp slashed over the pleading letter. **REQUEST DENIED** bled over the page, turning the heartfelt plea between husband and wife into a cold, formal rejection.

"What is it?" Josie's asked. The page felt heavy in my hand as I held it out for her to take.

My brain was a muddled and foggy mess. The tension headache that had been building was pulling at the muscles in my neck. Both my jaw and neck gave a loud cracking sound as I rolled my head from side to side and took a long, thoughtful breath. Every memory I had of Siana's and Nira's father was of him connecting devises and administering syringes full of dark fluid, his face turning red and angry whenever he didn't get a reaction he wanted. My brain couldn't reconcile that man with the hand that had written about protecting children. Could they possibly both be the same man? Could my memory of him have been wrong all this time?

That train of thought would have to wait. Instead, I focused my attention on the most important part of the letter. There was something that could be created to take away the mutation. In case of emergency. This had to be what Viteri had been working on in secret to give to the girls. And the reason they ran.

Josie finished reading just as I finished my thought. A look I hadn't seen since she had arrived was glimmering in her eyes. I could feel her heart speed up, beating out a hopeful rhythm. "Rhett. Could they really have created something to get rid of the shifts?" Her heart sped ever faster as her energy seemed to bounce all over the small room. "What do we do now? We probably need to see if we can find any more research about the specific plants Dr. Viteri was using." She continued to bounce around the room, her elated energy growing brighter and brighter as she went on meticulously searching through each pile of papers, "We need more…" she took a sharp breath in, "do you think there is more information on this at the beach house?"

"No. When they took them all, they raided everything. It's a wonder they didn't find the metal box that had the other serums in it. No."

A heaviness dropped into my gut. "If there's information about this emergency serum, there's only one place I can think of that it would be. RightCorp."

"Do you think you can remake it? Is there someone here that worked with the Rightleys or in the lab that can decipher it? There's zero reason for you to risk losing your head going there if we can't even make sense of what you bring back."

A cold shadow seemed to close in around us as I took in an icy breath. I knew exactly what we needed to do now. Who we needed. "We need Nira."

A claw raked against my heart as I stared at the page Josie was still holding. Her eyes shifted to the window. "But we haven't—"

"I know."

We had waited to see if there was something we could do to save Melissa, but we knew even then that there was nothing that could be done for her. She had amplified everything Nira sent out, and even now, you could see the toll it had taken on her body. The only thing tethering her to this world was Nira. We fought to keep both of their bodies functioning, but as soon as we brought Nira out of the shift, Melissa's mind would have nothing left.

My thoughts shifted to the pods that lined the border facing Hartlem. Dozens of bodies held in stasis to do exactly what Melissa and Nira were doing on their own. There was no telling what condition those people Siana trapped were in. The shift they were locked in was strong. Strong enough that getting close meant excruciating pain. My chest tightened as I thought of what else would be lost if we didn't deactivate it and soon.

"We've waited as long as we could, but now, we need Nira awake." It was time to say goodbye to my friend.

The room we had left them both in was full of warmth. Each day, the small amount of people allowed to be near them brought them trinkets and notes. The ones watching over them brought the items in, but our supply of anti-sense serum was running low. Unwisely, I had used more than I should have when the barrier first went up. I fought to get past whatever Siana had done. Even with the serum, it was too strong.

RightCorp had special suits outfitted in preparation for the subjects used for the barrier. Metal cages that tapped into a regulating system that sustained them. We didn't have anything like that. Nira and Melissa had to be taken care of by hand. Just like the people in Coranta had to be before they woke. A shudder went through me. We lost so many in the end. There wasn't enough to save them all. And now, the ones left in the city blamed us for it. Well, more specifically, they blamed me. They blamed Nira and Melissa. And they blamed Siana. My resolve hardened.

I would make sure that they all knew what they all sacrificed for them.

My finger brushed the foot of the bed that held my friend. The cushion underneath me flattened, and the bed creaked as I lowered myself down to sit beside her. It had already felt like I had lost her. I had mourned her already. But now, knowing that her breaths would stop. Knowing that whatever dream she was living through on loop, would end — It was like losing her all over again.

All we would have to do is move Nira and Melissa's tie to the living world would fade with her. The blue walls of the room gave an ethereal glow as the light of the fireplace bounced off of them.

I kissed her cheek. It was warm.

"Sir. The transport is ready."

"Thank you. Go ahead."

As they moved Nira to a hand cot and walked away, I held my breath. The warmth of her hand radiated through me as I rocked back and forth on the balls of my feet. Maybe we were wrong. Maybe she could still wake up from this nightmare, weak but alive. Melissa's body temperature dropped. I grabbed the blankets that had remained on Nira's bed and tucked them around her. She was the reason we could save anyone. I hugged her as the movement in her chest stopped. Her body had been through so much to sustain everyone's shift. It was done.

Icy shards cut at my insides as I swallowed back the sob that was trying to escape me. She could rest now. She deserved that. But I wouldn't. I wouldn't rest until I made all of it right.

The room went dark as a memory of another death curled its frigid and bony fingers around my heart. Another cold room where mine was the only heart that could still break and beat.

The muscles in my body locked up as my legs forced me to the floor. I made a promise to protect Nira and I wouldn't break that promise. The tears that slipped from my eyes stung as they carved an icy path down my face.

"Goodbye, Melissa. Rest now and I'll see you soon."

Coughing echoed through the room as the blocking serum we had hoped would work started tracing its way through her system.

"Where's Siana?" The rasp in Nira's voice was painful to hear.

"It's alright, Nira. Just take slow breaths. You've been asleep for a while and your body needs time to adjust." I said.

The sound of her body hitting the floor left an ache in my chest. I had tried to reach for her, knowing she wouldn't have the strength to hold herself up, but she was quicker than I had imagined she would be after weeks of sleep. She felt far too light as I placed her back on the bed.

"Where's my sister?" The sleepy haze in her voice was laced with panic.

"Hartlem."

She took a breath, placing her feet back on the floor and steadied herself against the side of the bed. Both the bed and Nira's legs faltered as she tried to push herself to her full height. "And the barrier?"

"It's up. Nira, you need to take it slow. We can get you caught up later. Right now, we need to make sure you're alright."

I nodded to the doctor, who didn't hesitate to take my place.

Her eyes began to droop again as she tried to remain standing while the doctor took all of her vitals.

"Everything seems normal." He spoke directly to Nira. "But that doesn't mean you can push it. You're gonna want to take it easy today just in case. Getting up and moving is important, but you need to listen to your body. Take frequent breaks and if you can, try to make it outside. The sun and fresh air will do you some good."

A moment later, a pained expression came over her as tears began to stream from her eyes. She slowly turned her head to look beside her. Where Melissa would have been when they fell asleep.

Her voice was no more than a whisper. "Were you able to save her?" The last word was stuck in her throat as she looked back up at me with pleading eyes.

No words came. Nira's legs were shaky as she made her way off of the bed she had been resting on. Her hand reached out for support and as her thin fingers wrapped around mine and I felt her body sway slightly. The loss I felt barreled down on me, becoming an overpowering storm as soon as she wrapped her arms around me. Much tighter than I would have thought her tired body would have allowed her. Time moved slowly as we stood there. Neither of us moving for a long time. Silently mourning everything that had been lost.

After a long while, I pulled her out to arm's length. Her head gave a gentle nod before bouncing back up. A chuckle bubbled up as I realized she had fallen asleep standing up. "I'm going to go tell Josie that you're awake. I'm sure she'll be happy to see you too. You rest and I will be right back."

"I'll come with you. I'm alright." I reached out and pulled at her senses. My chest felt hollow and sore, as if a hand clawed with jagged nails had scooped it out. A chill ran through every inch of my body, making it jump with shivers of cold and fear. Nira was not alright.

"No, you need to stay and heal."

"I'm alright. I promise. Besides, the doctor said I need to get up and move."

I gave a tight-lipped smile and a nod as she reached for my arm to steady herself.

The hallways were buzzing with excitement as we made our way to the cafeteria where Josie would most surely be. Whispers of Nira's name bounced around in a dizzying flurry as everyone took in the sight of her walking these halls again.

"You're famous." She ignored my small poke and instead stared forward.

"What's the name of what you do in Willulf? When someone dies, what do you do?"

I stared down but only got the top of her head. She was lost in thought; eyes fixed on some invisible point in front of her.

"A funeral. We have a celebration of the life they led."

She continued to stare out. I could see the gears working in her mind. "How many did we lose?"

"Too many to count, Nira. We did our best. What you and Melissa did was amazing."

She let out a tiny breath as we rounded the corner that led to the large cafeteria. "We need to celebrate them. All of them." Her brows furrowed and determination was written all over her face.

"We will. With time. But for now, we have work to do. I need your help to decipher some of the research we pulled. We're trying to find a way to break the barrier and—"

"Nira!" The excited screams that came from the kitchen made my neck pop as I whipped my head in that direction.

Gentle laughter came from Nira, standing beside me. The entire room erupted with cheers and laughter at the sight of Josie running toward us. A flood door had opened. As if everyone had been given permission in that moment to finally breathe. That's what Nira did. She gave everyone hope. And I hadn't realized until that moment how much they needed her. She would make an outstanding leader.

A realization dawned on me as I stood in awe, watching each person who had gotten the news of her waking and followed us to the large open space of the cafeteria crowd around her. They loved her. They had been waiting for the sign that she was alright. I took a step back. This was what the Continent needed. It was her.

Nira was the leader that these people needed. She was the lightning rod that called them to action. A grin pulled at my lips as I thought of Siana and I watching her lead. How proud she would be of her sister right now. My face fell once again. A hand rested on my arm. I hadn't noticed Nira step toward me, surprised she could move at all in that crowd.

"We're going to bring her back, Rhett. We're going to bring her home." Even without a pull at my mind, Nira could sense what I was feeling. "Now, let's go outside and you can fill me in on everything I missed. It's time we made a plan." A rosy warmth had returned to her cheeks.

Purpose.

"Here." Thakkar reached out his hand, a metal cup filled with a swirling dark liquid in his grasp. "I promise you will love it. And, as a plus, it's got enough caffeine to wake the dead."

He waited with excited eyes as I took the cup from him. The hot metal radiating through my black gloves left my fingers curling around its warmth. His energy vibrated as he waited for me to take a sip. The mission center was filling up slowly this morning. Apparently, several of the Sense Guard had been attacked along the far east border of the city. Word was they were still healing on the med floor.

The thick brown fluid had a peppery sweet smell. My nostrils tingled as my eyes shot back to Thakkar's face, still full of youthful excitement. "What is it?"

"Just trust me. You're going to like it. Everyone likes it." His smile glowed as much as the edges of my vision. I could sense he was truly happy to see me enjoy it.

After another quick sniff, I lowered my lips to the hot cup and took a gulp. The thick liquid was what I imagined lava might taste like. A syrup like consistency mixed with hot spices and fruit. I fought back the urge to spit it back out into the cup. A hot drip slowly burned down my chin as I forced the drink down. The heavy liquid sloshed in my empty stomach, and an almost immediate boost of energy went skittering out through my veins. "You do know that I'll kill you if you just poisoned me, old man."

A warm chuckle came from his belly as I wiped away the liquid still sitting on my chin. "There are more creative ways I could get rid of you if I really wanted to." His smirk was reassuring, but only lasted a moment before he lowered his voice so that only I could hear. "And just in case you're worrying, I didn't put anything about leaving the little girl behind in my report."

"Okay." I stared at his unwavering face. Did he think it had been some kind of test?

A murmur of voices and feet shuffled into the space as Robinson made his way to his usual spot. Thakkar gently nudged my arm, "You'd better drink that up quick. We're gonna be short handed today and Robinson already looks like he might rampage."

The aftertaste of the drink had turned into something more pleasant and the energy boost was more than welcome. Nightmares crept into my sleep. Even as I sat here, knowing that I was helping Coranta,

I had increasingly been racked with the urge to get

back. I wanted nothing more that to rush back to Henry.

He didn't deserve to give up his life in Coranta for me to be here. I had begun wanting to sit with my sister again and read a story. My heart lurched in my chest. I wanted to see Rhett. He had so much to answer for, and I wanted to make sure that he did.

My breathing quickened as I thought of all the possibilities of home that I would never get to experience again. Not if I wanted to keep the Continent safe. Worry fluttered in my uneasy mind. If I was starting to want these things, then something was very wrong. The serum that allowed me to ensure everyone's safety was waning. With each shift, I burned through a bit more. No more unless I had to. I couldn't risk it. The barrier had to be finished first.

A sharp squeal of the aging door cut through my thoughts as the last of the Guard joined us. I downed the rest of my drink, resulting in a full body shake.

Robinson started, a pained look sewn to his usually hard face. "As most of you have already heard, the rebels ambushed a large patrol last night. We will be suspending all mission related operations for today in order to give all hurt units time to rest and heal. Each of you will need to go give blood on the med floor before starting on your goodwill rounds today." I didn't miss his pointed look at me. "We have to make sure we are stocked up if anything like this happens again. And with the way they are organizing, It will happen again."

Thakkar shifted in the seat beside me. "Sir, Siana and I both already had a cup of Fools Draft. I don't think Dr. Madeline will take our blood today."

Robinson shot a dangerous look toward Thakkar. "Everyone is dismissed to their duties."

The sound of metal on concrete scratched out as everyone made their way off of the benches to exit.

"Thakkar." Robinson's voice reminded me of gravel being crushed beneath the wheel of our guard vehicle. "Get it done first thing tomorrow. No excuses."

"Yes, sir." Thakkar held the heavy metal door for me as we made our way back down the empty stairwell.

The clip clop of our feet on the stairs was the only sound for several floors. It bounced and echoed like the question that had been working its way around my brain. "Did you know they would be asking for blood today?"

A gentle smile tugged slightly at his peppered beard.

"If you knew, then why would you give me that cup of hot lava sludge, knowing that Robinson would be pissed with you?"

"Hot lava sludge?" He gave a small laugh, "It's called Fools Draft, and it looked like you needed a pick me up more than a needle today. Besides, everyone loves when I make it for them."

"You made that?" He gave a small nod as I sneered, though secretly loved the bouncy waves that it was sending through me. I almost felt like my full self again. My head hung low again as I stared at each weathered step that took us further down. Soon, I wouldn't have what it took to keep the Director happy. With each shift, the barrier was at risk and with it, all of Coranta. I couldn't let my mask drop. Not even for someone who might be my only friend here.

"What is a goodwill mission?" Short and to the point. I had to keep reminding myself that, even though Thakkar's father like warmth was a comfort here, I had to remain stone if I had any hope.

The shift in mood wasn't lost on him either, as he turned his tone back to business. "We go to the shops around Hartlem. Turney will probably be down in the lobby, already waiting to give us packs stuffed with money and trinkets for the people. It's usually a big event where all of Hartlem Proper comes out so that we can help them. They are grateful for each Gift."

"That's why they worship the Sense Guard. You buy them. Wait. Is this what the Gifts from Coranta are used for?" He couldn't be naïve enough to believe this was anything more than war propaganda. Could he?

"It's the Continents payment for keeping them safe as well."

"So Coranta needed to work nonstop and give everything so that you could keep your fan base?"

The hurt plastered on his face was awful. My hand picked at the red chord of my Guard uniform as he spoke. "Siana, whatever you may think of us here, we aren't out to hurt anyone. Our — my only hope is to help." We approached the bottom flight of stairs before he spoke again. "I don't believe that you are so cold that you don't care for the people here, too. If you didn't, you wouldn't have left that little girl."

The blinding morning sun burst through the doorway that connected to the lobby. Spots blurred my eyes as I rubbed them, straining to adjust to the oppressive light. Shuffling feet rasped their way around the lobby as blurry wisps moved in time. My face stretched in hopes of speeding up the transition from the dark, empty stairwell.

"Siana. Akshat." Turney's cheerful voice bounced over the space like it was competing with the light to fill it. An internal groan sank from my throat to the soles of my feet as I stared at the man with the too bright eyes. He had done a great job of avoiding me since our encounter at Hartlem Tower.

Something about him seemed off, and I fought against the urge to pull at his tethers and sense his real side. I had a feeling it would taste like pond scum and be just as slimy. As if to punctuate my thoughts, I watched as his eyes traced up and down one of the female Sense Guards that passed in front of us.

He straightened the front of his suit and strode toward us, his smile plastered to his face. "Let me go over everything with you. Your first Go0d Will trip is always so exciting and everyone has been waiting impatiently to see you." Turney shoved two large packs at Thakkar. "These are your Pro-Packs. They are filled with all sorts of goodies that you may distribute as you see fit. Just make sure they are empty when you return to the mission center." Turney's face was beaming by the time I could focus again.

His body gave an almost imperceptible jump as I spoke. "Is there an update on the barrier yet?"

His smile dropped for only a fraction of a beat while he tossed a quick side look toward Thakkar. "Everything is on track for completion."

"And when—"

"The Director will speak with you later about it." He grabbed the Pro-Pack still in Thakkar's hands and shoved it toward me. "Go have fun." Without another word, he made his way toward another group of Sense Guards.

"Let's go."

Turney hadn't been exaggerating.Cheering people lined the street, hands held outstretched toward the creeping black vehicle. The trudge forward had made our procession painfully slow for the past few blocks. "Where exactly are we going?"

"To Taliak Square."

No sooner than Thakkar said it, a large space opened up above and in front of us. Where buildings before had reached for the clouds and squeezed out so much light, there now was open air.

Colorful but tattered ribbons hung from lines that crisscrossed overhead, accented every six or so feet with a pendant of light. The lights, though off, still let off bursts of refracted light as they gently swung in the morning sun. It was beautiful.

My feet hit the giant cobblestone circle. It was so beautiful. There were people everywhere. Smiling and dancing while music held flitting notes in the air. Children jumped around without a care as they sang to whatever familiar song that was playing. I thought of Coranta. This. This cheerful celebration of life. This is what had been kept from them all this time. These people, despite the war and despite the death that loomed around them. They danced. They sang. They lived. A dark coil of smoke made my throat tight as I thought again of how everyone back home had been forced to live. What they had been engineered to be fine living without. I could only hope they could dance now. Did music ring out like it did here? Would Nira be able to sing? Would Josie be able to find love? Would Rhett twirl someone around while the tempo sped? My heart sputtered at the thought.

A warm hand rested on my shoulder. Thakkar leaned down. "We better move before they close in on us." In my awe ridden state, I hadn't realized that a decent size group had begun to push in toward our vehicle.

"Lead the way." I held on to his Pro-Pack as he pulled me through the now encompassing crowd.

Hands reached out to touch us as we surged forward. It was too much for the senses. A wave a nausea rolled through me as I struggled to block out the many emotions bombarding me.

"Thakkar, how much farther?" Heartbeats pounded, a series of bubbling drums wrapped at the space behind my eyes, along with a faint prick of electric yellow haze.

Before I had the chance to look around, the light from above us shifted to a much more muted amber tone.

The swell of the voices was still at its peak, but came from behind us instead of assaulting from all sides. My fingers ached, blood rushing back into them as I uncoiled them from the death grip I had on Thakkar's pack.

"I know it can be a little overwhelming. I passed out on my first Good Will mission. One step out on the cobblestone, and boom! Hit the ground." He gave me a reassuring pat on the back, "So you're doing great. And, to top that off, I won the bet."

"What bet?" I said as small voices excitingly chattered in the space. Thakkar's large stature was blocking.

"Some of the other Guards bet you wouldn't make it two feet before you hit the pavement. Which, I will say, is actually very optimistic of them. Most of the time, it's just too much on the senses all at once. It takes time to become adjusted to it. Especially since you have all five. It was a toss up whether that would make it better or worse for you." He shrugged his shoulders.

"That's so nice of you to warn me."

"That would have been unethical. Would've skewed the outcome of the bet." He patted my shoulder, "and besides, I kinda thought you would mute them all like you did at the docks."

My stomach turned at his words. It would be unethical to mess with his bet, but not to mess with the minds of hundreds of humans without their consent. The warm familiarity I had started to feel around him quickly dissipated, reminding me, yet again, that I had no family here. No one could be trusted.

Two large hands appeared on Thakkar's shoulders before moving him to the side with ease. "Siana, I am so happy to finally meet you!" There was such a light to the eyes of the large man that stood in front of me where my partner had just been. "I thought I would have seen you much sooner, but I suppose with such a Gift, the Director had some very important work for you first."

The mans accent was smooth and unlike anything I had ever heard. It had a melodic lilt to it that made the tension that had been building in my nerves immediately relax. His hands reached out to me with all the welcoming looks and pull of a worn leather book. His clothing was a fascinating swirl of bright shapes and pictures, a burst of color that told a story of which I had never seen or heard. I opened up just a crack, unable to resist tugging at his senses. I found myself enamored by the warm pink glow that emanated from him. The air in the shop we had entered was full of a smoky sweet smell unlike anything I had ever experienced before.

He gave a knowing smile and nod. "You are more than welcome to open your Gifts to anyone who passes this threshold. We have nothing to hide from the Guard here. We welcome you to this, our place of hope and learning."

Up until then, my view had been blocked, but as if to emphasize his point, he and Thakkar parted, revealing a warm and welcoming space. Low ceilings seemed to hold rows upon rows of shelves upright. Each of the dark wooden cases lined with books of all sizes and colors. Brightly woven carpets covered the floor and made a welcoming path forward into the maze of tomes. More strings with ribbons and lights, like those that hung around the square, framed the space. The familiar scent of paper, cloth, and leather replaced the smoky sweet smell from before. But here, the musty smell of mold and vinegar was completely absent.

This place was loved by many, made all the more apparent by the stack of broken and torn books stacked on a nearby counter. My body loosened as I leaned forward to run my hands down one cover, its pages slightly warped and stained. I lifted it to my nose. Someone had enjoyed their morning tea while losing themselves in these pages. A smile crept up my cheeks and filled my heart. I pulled it back and hoped no one had noticed.

"We were just about to have our story time with some of the children. We would be honored if you would care to join us."

I nodded, knowing that if I spoke, I would betray the feelings that were swirling in my chest.

The man with the lilting voice made his way to a large puffy chair. Tufts of fabric had been patched around it, the frays of what was underneath spread out like feathers. He didn't reach for a book. Instead, he looked around the room with a knowing smile. An excitement spread through the faces before him. Whatever story he was about to tell, they knew it. He began.

"Once upon a time, there was a little boy who lived at the base of a mighty waterfall. On days when the boy had adventured and played, the waterfall would use its bubbly waters to soothe him to sleep. On nights when the boys' day had been full of sorrow or pain, the waterfall would tell him stories of ancient heroes and give him petals from the blooms that grew at his banks."

The murmurs that had pulsed through the room were gone as everyone, including myself, hung to his every word.

"The boy lived in peace for many years and thrived off of the care given by the waterfall. But, as time changes all things, so it changed the boy. '*Waterfall. What is beyond our forest?*' The boy asked.

'*The world of men*' He bubbled in reply.

'*People like me?*'

'*People, yes. But not like you,*' Waterfall said.

'*I will go to see this world of men.*'

Several children's voices joined in hushed wonder as the story went on.

'*Remember who you are, my friend, when you feel and see things that are strange to you? Take with you the petals shimmering blue. When you start to forget me, place them on your tongue and return.*'

Something familiar scratched at the corners of my mind. Was this a story I had read before? I didn't make a habit of reading children's books. I made my way through the shelves of books as the story continued on in the background.

'*Thank you, friend*' The boy plucked the petals from the blue flower and climbed the rock face, trekked through the forest and entered the world of men.

As the sun was high in the crystal blue sky, the waterfall could sense the boy making his was back down to his home. Before he went inside, the boy waded into the water.

'*Friend, I've seen the world of men.*'

'*And what must you think?*'

'*I met a boy who was young as I. He laughed at my clothes but his thoughts were coated in green. He asked about my blue petals and I told them that they were if I forgot my friend.*' He opened his hands and the tiny blue petals danced on the water's surface. '*I did not need them.*'

"It's a story every child here knows by heart. The story of Taliak." Thakkar's voice was full of warmth and reverence. I didn't reply and instead let the words pull me back into the story.

"*The water rushed about him, 'Thank you. Sleep now, and tomorrow when you return to the world of men, take these and always remember me.'* The waterfall pulled from its clear depths a bright yellow plant."

Another strange feeling swirled in my gut.

"The next morning the boy went again to the world of men. When the sun shifted the sky to into shades of leaves before they fall, the waterfall could sense the boy making his way back down to his home. Before he went inside, he sat down on the bank with his toes in the water."

'I've seen the world of men.'

'And what must you think?'

'I met a man who was older than me. His face grew red as he spoke of my manners, but his thoughts were coated in blue. He tried to teach me the proper way to speak, and I found myself forgetting my home, but I took this and remembered.' His head hung in his palm sat a small bit of the yellow plant.

"The water rolled up on the bank and around his feet. *'Thank you. Sleep now, and take this and always remember me.'* The waterfall rushed at its highest point and a single purple and green fruit bobbed gently out of the water at its base, where it floated to the bank and rested at the boy's feet. *'This is the fruit of the Taliak tree. Take this and always remember me.'*

An earth shattering boom thundered through the small library, bringing a wave of terror with it as the little lights that had moments before twinkled now quivered on and off.

Cries from the children pierced through the ringing that was circling my ears.

"We need to go."

Thakkar nodded in response. I could feel the air thicken as he sense shifted and all the people calmly made their way to a doorway away from the direction of the blast. His powers were rooted in sight and sound. Whatever he was sending them, it sent a chill up my spine to see the fear wash away from each face and be replaced with robotic compliance.

The square was deathly silent as we made our way to its center, the other Sense Guards already having done their work to clear the space. The calm was eery and cold.

"Why aren't we moving?" I didn't stop my feet to talk to the Guards still waiting in a circle at the center of the cobblestone path. "Hello!" I couldn't drive well enough to handle these streets on a normal day, but that wasn't going to stop me now.

"Our directions are to hold and keep the peace." Only one of them spoke, but they all stared daggers at me.

"You're soldiers! You fight to keep these people protected, not to lull them into a false sense of security." The rage that was flowing through me was hard to tamp down. My hands shook as I reminded myself to keep it together. Stay cold. "We won't be able to access any type of threat from here. We need to go to higher ground to see where the blast came from."

Thakkar said. "She's right. We need to know if we need to evacuate the square. You all stay here and continue the Shift. We will alert you if action is needed."

We took off toward the tallest building in sight, not stopping until we had made our way to the very top.

The roof was a cluttered mess of garden and seating. Whoever used the space could have taken pointers from Nira. The withering vines that wrapped around decaying boxes of dirt looked brittle from neglect.

A cloud of smoke bloomed off in the distance. The explosion, that seemed to have been so much closer, was coming from the docks. A large ship, much like the one I had arrived on, was billowing out smoke as it slowly teetered to one side and began a descent into the dark water.

A final burst of air exploded in a watery blast from the ship just as another explosion racked my ears. This one farther down the shoreline toward the South.

There had to be multiple groups. There was no way the first explosion could have been by the same one. Which meant they may still be there.

"Come on. We need to get to the docks." I grabbed at Thakkar's sleeve before making a bolt for the door.

"We don't investigate any heavy fire. It's the Director's rule."

"That was the rule before I got here." Our footsteps were thunderous as we descended the building and emerged back out on the square. The other Sense Guards were still using their powers to calm the citizens in the surrounding buildings. Each one looking at me with stunned amazement as I began to shove them toward the SUV. "Get in! Now!"

Their feet held firm to the cobblestone. I swallowed a large lump that lodged itself in the back of my throat. The smell of burning plastic cut through the air and made my nose sting. "We need to get to the docks. There might be still be rebels there to apprehend." And people that can still be saved. Nothing. The anger I needed so badly to conceal from these people was bubbling up.

The smell of smoke and ashes had begun to burn my eyes as my heart ramped up. Nira's face flashed in my mind. I was here for her. I was here for everyone back home. I needed to help the people here so that they could stay safe. The only way to guarantee that safety was to stop this war. And these prim little brats weren't going to stand in my way.

The breath that I dragged down deep into my belly held a fire of its own. I pooled every ounce of my power, knowing full well I was so close to burning off every last bit of what made me cold to these people. This had better be worth it. My eyes snapped open as I pushed out a Sense Shift to the other Guards. When I had controlled Ethan, I hadn't felt anything but a pure thrill at destroying him. This. This felt wrong. The moment the thought crossed my mind, a loud gasp rang out from them as a collective.

The cords had snapped. I needed to focus, and fast. I pictured Hawthorne and Ethan and Melissa. I let that rage guide me. Each of the Sense Guard fell back into silence as I forced them to climb into the vehicle.

I sped through the empty streets. Everyone must have gone inside to wait out whatever horrific thing was happening. As the SUV careened around another corner, the shouting from the back seats became a deafening chorus as my focus on the road broke each chord I had pulled.

"Our orders are to stay away from direct fire!" A hand clamped down on my shoulder. We can't risk any of the Sense Guard just because little miss robot here can't understand orders."

"What's your name?" I threw the question back at him.

"You want to throw us into danger and you didn't even care to learn any of our names?"

Thakkar, sitting in the front with me, turned and grabbed the hand still latched on to my shoulder. "Kahill. Sit down. We're going to be fine." He gave me a pointed stare. "Viteri must have different orders. You said it yourself. She doesn't work off of emotion like us."

My chest tightened as Thakkar kept his eyes trained on me until we slid sideways into the metal gates of the dock, blocking the opened part of the entry as we spilled out of the SUV.

The smoke still filled the air, though the source of the flames was now a waterlogged tomb on the seabed.

"The rebels may still be here, so keep your eyes open. Start reaching out with your senses. Pull whoever you can. If you find anyone, bring them to me alive." The orders came from my lips but the voice sounded nothing like my own. It was hardened and absolute.

"We don't just go around killing people." Kahill whispered, following closely behind as we weaved in and out of the many shipment containers. "It's not right. Not that you know anything about right and wrong. What you did to Ethan Rightley—"

There it was. The reason for all the whispers and sneers when I walked in a room. Why, the only person that would even speak to me was my partner. They were still under the impression that I murdered Coranta's Saint. Well, if me being a murderer helped me sell this act, then so be it.

My feet stopped firmly as everyone else moved forward. My fingers clawed into the black leather sleeve of Kahill's Guard jacket. "I had no problem snapping his neck because he got in my way. Nod, if you understand what I'm saying."

A jerk upward of his chin was his response. The rest of the group was huddled behind Thakkar at the opening of the shipyard. One woman nearest him, a dark-skinned woman with hair that circled her sharp but warm face, said, "I can sense someone's fear spiking." Her own breathing had become erratic as she grabbed at her heart. "Their chest is on fire. No. Not their chest, their lungs. They can't breathe."

"Who here can sight shift?" I struggled to keep the panic that coursed through me from coating my voice.

A hand went up of another member of the Guard, this one a tall and very slim man with light skin and dark blond hair. He reminded me too much of the Rightleys. He didn't wait to pull in what he needed.

He staggered back against the container as if he were retreating from an enemy. "Water is rushing in." He broke from the shift and stared out at the air bubbles still escaping from the still raging water. Each of us followed his terrified stare. "There are still people alive on the ship."

My feet moved faster than my thoughts as I charged toward the scraps of wood and concrete that used to make up the dock. I stared in horror. There would be no way of hiding what I felt. So many panicked heart beats reached out from beneath the water. Screams that only a few others could hear echoed in my ears as the rest of the Guard made it to my side.

"We have to get to them." Tears ran down my face as I forced my voice out in one strong breath. "How do we get to them?"

Thakkar's voice broke. "We can't. There's no way, and besides that, anyone who survived the blast is bound to be hurt beyond saving. We would die trying to bring back bodies." Though his words were the harsh truth, the pain he felt speaking them rolled down his body and sank into each of us standing at the edge of the water.

Everyone looked out in horror. Each Guard pulling at a chord that would soon snap and cease to exist. "We can still help them. Everyone needs to shift something to help them while they — we can't let them go scared. If we can't pull them out, then we can at least take their away the suffering."

They all nodded as hand was placed in hand. I took hold, pulling from them and using the very last of my power to send out the only thing that I could think of. Hope. My brain tingled as I thought of Josie, laughing over spilled soup in her tiny kitchen. I thought of Henry, boosting me over a broken window sill and catching me right before I fell. I thought of Rhett, arms out, the only bright light in the middle of a suffocating darkness. I thought about Nira, alive and holding me in the courthouse.

Hope tasted like honey as its warm amber glow flowed out from the Guard and wrapped itself around the end of each line until, one by one, they began to fade in time with the heartbeats that gave them life.

Where the Guard around me gave them a sense of peace, I gave them the final act of it. There wasn't an ounce of fear that coiled around the sunken vessel as I cut the life at the end of each thread. I was death and in this moment; they welcomed me.

The water stilled. As if it had been holding its breath, waiting to release the lives it had just consumed.

My legs shook beneath me before completely giving out. The others stared at me with looks ranging between wonder and confusion as a guttural sob tore from my chest.

"What's going on here?" The arrival of Cole Turney's vehicle had gone unnoticed by all of us as he and Robinson made their way toward our group. "You are all supposed to be at the Square helping the people."

"No one says a fucking word." Thakkar ground out the order between his clenched teeth as the two took several steps forward.

"Did it not occur to you that we already have a large portion of the Guard still healing on the med-floor?"

My legs wouldn't have lifted me if I tried. My eyes blurred as the exhaustion of the shift threatened to pull me under. Not here. Not in front of them.

"What was that?" Robinson's voice sounded like it was underwater as he approached. I hadn't realized I had said anything out loud. The surrounding air closed in along with the darkness. The warmth of several sets of legs pressed in against me. Were they blocking me from view? Shielding me from Robinson?

The warm voice of a woman came from my right. "I was saying that we weren't supposed to be here, sir. We heard about some of the dock workers that were struggling to get resources for their families. We were on the way to bring them these when the explosions happened, sir." I could feel her transfer her weight as she pulled the Pro-Pack off her back.

"You were here when that happened?" I assumed he was looking out at the water.

Kahill's voice chimed in. "Nearly here, sir."

"So, were you able to catch who did it?" Turney's usually cheerful voice held a note of caution in it.

"No, sir. We only arrived after the ship was already sinking. The second explosion went off just before we got here."

"Viteri with you?" My whole body clenched as I tried to make myself as small as possible. If they saw me in this state, they would know I had nothing left of what made me vital to them. Yes, I could still use all my senses to Shift for them, but my ability to control was gone. Completely. My bargaining chip to keep Coranta out of this war had been gambled away. The very last of it drained into the vast waters that now lay still in front of me. I couldn't risk them going back on their part of the deal because they no longer had cause to fear me. Unfortunately, my fate and the fate of everyone I loved was up to the people who hated me more than most. The Guard squeezed in tighter around me.

"No. She remained with the others in Taliak Square." Another voice of the Guard covered me. Silence took hold of the space as the pull of a shift went out.

"Alright, well, let's move. We need to get back to the mission center and assess. Turney and I will go straight there, all of you, go rendezvous with the others and meet us before the top of the hour." The surrounding bodies loosened.

A rush of shuffling and whispers came from all around me as my weight rested over shoulders. The group moved together through the same maze of containers before depositing me just out of sight of our vehicle.

"Wait here. As soon as they're gone, we'll circle back and get you." Thakkar rested his hand on my shoulder as I looked at the rest of the Guard, the pain of what had just happened seeming to rest only on my face.

"Why?"

The woman that had first felt the people on the boat looked at me, tears filling her eyes. "I'm Geniah." She gave a soft smile as she seemed to be reaching for the right words, but instead she closed her eyes and a warm glow seeped into my veins. Hope.

The feeling was still radiating through me as I watched the Guards SUV pull away from the gate and another dull black vehicle pulled out behind it.

The base of my skull itched as I focused on the second vehicle, trailing behind the Sense Guards. Something wasn't right.

Chapter Seven

HENRY

My fingers traced the embossed lettering of the book. Siana would love this one. The words printed across the front shone gold under the soft glow of the kitchen lights. The kettle had long since whistled and gone cold.

Her footsteps sounded outside the door just as I was emptying out the water to refill for the second time.

"How was it out there today? Did you find anything interesting?" She smiled as she made her way over to me, exhaustion clear on her face.

"Nothing to worry about. My eyes are killing me, though."

I crossed the wooden floor and met her halfway to the kitchen. Her arms wrapped around me and I gave an inward sigh as I returned her embrace, though no warmth came from it. She felt strange ever since we had come here. Never the less, I knew that I could help her. I wouldn't stop until she knew how important she was.

"Do you feel up to reading tonight? I found a book that I really think you'll like." I held the book up for her to read the title.

"Shores of Gold and Sorrowful Tides. I think I've read this one before."

She always said that. I smiled as I crossed back to the kitchen island. "Can you get the tea started again while I finish dinner?"

"That depends. What's for dinner?" Her movement slowed as she made her way over to me working at the stove. I pulled the jacket I wore in tighter. I hated how cold it was here. She peeked around me to watch the vegetable soup I was making boil on the iron stove. A smile curled around her face.

A tired but satisfying "mmmmm" escaped her lips.

"And there are rolls in the oven."

She did her best to give a tired skip to the kettle and place it on the burner next to the soup. After that, she moved to the cabinets to grab cups. My hand-me-down cup was a worn gray one from a set that had been left when I first moved in. The worn wooden cabinets had been full of items from the previous owner. The shiny green mug Siana always grabbed was her favorite, and I made sure it was always there for her.

There wasn't much for me to do now that we were here. That was fine with me. I could help Coranta by helping her. I had no desire to try to be a part of the force anymore.

The outside was painful and despite the time that had already passed; I was still learning how to handle it all.

I bent to take the rolls out of the oven and move them to the counter.

"Henry, your hands. You have to cover them." A crash sounded along with a shatter as I tossed the pan of rolls onto the counter. Siana took a rag hanging by the sink, dipped it in the cold water, and wrapped it around my hands. A sad expression coated her face as she stared down at them.

"You have to be more careful with yourself, Henry."

"I know. I'm sorry."

Her head tilted down further to look at the floor. My eyes followed. Her green mug lay shattered and sprawled out beneath us. A large chunk rested under her bare foot. Drops of blood had already made their way onto the surface as a tear streaked its way down her cheek.

"I can fix it. I can fix all of it." I bent down, picking up as many pieces as I could find. If I got them all, I could glue it back. She had given up much bigger things than a teacup, but I wanted to give it back to her, all the same. She deserved that.

"You can't fix it, Henry. It's already shattered."

She was so tired.

I scrambled to pick up each piece, placing it gently on the wet towel that she had used to wrap my hand. With my newest task safely tucked away on the counter, I turned to her. Her face pleaded to me as I pulled her into a hug. She didn't hesitate to wrap her arms around me and I breathed her in. "Would you like to go sit on the couch and read for a while?"

"Yes, please." Her words brushed against my ear as a coiled feeling spread through me. Her hand was icy in mine as we walked to the old brown couch and sat. The cushions were flat from years of use. I had never felt more at home as her body relaxed against mine. She was strong. She could make it through this.

She laced her fingers in mine, tilting her face up so that our eyes met. The last of the daylight that had been peeking through the windows had finally been extinguished as she leaned in closer.

Chapter Eight
SIANA

My feet left metallic echoes bouncing off the walls of the stairwell as I made my way, yet again, to the mission center. The exchange at the docks had only been a few days before, but it had left my thoughts pinging back and forth ever since. The other Guards had parted without another word. They had all been very effective at avoiding me. The only time I could catch them all would be during mission assignments. Maybe if everyone else still thought me a monster, it wouldn't be a surprise to feel me rooting around someone else's senses. Or maybe I just needed to work on Robinson. If they told him what happened, he would have to have some kind of shift in mood toward me. However, one wrong slip, and I could completely give myself away. To everyone. This was my greatest risk yet. If I was going to be stuck with them, I had to know that I could trust them and I wasn't sure of that yet. I wanted to help Hartlem end their fighting. I also knew that, if given the chance, they would rush back into the Continent for more supplies. That included the people I needed to protect.

They were a threat to the ones I loved because they had sensed everything. In giving those people a moment of peace, I may have condemned the ones I loved to a life of pain. I was going to have to come up with a plan, and fast. Each day that went by, more and more people would become aware of the fact that the serum had leached its way out of my blood and burned off. My eyes watered as my thoughts pulled back to Coranta and everyone I left behind. I was finally myself again, and I wished more than anything that I wasn't. Everything sat heavy in the pit of my stomach. Josie, Nira. My throat tightened — Henry. More tears threaten to fall as I picture Rhett fighting on the balcony in the courthouse, a silent promise to keep my sister safe. I asked too much of too many, and they did the same.

My steps were quick as I realized someone had attached a tether to me. Ignoring how much noise my body was making between the labored breathing and the slamming feet, I pushed myself to create as much of a distance between the pull and my emotions.

"Damn it, Siana." My breathy whispers were a curse. I couldn't allow the people here to know that I was slipping. I couldn't allow them to see that the thing that gave me the power to be useful to them was evaporating, leaving behind nothing but a fake soldier in their war. This wouldn't be the first meeting that I missed because of this, but if they caught me, it may very well be the last.

The door was in sight and my adrenaline was charging through my veins as fast as I my feet traveled toward it. Somehow, despite weeks of covering and training myself to block everything, I had created a dam. And it had just burst.

My hand shot out to the handle just before it swung wide, connecting with my head.

Noises bounced around my pounding head. My conscious mind swirled around in my throbbing skull as the sounds grew louder. My body ached as I rolled to my side, trying to stop the waves of nausea and bile from running through me.

"She's waking up." Thakkar's voice was soft in my ear. Notes of relief and worry mingled together, followed by the unmistakable air of calm about him. "Siana, how are you feeling? Are you going to be sick?" He rubbed small circles between my shoulders as he spoke. "Do you need a bucket? It's alright if you do."

A guttural moan was all that my body would allow.

"Where's a bucket?" His shuffling about the space might have been comical in another circumstance. My eyes still struggled to focus, creating a blur of harsh light that stung and made me cringe. Thakkar was back before I could roll to my other side. He gently placed the small metal bin in my arms and helped me wrap my body around it. I silently hoped I wouldn't need the bin.

"Thakkar, where am I?" My voice was shaky.

"You're on the recovery floor." He turned to make a hurried request with someone else in the room. A quick snicker of laughter was his response before he continued talking to me. "You have a nasty split on your head."

"From the stairwell door." The sharp memory of the door connecting with my head made it throb as if punctuating the thought.

"Yes."

My entire body was screaming at me as I forced myself to a sitting position. The shaking felt like it radiated from my bones as I slowly slid my legs off of the well-used cot. The warm room swirled in shades of cream, gray, and green.

A heavy warmth rested on my shoulders just as the waves of colors and nausea began to slow. The gray and cream medical beds came into focus as the green walls of the room stopped spinning. Another trickle of warmth smoothed my nerves as a beautiful voice hummed in my ear.

I took a cautious breath and exhaled slowly, letting each muscle in my neck and back relax. The melody lulling the tension away and wrapping me in a calm that shouldn't have been possible. I could feel the pull as Thakkar continued to pass the memory to me.

A loud clatter of metal on concrete cut off the soothing song. My hands flattened against my ears, followed by an immediate jolt of pain that seared its way down the side of my face. A yelp of pain coated my tongue as my stomach twisted. I was going to need the bin.

"Well, well, well. I guess it is human, after all." An unfamiliar voice pulled my attention. Damn it Thakkar. This fatherly act was surely going to get me into trouble. My eyes, blurry again, darted around for the unknown voice. The room, although obviously meant for medical treatment, was nothing like what I had seen at Coranta or RightCorp. It was warm and worn, but it was a medical space all the same. I breathed in slowly while the person in Sense Guard, black and red, stared, crossed armed and one leg kicked back against a large section of wooded cabinets. Next to his feet laid a trash can, tipped over on its side and contents spilling out. My stomach dropped and threatened to do the same as I realized this man wasn't one from the group that already knew about what I had lost. Hopefully, he would resign any senses to the pain I was in and not the emotions that I was not supposed to have.

Thakkar spoke as I tried to focus on the Guard's face. "You're no longer needed. Report to the mission center before you're reprimanded for missing a briefing."

Thakkar's fatherly tone was gone and the words of a soldier replaced them. The Sense Guard made no hesitation to leave. "Don't worry about him. Jasper's still embarrassed about what you did to him when you first got here."

I had forgotten about that version of the docks. The one where I had arrived, cold and calculated. The memory of electricity, his jarring pain and clenched teeth. Jasper had every reason and right to hate me. Repulsion at what I could do when I first arrived mixed as recent memories of that place rolled through me. I fumbled to the floor to retrieve the bin. This time, I used it while Thakkar knelt to pat my back.

A female voice chimed in from behind me, followed by the familiar clinking of glass and metal. "I'm going to get these samples over to Hartlem Tower. Make sure she eats something. I'm going to tell Robinson that she needs to have a simple assignment for the day. She really shouldn't push it."

"Thank you, Dr. Madeline." A warm and familiar tone coated his words as a warmth filled the room.

"It's what I do." A door opened. "Oh and Akshatt, don't go hitting her with any more doors, please. The Director will be happy with the samples, but I don't think he will take too kindly to beating up his favorite Sense Guard." The door closed.

My head ached as I pulled it up to stare at my partner's face. A look of embarrassment and regret plastered his strong features. "I'm so so—"

"You hit me with the door."

"I did."

"And knocked me out."

"Also, yes."

"And now you're flirting with the doctor while I'm sitting here in pain."

"I'm not perfect." He moved to check the gauze bandage taped to my face.

"Obviously." His hands were warm and a soft chuckle came from his belly as he helped me up, patting me on the shoulder when I didn't immediately throw up again.

The hammering in my skull continued as Thakkar began to hum, the beautiful tune sounding slightly off key but still comforting in his warm tone. "The voice from before. Who was that?"

A smile radiated through him as he answered, "My daughter."

"Thank you."

He nodded and went on, "Looks like you're feeling better. And maybe you'll end up having a really great scar to go with that Super Sense Guard thing." He smiled as I reached for the spot on my face. It stung when I touched it. The bend in my arm felt stiff as I stretched it out. Another bit of gauze was wrapped around my skin there.

"Did I hit my arm too?" There was no pain as I pulled at the bandage there. A small cotton swab revealed a patch of red. "They took my blood?"

"It's standard any time someone comes in."

My eyes lingered on the small red spot.

"You hit her with a door?" Robinson's tone was a straight line and betraying no emotion. Although his senses let off the taste of something savory and sweet that I had never tasted before. Whatever he was feeling, it was something he enjoyed.

"Robinson, I would refrain from taking too much joy in this. I am still more than capable despite my injuries." I pushed the memory of a snaking tendril of smoke out to fill his nostrils.

"Siana." Thakkar whispered beside me, not a warning but urgent in its tone.

With a pop of my jaw, I cut off the shift. The mission room had already cleared out while I was getting patched up. We had just run into everyone leaving in a large mass, off to whatever assignment they had for the day. A few nods in my direction was all I got before they disappeared in all directions. Another day of waiting to see if they would give up my secret. "Fine. Where are we fighting today?"

Thakkar was quick to respond. "Dr. Madeline said she needs to go slow today. Take it easy."

"If the Dr thinks you need to take it easy, then you would be best utilized in the Outer City Market. The long walk and fresh air could be good for your recovery, although you seem to be making your way back to health very quickly." He gave a tight-lipped curl to the side of his mouth. "There's nothing there. The rebels steer clear of the markets. Our presence there is more of a show of strength than anything. A reminder to the people that we are there to protect them."

We left immediately after, grabbing whatever supplied Thakkar thought we might need, as well as my number one fan, Jasper. Jasper's hatred for me seeming to wash from his face the second the Outer City Market was mentioned. He chatted excitedly with my partner as we began our trek through the city on foot.

The dirty streets that formed the maze between Hartlem Tower and the outer city were treacherous.

Though Hartlem claimed the land, it was clear that it served a little purpose for them. Every thing was fire scorched and smelled of char long since extinguished and left to crumble. We had already stopped for several breaks before the large Tower was no longer looming in the distance. The haunted landscape of a broken city had been void of life for the entire trip. But the buildings here, though wasting away in different stages of disrepair, held heartbeats.

I pulled at a thread. A vision of myself walking through the streets below the shadow of a tall building flashed in my mind before the owner of the site retreated back into darkness. Anticipation laced my vision with an electric yellow glow as both my footsteps and the heartbeats became faster. Whoever was in the buildings, they were about to make a move.

"Do you feel that?" Thakkar moved his hand to his hip, where several dark metal objects hung from his utility belt. Jasper reached for the holster at his side.

I turned my focus from Thakkar to the anxious-looking Jasper, "What's that going to do?" My line of sight pointing to his weapon. The air began to fill with a thick uneasiness that was making the breath in my lungs burn.

"Sometimes there are too many of them, even for the sense guard. This ensures maximum eradication." A deep repulsion bubbled up through my chest as I stared at him. They were the enemies of Hartlem, but they were still human. I thought back to the Dires in Coranta. Following orders. Doing whatever the Rightleys told them because it was all they knew. Maybe it was the same here. Maybe we just needed to find whoever was pulling the strings. The image of Robinson shooting two rebels sends a wave of disgust through me again. If they were the enemies, why did all of this feel so complicated? No, not complicated. Wrong.

A sharp pain sliced through my forehead as I shook off the thought and repeated a new mantra in my head. Build the wall. Stop the war. Save the people you love. Build the wall. Stop the war. Save the people you love. A yellow haze surrounded my vision as my mind quieted. The still bodies of the rebels flashed in my mind again. Someone loved them too.

I narrowed my eyes at Jasper. "And how many of them can you eradicate with that?"

He patted the metal with a soft smile on his face. "I can usually subdue up to four or five with a sense shift and another ten with my weapon." His demeanor changed as he spoke. A cold mask rested over what had seemed like such a youthful face.

Thakkar's eyes were a sea of sadness as he looked over at the young man standing before him, but he remained silent. For all his talk about protecting Hartlem and Coranta, I couldn't help but wonder if he still felt compassion or even remorse for the rebels he 'eradicated'.

My eyes fixed back on the young guard as I pushed the gun he was now sweeping the buildings with down to his side. "Well, you can put that thing away. There are twenty-three of them."

"How could you possibly…"

"I counted the heartbeats."

"What do we do then, boss?" He kept the weapon down but didn't holster it. "Do I get to see that power of yours in action again?" He seemed almost giddy at the thought of seeing me slaughter so many.

The deep breath flowing down into my chest was cooling as I pulled at a memory. Now that the serum was finally gone, I found myself looking forward to sending out a sense shift that I knew wouldn't end in death.

Well, at least if Jasper stayed in check, it wouldn't. My eyes fluttered as I sent out the full sense shift.

Nira picked mint leaves for me to chew on while she worked in her backyard garden. The soft blanket, newly washed, smelling of lemon and soap, draped around my shoulders as I sat on the dark earth. The feel of her fingers brushing through my hair and placing small blooms as she braided it.

The yellow slowly faded and flowed into a pale turquoise. "Let's keep moving." My body swayed as the shift took a toll on me as I held it in place.

"I thought this was easy for you. Shouldn't you be able to do a little shift without falling apart?" Jasper gave a look wrapped in dark realization. "You know Robinson—"

"In case you forgot, she experienced some head trauma this morning. The Doc said she needed to take it easy." Thakkar took my elbow to help keep me steady as he stared Jasper down. "Would you like to try a full sense shift? Oh, that's right, none of us can. She's the only one with that kind of power. So, why don't you pull your weight and do a sweep ahead? Clear the way to the market. We'll meet you there."

I held on to the shift as Thakkar sent Jasper on. It was a slow trek through the dilapidated part of the city. The heartbeats kept pace as they followed, each now a gentle but steady pace as a calmness descended and the last bit of towering buildings gave way to open sky.

"We need to talk about what happened at the docks." My voice was quiet as I juggled holding the shift and a conversation.

"I've spoken with the others. You don't need to worry. I trust them."

"And you? Can I trust you?" I paused, not wanting to take another step until he answered.

"What you did for them? It was unimaginably selfless. To take a life is one of the worst things anyone could do in this world. But that's not what you did. You took their deaths for them. You helped guide them and at great expense to yourself." He looked down at me, a deep pride shining through his eyes. "The other Guards and I that were there... I can't explain how what you did pulled at us." He looked around as if searching for listening ears. "We've already decided. We may work for Hartlem, but from now on, we follow you. You're going to be the one that stops the rebels and keeps everyone safe. We follow your orders from here on out."

I dropped the shift I had been holding and reached out to him with my senses. There was that amber glow again. Warm and bright like honey.

We made it to our destination completely unscathed. Physically, at least.

The bustle of the OuterCity was jarring compared to the hollowness that encompassed the way behind us. The twenty-three heartbeats mingled with the vendors and people that inhabited the OuterCity. Both Guards faces glowed at my side as we met back up at the entrance. The excitement that coursed through both of them was intriguing.

I spoke to Jasper from the corner of my mouth. "Are these not the enemies of Hartlem?"

His brow furrowed as he turned to me. "These people are not our enemies. Yes, some of them have been brainwashed into thinking that we are here to hurt them, but most of the people here are bright and hopeful. They appreciate what is being done for them. They respect the Sense Guard. You can feel it."

As we walked past vendors of men, women, and children, I could sense what he had meant. At first, a whiff of bitterness mixed with a sharp, salty hatred lingered on the air before something else overpowered it. An almost floral like smell accompanied a purple glow that filtered its way through the marketplace. A rhythm less tune weaved its song around the market, but the players were completely out of sight. My eyes wandered around as several nervous looking merchants glanced our way. Each stall boasting different wares from fruit to items of clothing. But at this moment, several seemed to have switched to hawking bottles of what seemed to be perfume, spraying a healthy dose into the air as we passed.

"The market is my favorite place in all of Hartlem. It reminds me of home." A wide smile covered Thakkar's face as a familiar taste of cotton candy bounced around my mouth. A pleasant memory of Henry swirled in my head.

Clever. Very clever.

"Would you like to buy some tea leaves?" A small voice belonged to a young boy standing at my elbow. "My family grows the best herbs and spices in all the OuterCity." He held out several sachets of tea for me to inspect. The brittle leaves scratched against the palm of my hand as I brought the bag to my nose and inhaled the scent. Something about the mixture of smells combined with the music still swirling around the market seemed to weave webs into my mind. Colors played around my vision, casting a radiant glow and made everything more saturated. I looked at Thakkar, who was walking toward another stall full of fish and other creatures from the sea.

An alarm went off in my head as someone tried to pull me into a sense shift. One glance at Thakkar and I could tell he was already under. What was meant to be a calm day of recovering had spun into a trap. Horror rippled through me as I watched Thakkar be escorted even farther away from me. No.

They would take him. He was on my side. He protected me. Believed in me. The cut on my head stung as I pushed a sense shift of my own out into the crowd of bodies. I may not be able to hurt them, but I could still scare them. Visions of what I had done spread out like tendrils of black smog. The crowd that had been bustling around me was now staring in wide-eyed fear as some shuffled or barreled out of what I'm sure they thought would be the distance of my power. Even with my normal powers, they wouldn't be able to get away fast enough if I chose to make a spectacle of them. My stomach rebelled at the thought of hurting anyone again, but these were the rebels and I had to end this war. My new partner was still entranced several stalls away as a group of bodies surged forward. Twenty-four, to be exact. The sickly taste of fear and repulsion closed in on me, accompanied by the familiar yellow fog from before. But this time, there was one more — One heartbeat that didn't race like the others.

A woman walked forward from the swirl of colors that the tea and mist had left suffocating my vision. Her skin seemed to swirl like the light brown sand of the seabed and her long shadowy hair flowed like familiar dark waves. The effect of the sprayed mist and tea was strong and my body struggled to fight the pull of a shift as she made the last few steps to meet me.

"We don't harm the sense guard here in the market. There's no need for you to fight us." Her words came out in a beautiful rhythm, which may very well have just been whatever drugs they had pumped into the air.

"Really? Because it really seems like you are trying pretty hard to force a shift right now."

"True." She nodded her head toward me, but the pull I was feeling didn't go away. "Why didn't you kill the people that you felt on the way here?" She stared at me through the fog that continued to cloud my vision.

The pull was becoming even stronger as I struggled to stay above water.

"It was faster that way." Nausea bubbled in my chest as I fought to focus. Trying to stare at a fixed point wasn't helping very much though, since even the rocks at my feet blurred into a mess of light and dark gray swirls. I gulped down the knot that was forming in the back of my throat. "You're making me regret that decision right now."

"I'm sorry you feel that way. We only want to help the people."

Rage built in me, her words bringing back the memory of the docks again. The shift I wanted to send out seemed trapped inside of me. A storm inside a fragile glass bottle. "You're trying to destroy everyone. What you did to those people on that ship. If you knew what they felt as the water rushed in on them—", my speech tapered off as I released a slow breath, trying to steady the dizziness of whatever she was doing. I had to get away from whatever mist they were pumping into the air if I had a chance of leaving here. A panicked glance around gave me no clear path to safety.

"We have no desire to destroy anyone. But we will defend ourselves from those who want our, what was it your friend said? Eradication." Her eyes shifted to the side, the daggers she was staring focused on Jasper. She reached out a hand to close the distance between us. My body gave a defensive jump. How had she gotten so close? My head swirled again at the quick movement and my knees buckled under me. She caught my hands before I could fall. My eyes narrowed on hers. There was something so familiar about her. Even with the world around me blurring together in a swath of brightly colored waves, I could sense it. She didn't let go of my hands as she spoke. "The people that Hartlem calls its enemies, these rebels, are fighting to live."

"Last I checked, you were the ones ruining the peace. You want to live, stop killing."

"We don't choose to live like the Director wants us to, but how we choose. Hartlem sees that freedom as a threat."

"Then you choose this violence. You choose to put all the people of Hartlem in danger."

Her mouth pulled up in a snarl as she leaned in further. "All Hartlem does is spread lies and kill. Not us."

I could sense the anger rolling off of her in deep red swirls. She really believed what she said was true. "Why trust me then? Why even tell me any of this?"

"I saw what you did at the docks. Both times. I have no desire to make an enemy of you and I won't lie to you. You have a greater hold on the Gift than any of us, including myself." She dropped my hands and took a step back. Something about the way she moved was so familiar, there was a graceful flow to it. The others that had been waiting on the edge of our conversation were pulled in with her. "Your gift is stronger than any we have seen. We would like to make a kind of truce with you- with the Guard, if you can sway them." She looked around, "And from what we hear, you already have sway over some of them. We don't want to be Hartlem's distraction in its propaganda machine and I think you could be the one that helps us do that." She signaled to someone out of my visual.

The surrounding vendors were still spraying their bottles at intervals. The contents building in the air and creating another wave of swirls. "It's going to be difficult to agree to anything when you keep—" A final thought that this felt all too familiar passed through my mind as darkness covered me again.

More beautiful and bright colors circled my vision as I pulled my blurry eyes open. My head, thankfully, was no longer spinning. The chair they had slumped me in was large, wood carved and tufted with a soft padding of fabric. My hands were free to trace along the intricately carved red stained wood. "I'm fine."

I took in a slow breath as the room slowly stopped spinning. "Go slow, stay calm, get yourself out." Even whispering, my voice was loud in my ears. A slow, uneven pounding in my chest played in my ears along with the sounds of the market outside the room. After looking around for a moment, I realized that the colors I had thought were a reaction to the spray were actually beautifully woven tapestries and lengths of fabric that someone had hung to create walls.

"You should be feeling much better by now." My mind snapped back at the sound of the female voice just as she tossed a leather pouch toward me. It bounced off of my arm and landed with a slosh in my lap. "I'm Adilah." She had made her was through the fabric doorway in complete silence.

"Where's Thakkar?"

She gave a warm smile. "He's fine. He and your other friend are having a great time shopping in the market. They don't even know you're gone." She rested her hands in front of her and continued, "I hope you understand why we are doing everything this way. I know you have a good heart. I feel like you can be trusted. However, we do have to be careful."

They did not tie my hands down. Or my feet. Either she really believed I wouldn't try anything or she was waiting for me to. I took a steady breath, placing my hands over my legs. My nails picked at the hem along the side of the rough black fabric. "And how, exactly, do you know you can trust me?" A tremor was building in my right leg as my nerves were set on edge.

Her dark hair fell in soft waves around her, complementing the bright blues and greens of her flowing shirt. Her eyes, though piercing, seemed to hold a spark of kindness in them as she kept them trained on me while she spoke. She nodded her head toward the pouch still resting in my lap. "You should really drink that. It will help get rid of any lingering effects of the mist."

The leather pouch squished in my hands. There was no way I was about to drink something from the enemy. And I was pretty certain that was exactly who I was facing. Although my aim hadn't been as good as hers, she caught the pouch with ease before sitting it down on a table and taking a chair opposite me. "Suit yourself. However, I don't envy the headache you're going to have in a few hours."

"What am I doing here? What could you possibly want with a Sense Guard?"

"You're not a Sense Guard. That was made evident by your work at the docks."

My every vertebra was stacked in a straight line. "You were there." Not a question. An accusation and a dangerous one at that. If she knew what happened that day, then she must be one of the rebels responsible for the lives taken there. I was sitting across from a murderer.

She went on. "You could have left those people to suffer on that ship. To show them a genuine kindness that so many would deem a waste of your Gift, it was inspiring. That takes a compassion that most of the Guard no longer possess.."

"That's a lot of kind words from the person that put those people there to begin with." My body felt heavy as I leaned forward, my mind taking a mental inventory of every terrified heartbeat that had been snuffed out in those deadly waters as I readied myself to charge at her.

"Will your Director be so kind when he finds out what you gave up for a handful of people that were about to die, anyway?"

I lunged. My hands collided with her neck, nails digging in as I tightened my death grip. A muddle of red and green flames whipped and intertwined at the edges of my vision, throat tightened as the taste of iron and char dripped down the back of my tongue. Rage consumed me as I watched her struggle for breath.

My stomach dropped as my body was hoisted back, thick arms wrapping around my body, pinning me to the person behind me. My foot caught the side of Adilah's head as I kicked my legs out wildly. A fiery hatred surged through my veins as I threw my head backwards, letting out a visceral yell when my head connected with the person's teeth. A sharp ache pulsed through my ankle as I fell to the floor. Heavy hands shoved my shoulders down while a knee landed solidly on the middle of my back, pushing the air in my lunges out in burning streams as I screamed, "Why? Tell me why?"

Adilah moved at the edge of my vision, a deep rattling cough punctuating her pained movements. She didn't answer me. Instead, she took small pained sips from the pouch she had offered me just moments before.

She let out a sad laugh before another round of painful coughs racked her body.

A deep, worried voice came from above me as the knee of its owner dug deeper into my back. "What do you want me to do with her?"

Adilah cleared her throat. "She's fine. I can't blame her for not knowing."

"Not knowing what? That you and your people are trying to destroy Hartlem? That you enjoy killing innocent people? Or that you're a fucking psycho bitch!" Another pained cry escaped me as the man holding me down pulled back on my arms and forced me into a kneeling position in front of her.

Red veins webbed the whites of her eyes as she shot the man a stern look. "Do not hurt her again." The arms holding me back loosened only slightly as she knelt just a few feet from me.

The pull at my senses was a familiar feeling now. Her eyes closed just before another round of coughs rolled from her. The sound of it echoing down through the shift. A full sense shift.

How was it possible that a rebel had the same power that had been engineered in me?

Everything faded away as the memory settled in my mind. My heart thudded uncomfortably as I looked out, seeing myself and the Sense Guard standing at the edge of the water.

My eyes moved to each person in turn. The Sense Guard were ruthless soldiers, set on our destruction. Tears rolled down my cheeks as a realization of what they were doing washed over me. A wave of gratefulness rose up through my chest and a small sob caught on the breath that I let out. My ear twitched at the sound of crunching gravel. Someone was approaching from the left.

"What do we do about them?" The worried voice was unmistakably Cole Turney.

My feet moved silently as I backed away, a small thud bouncing off the metal container I squeezed my body against. The cold of the metal seeped through the worn brown material of my jacket. I willed my body to be as small as possible as I committed my shivering body to the shadows just in time to see both Turney and General Robinson make their way to the place where I had just stood. Steady beads of cold sweat trailed down my face as I watched them watching the Sense Guard.

"I don't know. They just showed up not too long ago and went straight to the ship."

"What are they doing? Is Viteri with them?" Turney started forward before Robinson gripped the arm of his gray tailored suit jacket and pulled him back sharply.

"She is. She was leading the charge in. Whatever they're doing, let's let it play out." He stepped back toward the space they had came from. "besides, it will look better if we come from the gate. We don't need to arise their suspicion as to how we got here so fast."

Their footsteps crunched on the path between containers. The last of their words almost lost in the sound, "Will she stay in line knowing that we just — the rebels just blew up the supplies meant for Coranta's barrier?"

"If she truly believed we could build a wall of that magnitude in the span of a few months, she'll believe anything. We'll tell her it's just a small setback. Besides," A cruel happiness hung on Robinson's voice, "She seems to be caring an awful lot about what is happening around her. We can use that to get the Director what he really wants."

Silence followed as my body escaped from the shadows and stared out at the Guard.

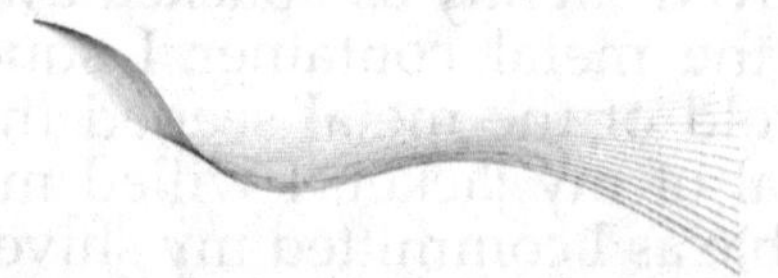

Hands no longer held me down as I settled back into my body. "They set off that explosion." The words felt heavy enough to hit the floor as they fell from my mouth. "Why? Why would they hurt their own people like that?"

"They are trying to hit us where we live. They don't care if they're wrong. In fact, when they are, they use it to drum up more fear and hatred by blaming it on us."

"The second explosion. Was that them too?" I held my breath, not wanting but needing to know how many others had been sacrificed.

She nodded. "A warehouse that we once used long before the Director started to use the Good Will trips to unwittingly recruit people." I furrowed my brows in question and she continued. "The Pro-Packs of bribes. They're riddled with hidden sensors and devices made to listen in and track us." She smiled. "We've been using it against them. Setting them up in places far away from us and innocent people." Her face turned sullen as she looked me straight in the eyes. "After the docks, it's not a tactic we will use lightly again. And it made it very clear to us that we needed to change strategies. We don't take death lightly and we don't kill anyone without reason."

"What do you want from me?" The question seemed simple, but so much hung in the void between its asking and the answer.

"The Director has been having your friends round up the city's children to see if they have the Gift. You have been leaving them behind. Bring them to us instead."

My mind was still reeling after what Adilah had showed me. I knew the rebels weren't the enemies that we had been made to believe they were, but that didn't mean they had the right to hurt children. "No. They aren't pawns. They don't deserve to be taken to the Grey Forest or Hartlem Tower. If you use children to fight your battles than you are no better than—"

"This is not a battle we should have ever had to fight!" The anger seeping into her voice was predatory. "We do not involve the children of this community in anything! Do you think, if we actually had a way to send anyone home, that we would stay here?"

"Hartlem isn't your home?" I stared at the tapestries that made up the tent walls again.

Woven stories of beautiful bright blooms wrapping their way around ancient mossy green tree trunks. Cerulean blues interweaving in and out with a cloud of white foam at the base of a flowing waterfall. Thin trees with plush tops that hung low from the weight of the fruit.

"I've lived here my whole life, but no. Hartlem is not my home. Taliak is my home. The Grey Forest is the name given it by Hartlem when they forced everyone out."

"Why?"

"Because they can't make money off of something that already belongs to someone else. The Gifts come from Taliak, but they are fading with each generation." She stood and brushed her hand over the images, the fabric seeming to flow at her touch. "The waterfall and the flowers and plants — they're like none other anywhere on any continent. Hartlem and RightCorp stole our home for this, and we've been fighting for over a century to get it back." A deep sadness shone from Adilah's eyes.

"Your powers are pretty strong, though. How is that if you've lived here your whole life?" I wanted to trust her, but a seed of doubt was buried deep in my brain. Something about her was so familiar I just couldn't put my finger on it, which meant I couldn't trust it.

She went on, "Before RightCorp moved their experiments to Recreor Island, before the fighting really started amping up, they did them here in the city. My mother was part of them."

"Your mother worked for RightCorp?"

"No."

My heart collapsed as I took in the meaning of that single word.

"My father lived on the Continent, but he would come once a year with others." She offered me her hand, and I took it. She pulled me up and led me to the opening of the tent as she continued. After they shut the lab here down, I saw him for the last time. I hadn't shown any progress, so they had both me and my mother thrown out."

My eyes watered as the bright daylight beat down on us out in the open market. We walked between stalls, close enough for anyone to hear our conversation, but she didn't seem to mind. "The last time I saw him, I had finally been activated. No better trigger than war. I hid while sending him a memory—what you would call a Sense Shift — but he didn't care. The horrors that I had seen, the things that they did to us, he didn't care. He just kept walking."

I didn't say a word as we walked in and out of the market stalls and she told me everything. She introduced me to vendor after vendor, each with their own story and heartache. She spoke to me as if I were a trusted equal instead of someone who had just tried to kill her. My head throbbed as we made it back to the entrance of the market. My temples held a warm sting to them where my fingers had rubbed at the skin there. A knowing look pulled at her face as she spoke to the nearest vendor, who disappeared into a tent for only a moment before returning with a cup of swirling blue liquid. Adilah gave her a warm smile before taking the cup.

"Last time I'm gonna offer." She held it out to me.

This time I took it and drank. The cold liquid tasted like nothing I had ever tried. The floral drink felt light on my tongue and seemed to disappear before it hit my empty stomach, taking the pain in my headache with it. The pain from my run in with the door still stung though.

"How do you know I won't just go straight to the Director and tell him everything? This puts a lot of weight on my shoulders. Not to mention, what will happen if I'm found out?"

She exhaled a puff of breath. "If you allow me to, I would like to give you my memories. It's similar to a Sense Shift, but it takes a lot. And you have to allow it. It won't work if you aren't open to it."

I could feel my eyes go wide for only a split second before answering. "Alright."

She gave a gentle smile as she nodded and placed her hand over my heart. What felt like a lightning bolt flew through my chest to my head as if it were racing through the palms of her hands. This wasn't like the electricity I had felt in Hartlem's lab, or what kept the barrier up. Her Gift was spectacular. In a matter of seconds, I had seen everything she had. Flashes of her father and the RightCorp lab. Explosions shaking buildings apart. Fighting like nothing I could have imagined in any of the books I had read. It was all burned into my conscious as if they were my own memories. Strangely enough, one of them already was. At least, it was one that someone else had already shown me before. I focused on that memory. A flash of pure chaos split my vision. I couldn't raise my voice above a whisper even if I had wanted to. My throat was raw with tears that weren't mine.

I was looking at the owner of that memory that had been shown to me in the library at Rightly Manor. "Who are you? I know you." She had seemed so familiar to me. A familiarity that had scratched at the edge of my mind.

"Yes, I know you." My footsteps were heavy as I closed the distance between us. Genuine confusion was clear on her face.

"You may not have been able to get through to your father, but you certainly made an impression on someone very close to him." It all made sense now. The visits to Hartlem.

Her having such a powerful gift. "Does he know that you are here?" The men and women whose heartbeats I had tracked earlier were moving in toward us. Whatever connection she had with them was being pulled on as my heart raced and everything clicked.

"Does who know I'm here?"

"Rhett. Does he know that he has a sister in Hartlem?"

Chapter Ten

RHETT

The gates to Coranta were closed. The Dires that had been left within the city walls were hundreds less than before what they were calling the Awakening. Too many of them woke to bodies of the people who couldn't handle the transition or withered away while they waited to wake up. I would forever be haunted by the fact that we didn't save them all.

When the ones that were left were in a place to talk, we tried to explain what had happened. They didn't take it well. Before we could do anything to really help, they had chased us out of the city. Sheridan had several officers on the inside that would relay news about what was happening and it wasn't good.

They had gone from confusion to hatred as they vilified Nira, Myself, and Siana. They deemed us all traitors to the Rightleys, refusing to believe the Rightleys had put them all in danger.

Whoever was acting as their leader was adamant about their hatred for us. We had tried to gather intelligence on them, but none of our people on the inside had come back with any solid information. That's if they came back at all.

The once busy streets of Coranta were bare. Hardly any movement was found on the dark streets, but coming into the city during the day would have been a suicide mission. Everyone here knew that I was a sense shifter, and because of my work with the Rightleys before the Awakening, most knew my face.

The smell of charred stone and wood hung in the air as I walked along another empty street. My body hugged the concrete building as I stared down at the source of the smell. A building across the street still had glowing embers at what was left of its base. The fact that they hadn't burned the entire city down was a miracle, but it was still possible.

My heart pounded as I made my way further into the city, steering clear of any movement. The Rightley's mansion on the hill still seemed to be intact as I stared up at it from the edge of the burrows. Sheridan's insiders had told us that the remaining dires were taking up residence in the larger places like the med borough, storage facilities, courthouse and library. Even they steered clear of my target: RightCorp Labs. According to the last correspondence from Kindolf, they were still keeping most of the dires that had been experimented on there.

My feet ached as I skirted the last of the boroughs. A glass bottle crashed down on the ground in front of me as a small group of dires moved a small distance ahead on the dark street. My chest tightened as I rushed to cover behind a stack of boxes.

"How long do you think they'll wait before giving the order?" The men approaching hadn't seen me. I hunched down in my hiding place as they continued their drunken conversation.

"Not soon enough. If we know where they are, we should be moving before they have a chance to leave."

A third voice chimed in. This one sounded younger than the rest. "We don't know the extent of their powers. I'm pretty sure they're just being cautious."

"I heard that these Sense Shifters could peel the skin off of your body just by thinking about it."

"That's ridiculous." The short one said, but an obvious tremor feathered his voice.

"According to some of the papers they found before they locked down the lab, the Rightleys had been shipping sense shifters away for decades just to protect Coranta from them."

My blood was beginning to boil. How had these idiots gotten everything so wrong? After everything that we had done for them. Melissa and Siana had given up everything for them and now here they were, trashing their names and acting as if they were the monsters that put them here. My head told me to stay out of sight, but my anger didn't know how to stay down and shut up.

I focused on my time in RightCorp labs as I sent every bit of fear I had felt there down the line that was now connected me and these three assholes. The pull of the sense shift went tight as I felt their pulses begin to race. The three started to turn their heads this way and that, looking for something that wasn't there.

"Did you hear that?" The man in the faded red shirt didn't look to his companions for confirmation as his gaze surveyed his surroundings.

"What is it? What's out there?" The idiot in all black asked.

Their friend didn't dare to speak. He just stared around with wide eyes and looked very much like he was trying his hardest not to crumble in on himself. I remembered that feeling.

117

My eyes began to blur as the senses I was pulling from the memory reopened wounds that would never heal. It was worth it. I thought of Siana's father getting closer and closer as I was strapped to a chair; the light glaring off of the walls of the sterile white room. I thought of the terror I felt hearing my mother in the next room, pleading with my father to stop all the testing. I thought of Siana, on the other side of the glass, already sick and pale with what they had done to her. The injection they had given me burned as it entered my bloodstream.

The men in front of me could feel it, too. They began to scream as they tore at the fabric covering their arms and then their skin.

I severed the connection.

These weren't the people I was after. These were a couple of confused jackasses who didn't understand that they were being manipulated. Again.

I let the shift fall. The fear and confusion that rolled off of each of them was satisfying but still brought pangs of guilt to my gut. I wouldn't control people with fear and manipulate them like Ethan had done or like whoever was running Coranta was doing now. These were people that still needing saving, too. True, they weren't the children that had been forced to endure painful testing, but they were humans none the less. They deserved a free life.

The bottle was slick in my hand as I raised it up above my head, still remaining hidden in the shadows. I threw it, hoping that the men wouldn't see where it had come from. It soared through the air before shattering on the opposite side of the street. All three men took off running, not glancing back for a second at the monster they thought they were running from.

I wasn't sure how many hours had passed since I entered the city, but I wasn't sure if I was going to be able to find what I needed in the lab and get back out before light washed over Coranta.

My mind was still going over every possible scenario that could greet me when I entered the lab.

According to Kindolf, they had all but abandoned it. The horrors that were beyond its doors were boarded up and left to rot. When I turned the corner, I saw how wrong he had been. Lights shone through the windows of the lab and the white marble gave off an eery gleam in the moonlight.

My body cringed at the sound my footsteps made as they took me closer to the marble arches.

This felt like a trap. Clear signs of use shown outside and throughout the RightCorp lab. How had Kindolf been so wrong? It was clear that they had started using the lab again, but for what? The thick leather of my boots crunched the ground under the marble arches. The last place where Melissa ended her fight. I would make sure these people knew what she did for them.

I knew better than to enter the front doors and made my around the building. The wall was dark behind the dreadful place. Giant metal boxes covered the ground behind the lab. They growled and slammed as the fans and gears inside spun and clashed. They had every power cell and generator up and running. The whirring sound was deafening as I climbed my way on top of one placed below a window. Hopefully, they would be strong enough to hold my weight as I made my way to the roof of the facility. My weight made it difficult to climb over the ledge of the roof silently and I gave a muted thank you to the cacophony of metallic chaos below on the ground. An access door was just a few yards away, and I made my way to it in the darkness.

I wasn't prepared to come in contact with anyone on this mission. My breath felt heavy and came out in a thin current as I scanned the area. Nothing seemed to be out of place. But it still felt like I was walking into a trap.

The handle opened smoothly as I made my way through the metal door. A dark stairway led down and pooled light spilled over from another hallway on the bottom step. For a while, I didn't move. I pushed out my senses. The few bodies that I could feel were calm. No raised blood pressure or anxiety flowed out from them, so I continued toward the light.

Each room I passed sent waves of confusion out from me. The rooms that had last held the test subjects of the RightCorp were now transformed into living areas. Beds were in different level of use, clothes laid out on the chrome colored counter tops and every so often, traces of dinners could be spotted on small tables. They hadn't abandoned the lab. They were living in it.

With each level I descended, I could feel more and more of them. Deep in the underground floors of the RightCorp lab were the people that they had failed to protect. However, as I continued to reach out toward the dozens, if not more, bodies that moved hastily around, it was hard to hone in on any particular sense. All were a whirl of quick heart beats and dizzying breaths.

I was stuck. There would be no way to get down to the final level to search the main lab without someone noticing me. And seeing as how I was a part of Coranta's hit list for Sense Shifters, I very much wanted to keep it that way. A slow, exasperated breath of air escaped my lips as I looked around the wide space. The lower levels forwent small, glass encased rooms for wider spaces. Whatever dark deeds the open level used to be for had been abandoned and now large stained areas of the floor were covered in tables and chairs.

A mismatched hall of furniture that mirrored the Coranta that had, until recently, existed on the surface. The surface that sat far above the room I moved around.

My hands froze on the cold, scarred surface of a worn and beaten table. Gouges that had surely once been riddled with splinters were now worn down by what seemed like decades of use. A hallway on the far side of the space stole my attention away. An unseen door had been opened and closed, letting a sliver of sound and light escape for a fraction of a moment. Just long enough to start my heart thrashing inside my chest. I shrank under the table hoping that the darkness and cover would keep me from sight of the multiple pairs of footsteps. How many pairs there were I didn't know?

"I don't want her pissed at me. Just find the damn thing so we can get back." The voice of a younger man found its way to my hiding spot under the table.

"I really don't want to spend my night looking for some stupid battery when I could be down there having fun."

"Then you can go back down and enjoy yourself until I come back with it. I don't mind taking all the praise." I could hear the smile in his tone as he teased his search partner.

"Yeah, I don't think so."

Footsteps continued to move around the hall as they searched. The sound that alerted me to their presence had been from a celebration happening on the floor below. My gut clenched at the thought of what they could be celebrating. The feeling became a vice on my insides as they inched ever closer to my hiding place. There was no cloth draped over the edge to cover me and my skin crawled with the thought of them spotting me. All it would take is one of them looking in my direction and I would be done for. My fingers itched for something to throw, but there was nothing close.

"Get back in there." A familiar voice joined the sound of the searching.

Kindolph. He was here. Had they caught him? No. That didn't make any sense. If they caught anyone that even worked with sense shifters would be killed. But here he was, walking around. That smart bastard was working undercover.

No wonder we hadn't heard anything from him for days. But why was he still here?

My heart was still pounding beneath my rib cage as I thought of a way to get us both out of here.

My eyes darted to the other end of the room again as another set of footsteps made their way towards us. These, lighter but walked with a steady confidence.

"Jack." A pause as he adjusted himself to face the voice. "Come check the records room. I need to reach back out as soon as possible." There was no affection or familiarity in her tone. Whoever she was, she meant business, and Kindolph was about to be the focus of it.

Kindolph's voice was sharp in reply, "Boys, get back to the party now. I will take care of finding the battery for the comm.

Footsteps retreated in different directions. Two made their way back to the hallway door around the bend while the other followed in the direction of the unknown woman to what I assumed was the records room.

My knowledge of the RightCorp labs was limited to decades old maps and my short memory from being here right after Siana shifted Coranta. And that hardly lent itself to familiarly except for the many nightmares it had taken root every night.

From what I did remember, besides the large open space that I was hiding in now, there were a small amount of offices. Eyes adjusted to the dark space, I moved around each piece of furniture with ease despite the pounding of blood rushing through my ears.

The sound blocked out any other noise as I fought to calm myself and hear. I couldn't risk a sense shift. On the off chance that someone did find me and didn't know who I was.

The handle on the door beside the one marked "Records" opened smoothly and gave a barely audible click as I pushed it closed. The walls couldn't have been that thick, but their voices came through as indecipherable muttering all the same.

The room I found myself in was too small to have been a lab. It could have existed as an office once, but now the dark shelves had been emptied and scratch marks marred the floor. I hoped that they were from moving out the old office furniture to make was for something else, but my stomach clenched as my brain knew better.

The other room had gone silent as I waved the gruesome thought from my mind. My body froze, waiting for any sign of life from the next room. The effort of slowing each breath was becoming excruciating as I inched closer to the wall. It was cold to the tough when I pushed myself up against it, struggling to hear anything that might mean Kindolph would be fine. Another breath, and another. Nothing. Nothing, until a crash sounded against the other side, followed by another and another. I couldn't leave him in there by himself. Coranta had always had this habit of underestimating its women. I didn't share that same weakness. Whatever was happening, it wasn't pleasant. The dropped tile ceiling seemed like my only hope of helping my friend. The large shelf creaked under my weight as I pulled myself up to reach the tile ceiling. My hand brushed the rough edges of the tile aside as a cloud of dust flowed down. I stifled the impulse to sneeze and squeezed myself into the dark, dusty space.

Their voices were clear as I crossed the space that connected each room.

"It doesn't matter if you think they have an army with them! When I say I want something done, that means that it is happening. Do you understand me quite well, Mr. Kindolph?"

"Officer Kindolph."

"Not here. Not anymore. Now you're mine. You work for me. And you will do very well to remember all the things that I have done and will do if you ever find yourself forgetting that."

Purposeful footsteps tapped their way toward the wall where I had been trying to listen only minutes before. The shattered glass crunching under each step forward, ending in a final punctuated twist.

"Trust me, Jack, if you think you're afraid of what your friends at the Sector will do to you when they find out what you've been up to, you are living in a state of unsettling delusion. I like you. You've provided us with an unmatched advantage. However, I will not hesitate to make what Siana Viteri did look like child's play. So next time I say go..."

She waited for an answer, but only for a second. "Then I go."

"I'm glad we understand each other."

The ceiling tiles gave a stomach dropping crack. Shit. Shit. Shit. Shit. Shit. I stayed as still as possible, not wanting to break them any further or alert Kindolf or his mysterious friend of my hiding place. Unfortunately for me, the ceiling would not be cooperating.

A final crack split the tile along with its metal housing. There was no recourse but to commit now. My body thudded off of the top of several large metal filing cabinets before finally slamming against the hard concrete floor of the records room. As I lay covered in the debris and filth that had been rotting with age in the ceiling, Kindolph and the woman looked down at me. The fear in Kindolph was palpable as I pushed out a sense shift.

No point in hiding it now. He cowered on the floor and gripped onto his knees, that were pushing into his broad chest. The woman, however, didn't budge. Instead, she glared down at me with annoyance coupled with disdain dripping off of every feature.

My skin itched as I studied her tall frame from toes to top. Her feet seemed nearly bare as her pitch black baggy pants flowed in a straight line from her small hips down to where only a small peek of her long toes inched out.

The shirt she wore was stark white, that, if not for the veins that traced her skin, would have nearly blended in with her ghostly pallor.

A nauseating pain started to build in my chest as her resemblance to Melissa was undeniable. Even her clothes seemed very close to something I had sworn I had seen Melissa wear before. I wondered if they had raided Rightley Manor after the Awakening. I was under the impression that they still held reverence for them and left it untouched out of respect. Perhaps I was mistaken. Her dark hair was slicked back tightly and gathered into a high twist atop her too pale scalp, but little wisps of hair had managed to escape and flowed out in flat tendrils. A knot plugged my throat as I struggled to swallow. Her piercing pale blue eyes were both mesmerizing and frightening as I tried and failed to avert my stare.

"How unfortunate. I was hoping to get news of you falling in your little hideout. Looks like I will just have to see your reaction first hand when my people come back."

"Who are you?"

"Oh, the great Wolf doesn't know everything, I guess?" She picked at the dirt under her short, jagged nails before crushing another piece of glass under her foot. The same glass lined the side of my right arm from the fall. Not enough to cause serious damage, but it fucking hurt all the same. Small droplets of blood trickled down my fingertips and fell to the cold floor.

"You still haven't told me who I'm speaking to." My voice was punctuated by Kindolph's whimpering in the corner of the room. My shift was pushing out into the hallway. No one was coming. Tendrils of my power snaked their way down to the floor below.

My body tightened like a cable as I felt the pulsing of a hundred heartbeats. Fast-paced pounding, but no one was alert to what was happening just above them.

She moved to pick Kindolph up from the floor. A motherly annoyance plastered on what seemed like a young face. "You know what Mr. Willulf? I never had to hate you before. Hate is an ugly emotion. Along with heartache, anxiety, fear. I never had to worry about any of those before. I knew they existed, of course, and I felt them in my own way, but they never hurt me."

She continued to pull her fallen comrade up to a sitting position. "Do you know what it's like to wake up one day and be surrounded by bodies? To be trapped and unaware of what you feel or why you feel it? I do. Did you or your little friends even consider what might happen to the Dires here in Coranta when you set your plan off? Huh? Or were you just so short sighted and blinded by power that you didn't care?"

"We fought for the Dires of Coranta. People died to save all of you. To give you a better life."

"And who were you to say that we needed a better life?"

"The Rightleys were poisoning you! You have no idea what they took from the people."

"And they didn't want to know. Everyone was content to live with that calm and you all threw us willingly into chaos. Imagine earth shaking fear permeating the very core of your bones. That's what you, Melissa, Nira, and Siana put us through. You destroyed our way of life. And now, we will return the favor. We will not stop until every single Sense Shifter on the continent is dead."

"They will still come. Hartlem won't be shut out forever."

"Oh, yes, Hartlem. Our friends across the water. Jack's told me all about them and the deal Siana struck. Again, without thought for the rest of us, that would be affected." She shrugged and threw the piece of glass toward Kindolph's feet.

Another look of disgust rolled over her face as she glared in his direction. "As long as they keep that barrier going, we have no problem with them."

Music trickled its way through the gap under the door. A slight smile slid its way across her mouth as she heard it, too.

"All this complaining about emotions, you seem to enjoy whatever you're feeling right now."

Her face dropped into a deadly glare and fixed on me. My brow furrowed as I focused on her. Every ounce of my power seemed to seep away the second I directed everything to her. An emptiness raked its way down my body and seemed to pool like the little puddles of my blood that had grown and were now soaking into the fabric of my shoes. My power surged for only a moment more before a defining snap rang out through the room. Her only answer to the sound was a slight raise of her chin.

Every nerve in my body was screaming at me to get out while I still could. "You're a Sense Shifter."

Her sharp eyes were like daggers as her stare pinned me in place. "No, little Wolf. I am something so much more."

The crack of the wood splitting from the frame of the door sent my nerves charging through my body again. She took a single step back while four men lunged at me. The power I had held just moments before was gone. With no weapon to fight my way out, I stood trapped, unable to escape or warn the Sector of what was coming.

Chapter Eleven

RHETT

This room had been a reoccurring setting in my nightmares for years. The sterile walls, bright lights, and large wall of reinforced glass window took up enough of my waking thoughts as well. The space took on a strange tone now. The large shelves and sharp instruments that had once seemed so large now just looked small and insignificant. Where they had once gleamed in the harsh light, they now lay in disarray and disuse. Everything seemed — small. Then again, the last time I was in this particular room, I was much smaller. The company I had then had been infinitely better than well. The thought of Siana had me glancing over to the medical chair that had been shoved to one corner of the room. I couldn't make out the right arm from where I stood, but I knew there would be a worn spot where she had rubbed her small fist against it so many times before.

My focus snapped back to Kindolph, who was standing by the glass windowed door, staring at something on the other side. A satisfying pang of adrenaline spiked through me as I clasped my hand down on his shoulder and dug my fingers in before slamming him to the ground. I knew his heart was pounding in his chest, even if I still couldn't sense it.

"I should rip you apart. You know that, right?"

His elbows slipped out from under him as he tried to sloppily push himself backwards away from me. At least he was sane enough to know that I wasn't bluffing.

"Eilith!" Panic coated his voice while he sat in a pitiful lump on the floor. Henry had his annoying qualities, but he was leagues better than this pitiful mess.

"We've been searching for you. Prue almost got herself killed coming to Coranta to make sure you were alright."

"Eilith, please!"

"Is that your friend, Jack?" I mocked her tone in the records room as I closed in. "Good. You're going to need a friend by the time I'm done with you. You fucking traitor!" I lunged at him, landing a sickening blow to his chest and another to his face. The sound of cracking was punctuated by his scream. Before I could land another, I was being pulled off of him. Cold metal cuffs snapped into place, pinning me to the medical chair and out of thrashing distance of Kindolph.

The man and woman walked back to him, but instead of helping him up, each gave him another hit to match the ones I had already left on him. "She says to stop yelling. She doesn't like the noise. And you," the woman turned to me and pointed a finger in Kindolph's direction. "She said to have fun." They both left without another word.

"Kindolf, who is she?"

Pitiful groans were his only answer. Images of a past life flashed through my head as I stared around the room.

How many times had Siana and Nira's father run his tests on us from this room? And at the order of not only the Rightleys, but my father as well. Eilith.

The name didn't sound familiar, and neither did her face. She must have worked in the RightCorp lab before the fall of the Rightleys.

The metal cuffs rubbed at my wrists. They had cuffed me to a moving object. Heavy and clunky, but movable. The sounds of screeching metal on the tile floor made Kindolf jump. Another satisfying groan came from him as he obviously regretted his reaction.

"Looks like you are on your own now." My wrists ached as I pulled the chair around to sit, my arms bent awkwardly to accommodate my cuffed hands.

"You think you're so high and mighty, don't you? Like you should have everything just because your family ran a fraction of the continent? You deserve to pay just like the Rightleys did." His voice was low; a combination of pain and, most likely, fear.

"Not so high and mighty that I would choose to betray everyone who ever helped me by planning to attack and kill innocent people."

The cough that shot from his mouth was accompanied by small flecks of blood that peppered the tile floor in front of him. But besides the pained hacking, he remained silent.

"Let me guess. You got a thing for this Eilith person, am I right? What is it, Jack? She toss you a smile and you fell hard and decided to take everyone who ever meant something to you down too?" My head felt cloudy as a pull began to tug at my mind. Someone was prying.

And I had a feeling I knew exactly who it was. My neck began to itch. Made worse by the fact that I had no way to scratch it. A staggered breath left my chest as Kindolf let loose a chain of ear grating coughs.

131

I raised my voice so my words wouldn't be drowned out by it. "Do mind cutting that out?"

"I can't help it. You try getting your lungs punched in and see how you feel."

"First off, I have. Second, you're a waste of a good beating. And third, I wasn't talking to you, you worthless piece of shit." My eyes stared daggers toward the source of the pull.

There, peering in through the small glass window of the closed door, was a stone face Eilith. Her words were only slightly muffled by the glass that separated her from the room. "I've never encountered someone with Touch before. It's taking me a bit longer to adjust to it." Every word that she said she spoke as if it were a fact. Logical and tested. "I'm going to need to hang on to you for a little while to see what we can do together."

"I'm very sorry to disappoint you, but I do have other places to be."

"You mean at your stolen facility? Don't worry, we will take good care of all of your people."

"If you harm a single hair on any of their heads, I will end you." The growl in my chest was visceral as I let every ounce of venom I could muster letting it pool into my voice. "It will not be fast, but I swear it will be painful."

"Hm." She tilted her head toward me. If she had been afraid of anything I said, she didn't show it. Instead, my heart raced as an overwhelming feeling of fear took over me. Every part of me felt small and insignificant as my vision tunneled and the room blurred. Invisible hands gripped and scratched at my skin as I struggled to fight against them.

A heavy weight descended onto my head just before piercing hot pain shot through my skull. I couldn't hold back the scream that was ripping itself from my throat.

A woman's voice faded with the shift. "Shhh. Warriors don't scream. Aren't you a warrior?"

The weight of whatever was happening was gone, but a shadow of pain lingered behind. Blood had begun to drip from my wrists again from where the cuffs tore at my already broken skin. Hot tears trailed down my cheeks and landed on my shirt as I refused to avert my gaze from the woman standing at the door.

"Who are you?"

She pushed another tendril of senses toward me. This time it was a blurry image. Almost like pictures bring flipped through slowly. Three small children playing hide and seek in one of the living quarters of the lab. I could just make out the drawings that Siana had made for each of our doors. The picture of the wolf that I knew was hanging on one of them was a strange blur as I struggled to focus. A frozen coil closed around my throat as I watched the images. This wasn't something I had seen before. This wasn't my memory.

The image fell before she spoke again. "I am what was left behind. I was left to endure the pain that we should have all shared. But no, you and Nira and Siana; You got to go on your little adventure out into the world and you left me behind with the Doctor."

"I don't know what you are talking about. Dr. Viteri left RightCorp that night as well."

"No. She wanted to stay behind with me. She gave me what was meant for her daughter. I really thought she did it out of love. I loved her like a mother, I suppose until I didn't."

The confusion I felt was overpowering. Blood continued to drip from my wrists as I stared into her unfamiliar eyes, certain that, although she bore the same telltale traces of being experimented on as Melissa had, I had never once seen this woman.

I asked the same question that I had been repeating for what felt like weeks now. "Who are you?"

The first real flash of emotion crossed her face. Not a sadness or contempt, but as if she were remembering something. Her face settled back into its cold mask as her gaze met mine. "I'm no one." A hint of warning lurked behind those words as she regained her calculated composure. "No. I'm what's possible when science and logic are allowed to flourish beyond emotion. You were failures because you were treated like children. And I'm going to destroy everything that made you that way."

My head was racing. My memory of this place hadn't faded over time. I remembered every test, every word, everything about his place. But I didn't remember another child. "Taking out whatever ill conceived grudge you have against me and the Viteri's is one thing. But killing hundreds of innocent people at the rehab facility isn't going to help you."

"No one said anything about killing them. Thanks to you and your friends, I find myself in need of a few more bodies." She smiled. It could have seemed genuine if not for the circumstances. "Move Jack back to the glass room, please. It seems little Rhett won't be playing today, and I need space to really practice."

The two guards from before came back as Kindolph scrambled to move away. "Rhett, help me. Please, I can make it right. Please, just help me."

I sat in shocked silence as they dragged him from the room.

"What are you going to do with him?"

"Don't worry, Rhett. We aren't going far. You should still be able to hear our progress." And with that, she closed the door, leaving me in darkness to brace myself against what I feared would come next.

Kindolph's screams echoed through the hard, tiled space. His pain was etched onto every syllable that left his mouth with a horrified scream. A weight slammed against my chest with every sound. Somehow, Eilith had taken my power. She had drained everything that I could have used to protect myself and turned it into a scythe against someone who I had once thought of as an ally.

The blood in my veins turned icy as another scream ripped through the open space above that connected each room. Even if she had taken him to another part of the lab, I wouldn't be able to avoid his terrified calls for help.

My heavy lids searched the space for anything I could use to defend myself. I wasn't sure if she would use my own powers against me again but, by the sounds coming from Kindolf, I didn't want to risk hanging around and letting her try. My lids hung heavy. My veins should have been coursing with adrenaline, but instead, I was struggling to stay awake. Whatever she had done; whatever powers RightCorp had given her, it had taken my energy as well.

Another scream rent the heavy air. I could feel her. Eilith. Why would she torture Kindolph if he was working with her? Did she think that he had let me in? That he had helped me in someway? No. She knew. I could sense that she knew. So why put him through whatever horror was happening to him?

He stopped.

The screams that had pierced through every nerve in my body had stopped. Abruptly. A tug at my mind was followed by silent images of Kindolph laying beaten but still breathing, his blood cooling in a puddle on the bone white tile of a lab and on the wall behind him, in the same dark red, someone had painted a sickening message.

WELCOME HOME, RHETT

Chapter Twelve
SIANA

Thakkar sat across from me in the waiting area on the 8th floor of the Mission Center. His face pulled into a tight stare that I could feel only had a little to do with what was happening outside. I stared out the soot covered window as ash began to float down through the morning air. A plume of smoke making its way into the vast Hartlem sky blocked out the morning sun.

"Do we know yet what the target was?" I said.

Thakkar worried at the cuff of his sleeve, his chair creaking as he leaned forward. "According to our sources, it was headquarters."

"Have they ever made it this close before?"

"Not since I've been here. We should probably get going." He stood, straightening his jacket before trailing his fingers thoughtfully through his beard. "It's a bad idea to be late to an emergency meeting straight from the Director."

"I have business elsewhere. You can fill me in when I get back."

"He and Robinson are going to be angry if you miss another briefing. Especially one like this."

"Well then, they'll be angry."

I could feel Thakkar's annoyance float in pale green spots around me. He had made it clear at the market that he and some of the other Sense Guards were with me. But that was a week ago when they thought they would be following me in their fight against the rebels. Would they still follow me when they found out what Adilah and I had planned? I had to know for sure.

The stairwell was cold and goosebumps popped up over my arms as I made my way down to the first floor. The small few that were at the docks had warmed up to me, but the rest of the Sense Guard did their best to avoid me. With everyone scrambling to make it to the briefing, I made it outside headquarters completely unhindered.

I let out a slow breath as the smell of smoke left a red rim around my vision. Keep moving.

My body moved carefully between buildings, weaving in and out to avoid unwanted attention. Only someone in the Guard would have been able to follow me. The tall but decaying buildings peered down at me. I would have shuddered before to think of being watched.

By the time I reached my destination, the effects of the morning's attack were far behind me. Standing at the door, I pulled at the senses still hiding in the old building. I had avoided coming back here. I had seen firsthand through the last few weeks what the rebels provided for these children and it was an infinitely better option that what awaited them if brought to the Sense Guard. Still. The last time I had been here, I was still a monster. No more so that the man whose life I had ended here, but a monster all the same.

Two hearts beat rapidly from the shadows. They knew I was coming.

"Are you going to take me in?" The voice, though quiet, didn't come from a small child this time. It was male, but still had the timber of youth to it.

A tall silhouette stood at the opposite side of the crumbling building. A youthful face that couldn't have been more that seventeen, warred against the image that I could pull from his mind. He had seen far more than anyone his age should have to. But that was no different from anyone else in Hartlem. Except that he was here, standing in front of a Sense Guard, although not without fear. I could feel it radiating off of him as he fought the urge to run. He wouldn't run, though. That much I knew.

"Did you see the attack this morning?" I closed the distance as he took a cautious step toward the other heartbeat, still hidden.

"We heard it." The lump in his throat moved up, and down as he swallowed down his fear. His shoulders squared as his body shifted back and forth. "I mean I heard it."

"And you're all by yourself here?"

"Yes." He lied. I could taste the bile he was trying to hold back as fear coiled itself around his heart. He was terrified of me, of what I could do, and yet, he lied. Good.

"Why are you here? Why did you remain when the others you were hiding with, the ones who would cower beneath a child, have fled?" The fire in my chest flared as the girl's face flashed in front of my eyes. "Do you know what the Sense Guard does with children left alone?"

His back hunched over as the need to make himself smaller overwhelmed him. And yet, he remained silent. He was stronger than he realized.

"You collect us. To be sent to the Golden City." The little girl from the day before emerged from behind a wall of decades old garbage. Where the young man cowered, she stood straight and looked me in the eye. However, the look she gave me was not one of resentment like so many other in her place had given me. Hers was one of reverence. The boy kept his eyes fixed on me as he rushed toward and using his body to block her from my sight again.

"There is no Golden City." I replied.

She peeked around his arm. "There used to be. Back before the war, the ones with the gift would be taken to the Golden City to protect the rest of us."

Another fairytale that Hartlem and RightCorp had fed these people.

"No. There is no Golden City. No Utopia. No fairytale kingdom. There is only Hartlem and the Continent." At that, she stepped out from behind the boy who held fast to her shoulder. A gentle sheen closed in around us as a slight tickle feathered its way around my mind. This little girl had the Gift.

Garbage crunched and shifted under the weight of my movements as I took one knee slowly to the floor. "But let me tell you a secret. Both are still just as much worth fighting for."

The look in their eyes was priceless. Full of confusion and hope.

I kept my words soft and slow as I spoke. "I need your help to make that happen."

"Why would we help the Guard? What you did before. It was awful."

My gut twisted in disgust. How many times had they had nightmares about what I had done?

A slow breath calmed my racing heart before I continued. "And yet, you're still here. You showed up when everyone else ran. Why? Is it because you know what is happening is wrong?" I fixed my sights on the boy. "Did you know that it was predetermined that he leave her out in the open for us to take? That she was his bargaining chip?" Disgust rolled over me in waves. Without the toxins to dampen my repulsion this time around, the memory left me feeling a combination of anger and sorrow for them.

He held his head down but there was no shame that radiated out from him, instead anger boiled under his skin as well.

The little girl took his hand in hers. "Jesse. I think we should help her. I feel like she's good."

The rage that was still brimming off of him gave off a metallic taste as he knelt down beside her. "Is she telling the truth? Did they really shut you out on purpose?"

She shrugged.

"Lissy. Why didn't you tell me? I promised mom to keep you safe. You have to help me do that. If you don't tell me— "

"You seemed happy with them. I didn't want to ruin it. We've been alone for so long because of the Gift. I thought if I hid it, and we stayed, you could stay happy."

"You make me happy. And I will do whatever I need to do to make sure you are, too."

I took a few steps forward. Jesse took a startled step back, holding on to Lissy's shoulders. "If you've made a decision, follow me."

Lissy smiled, "We can trust her. She isn't like the others. I can feel it, Jesse."

The piles of trash and debris only grew as we made our way toward the coastline of Hartlem. We were far enough away that the tall building that housed Hartlem's Director no longer lorded over us. Its tall frame wiped clean of our field of view. Lissy had gotten tired along the way and was now perched on her brother's back.

Her little face turning now and then to scan the steps we had already left behind. "I can feel someone."

"I know. He's been following me since I left headquarters this morning. Just continue on. We don't engaged with him yet."

The sounds and smells of the ocean had been on repeat for a while now as we approached the old shipping dock with its many large containers. I brushed my hand along the one that read, Dark Sheep Construction, on the side.

We made our way around to the side that faced the waves, its door blocked from view of the rest of the city behind it. I opened the long metal handle that released the pipes from their resting place on top and bottom of the door. The earsplitting squeal that the door let out as I pulled it away from the metal frame made both the girl and boy shiver.

Jesse plopped his sister down before giving me an uneasy look. "I'm not going in there with you. You're not going to trap up in there."

"If I were going to trap you, I would have saved myself all the walking and called someone to drag you in."

Lissy went inside before her brother. "If you hurt her. I'll kill you." He said it on a shaky breath, but it rang true. I nodded.

"I'm going to introduce you to someone who can help you and your sister and others like her."

The sound of metal crashing behind me sent both of them into hiding.

The clatter of the vibrating metal had finally come to an end as Thakkar approached with heavy footsteps.

"I knew it! The bombs going off so close to headquarters. Not bringing in the children for questioning. Going off on your own all the time. You're working with the rebels." His hands reached for mine. "Siana, you are going to get yourself killed. You can't do this."

"You saw what they did at the docks. The other Guards, too. There was no way that Turney and Robinson weren't already there. Which means they either had time to apprehend the rebels—"

"Or they set the explosion off." He rubbed his brow. "I — I thought of that, but it makes no sense for them to hurt anyone. There has to be a reason they were there."

I let out a slow breath as Lissy and Jesse shuffled around in the container behind me. "You said that you could trust me, Akshat. That you would follow me. I would have loved to trust that you wouldn't say something to Robinson if I had just told you about this, but I can feel how much you respect his position. I needed to show you."

"I can't let you put the Guard in danger, Viteri. These people you're helping would destroy both Hartlem and Coranta if given the chance."

"You mean like they destroyed that boat?"

A deep blue wrapped in sickly yellow pulsed around my vision. He was remembering the docks. The smell of sea water churned in the air. The doubt that had burrowed into his mind was starting to bloom.

"You're wrong about a lot of things, Thakkar."

The sound of metal scraping on concrete was his only warning as I took the advantage of his deep thought and pushed him into a shift.

His body hit the ground hard. He would be bruised when he woke up, but besides that, no worse off. Several people came in from the door hidden in the back of the container while I escorted Jesse and Lissy down into the tight space. A hallway, created from the space between a long row of containers. We moved in complete darkness as we approached the end of the tight space, a hatch leading down into the rebels base in the bottom of Hartlem's biggest water filtration plant.

Jesse held tight to his sister, who looked around in wonder. The cavernous room was filled with people. They both looked around with cautious optimism as Adilah approached us. Her long, dark braid rested over her shoulder and fell to her waist as a welcoming smile greeted us.

"You never cease to surprise me, Viteri. Who do we have this time?"

"This is Jesse and Lissy. Siblings. Lissy here is a Gifted."

Adilah turned to the people who had come up behind her. "Take them to get some clean clothes and food and then give them somewhere to rest." She bent down to Lissy. "Can you trust me when I say that I will keep you safe?"

Lissy was focused as she closed her eyes and took a breath. When she opened them again, there was a smile resting on her face. She nodded.

"Good." Both were led further into the room for some much needed rest.

"Well, this is certainly a new one. I don't think anyone has ever brought me a Sense Guard before." She circled around the passed out Thakkar.

"He's a good man. Once he knows what's really going on, he'll help." My vision spun. The air in the room was heavy in my lungs as I went to my knees on the hard concrete floor. I still was getting used to the toll shifts had on my body again.

Thakkar let out a startled gasp as the hold I had placed on him wavered.

"Get him to a holding cell now." Adilah gave orders to the men holding Thakkar before turning back to me. "How often is this happening?"

"With most shifts. Now that the serum is completely gone, I feel like something's eating away at me every time."

"You have to slow down. You need to be able to give a show to the Director if it's called for." She smiled, her hand warm on my shoulder as she comforted me for the hundredth time.

A group of excited kids surrounded Lissy before they made it very far. A deep set smile made her face glow as Jesse stood, still protectively close by, but smiling as well.

"We're close. Hold on, and we'll have you home before you know it."

My eyes watered as I thought about Nira and Josie. Rhett would protect them. I knew he would. He made a promise. No matter what may have happened, I knew what he felt for me wasn't a lie. They would all be safe together. My mind wandered then to Henry. I had to find a way to get him back home, too. A deep guilt ate away at me a little more every time I thought about what I had taken from him to get here.

"Where are you right now?"

"Here. I'm here." I nodded my head toward her, wanting more than anything to get home. If everything went as planned, soon I would be.

Adilah made her way toward the doorway where they would be holding Thakkar.

My feet pulled me gently forward as I tried to blink away the woozy feeling that the shift had weighed on me.

"Siana!" Several voices rang out around the large room. I stopped, heart soaring at the question I knew would be asked by the group shouting my name. I smiled and shrugged at Adilah.

She made an exasperated sigh. "Make it quick, Viteri." A gentle laugh trailed behind her as she disappeared through the doorway.

The filtration center above us was loud enough to cover any amount of chatter, which was good because everyone here loved to celebrate. The small owners of the voices were closing in on me, bringing a flow of excitement and bright energy with them. Only a few weeks of working with the rebels and I already felt more at home with them than anywhere else in Hartlem.

"Siana, can you tell us more stories before you leave again?" Little hands pulled at my clothes as a warm smile did the same to my lips. Without an answer, they led me to a corner area that was covered much like the tent where I first spoke to Adilah. Woven works of art to set the scene for tales of adventures and heroes.

If I could stay anywhere, it would be in this small corner of the world. Storytelling had always been a love of mine, but having the gift to let them sense everything that I did was beautiful. The smell of the salt water lapping the side of a pirate ship, the sounds of bells as they softly chimed outside a fairy village, the feeling of rain as it pings off of the hammered metal helmet of a knight forging into battle. Not today, though. My head was still heavy, though the quick jolt of happiness was doing a pretty good job of holding back the headache that had been building.

"I'm sorry. I'm a bit tuckered out today." The collective groan made a laugh bubble up in my chest. "Hey. I'm not the only one here that can tell stories."

A worn hand patted my shoulder, and with it warm waves pushed out over my body and mind. The tension and pain that had been building pulled away as its tide rushed back to the old man beside me. I let out a relieved breath. "Thank you."

"It's my pleasure." He gave me another pat of the shoulder before slowly making his way to the bench that sat tucked in to the brightly colored corner. I wanted nothing more than to stay and listen to his story, but Adilah was waiting and it would help Thakkar if he saw my face when he woke up.

"Are you alright?" My legs hurt from having one knee on the concrete floor the whole time Adilah had been using her Gift with Thakkar. Several tears had already fallen and been lost in his beard. "Whatever questions you have, she'll answer them truthfully."

He stared into my eyes as if the answers to the questions he was thinking might be found there. "My daughter. Coranta. All of these lives lost. Over what? Some plants?"

Adilah waved the others out of the room before pulling two chairs toward Thakkar. We each took a seat before she spoke. "No, Akshat. Everything that has been lost is because of greed. We are not the monsters that they have painted us to be. The land gave us the Gifts. Our people offered to share them when Hartlem came, but that wasn't enough. So we were driven out."

"Then how do you still shift? I'm sorry, I mean, the Gifts: how do you still have them?" Thakkar asked.

Adilah's voice was firm but kind as she answered. "It's in our blood, but it's dying out. Very few are still born with it because we have been without it for so long."

147

I placed my hand on his arm.

"Why don't you show these to the entire Sense Guard?"

"You're a good person. Siana is a good person. That is easy enough to spot, even without the Gift. Not all the Guard is the same. With so much hatred and propaganda circling, it's difficult to pick out the good from the bad. But what happened at the docks. That was the sign we needed to know we could reach out." She gave me a pointed look, "Which was much better than the alternative."

"Alternative?"

"We'll talk about that another time. For now, I need to know that you are with us."

Thakkar looked down at his hands. They weren't bound. The door to the room was wide open and the men that had escorted his sleeping body in were nowhere in sight. "I'm assuming that I'm not actually allowed to just walk out of here?"

"You assume correct. You are free to make your own decision. And I am free to make sure that decision doesn't hurt the people I'm trying to protect."

I leaned back, a spectator in their conversation, but very much invested in the outcome.

His face turned toward me. "Do you trust them?"

"I do."

"Then I follow."

Chapter Thirteen
HENRY

The door to the living room opened slowly as Siana made her way home carrying several heavy looking bags.

"Do you want me to help you with those?" I reached for the items, but she pulled them back.

"No, I can handle them on my own." She took a deep breath before wrinkling her nose. "What's burning?"

"Oh, shit." I rushed to the stove as she let out a gentle laugh. The pan clattered in the sink as smoke and steam rushed up from our burnt meal. "Sorry. I guess I got distracted."

"No, Henry. I'm the one that should be sorry. You shouldn't even be here. Holed up in this little space with nothing to do but cook and keep yourself company. It's all my fault." We had this same discussion too many times to count now, and every time I assured her she wasn't to blame and every time she would get so angry with me.

I already knew what was coming next. She pulled the curtains back and stared outside, but no light came through. It was always dark when she got home.

"Please, Siana, just let me take those from you. Sit down and I'll get you some tea." A small tapping sound came from the roof. She stared up at the empty white ceiling. "What is that?"

"I'm not sure. It started just a little while ago. I'm not gonna lie, it's had me on gritting my teeth on several occasions." The small space where we lived had started to feel increasingly cramped as each day went on. The random tapping sound wasn't helping the already depressing mood. "If it wasn't so random, I might not mind it. I don't like that I never know what to expect here. Or when to expect it."

She wrapped her fingers around mine, giving me a gentle smile as she spoke. "Do you want to go check it out? See what's driving you crazy?"

"No. No, it's fine. It'll stop here in just a minute. Besides, it's so dark out there, we wouldn't be able to see to fix it, anyway."

We both made our way back over to the kitchen counter, where we spent so much of our time. She made a pained look and chuckled at the soup that would have to be made again. We both worked in silence as we bumped around each other, grabbing things we would need from the small space. The bags that she still had hanging off her shoulders were making it even harder to avoid being in each other's space. I grabbed one strap, and she gave a small protest. "You don't have to do that."

It was far heavier than I imagined as I slung it over my shoulder. "I know."

As I slid the other bag off her shoulder and onto my own, a one-sided smile graced her beautiful face. I traced my thumb over the side where it was missing. She smiled at me it full earnest and a warm glow filled my chest. My heart beat fast as she closed the distance between us. My heart raced out of my chest as our lips met for the second time. My hands reached for her face as one strap fell down my arm, pulling it to the ground. Her unwavering stare remained fixed on the bag now resting on the floor.

"Stop acting like you care for me, Henry. Stop acting like I'm not the one that put you in this position in the first place. Like I'm not the one that messed with your head. Like I'm not the one that handed you that vial and asked you to stand by while I destroyed our lives." All the emotions she had been holding back were bubbling to the surface. It had finally hit me. It was too much. Whether she knew it or not, I was about to break as well.

"Stop lying to yourself thinking that you're the only one to blame! Everyone has blame, and you don't get to take that. You don't get to carry all of that yourself. I can handle fixing the harm that I caused myself." My body sunk to the stool. The cold of the metal seeped through my clothes and leeched into my bones. My voice came out as barely more than a whisper as she stood in front of me, eyes now level with my own. "How can I forgive myself if you don't let me make up for what I've done to you?"

The loud thud of the bags dropping to the hard floor echoed throughout the room as a warmth began to web out all over my chest and torso.

Chapter Fourteen
SIANA

Days of meeting in secret with Adilah and planning had been exhausting but necessary. What had felt like weeks of waiting were finally about to end. A rush of adrenaline burst through my body as Robinson escorted me to the Director after another morning of reports from the mission center.

The drive to Hartlem tower had been a silent one. Thakkar stared out the windows as we closed in on the giant building while I stared down at Robinson. The hatred he had for me pulsed around him, but an orange glow accompanied it along with a familiar savory sweet smell. The same taste and smell as when Thakkar hit me with the door. He was deeply enjoying whatever he was thinking of. My heart sank, not knowing if it would bode well.

The lobby was bare of life or warmth, the morning sun just hitting the back of the building as our vehicle came to a stop and we made our way inside.

I fought the urge to shrink away as Robinson sat on one of the metal chairs in the lobby, but not before dragging it slowly against the hard ground. He gave a sly smile. "Viteri, head up."

Both Thakkar and I moved in unison past him toward the stairs. A hollow thud shifted my attention as Robinson stood and slapped his arm over my partner's chest. "You stay with me. We have some mission prep to take care of."

For the first time since I had come to Hartlem, I saw the briefest look of disgust flash on Akshat's face before he placed a smile back on. "Lead the way."

He gave me a small nod as I made my way to the elevator alone, before the doors cut him completely out of sight.

Each floor the metal box climbed added another wave of apprehension. My fingers gripped the dark leather cuffs of my jacket as a slow trembling breath rushed past my lips. Adilah knew these people well. And with all of Thakkar's knowledge, the chances that we were right about what was about to happen were high. It still had me on edge. My body gave a small jolt as the elevator came to a stop. The gentle ping going out just before the doors slid open again.

I took several confident steps forward, surprising myself at the steadiness of my limbs.

The Director stood at his desk, his gaze seeming to go through me as the doors closed at my back. "Do you see all those people down there, Siana?" He gestured toward the window without taking a step closer himself. I nodded in reply but stayed silent for fear my voice might shake.

"We protect them. They are able to live their lives because of the battles that we fight. They know the danger and they're grateful to be able to live despite what they know surrounds them."

His eyes focused on me. "They are grateful to you. To the entire Sense Guard for what you do."

"Yes, sir." My heart was slamming against my rib cage, but I stood still, my nails digging into the skin on my wrist as I gripped both arms behind me.

His gaze left me for a small box that rested on the edge of his desk. It made a slight swishing sound as he gently shuffled it about on the glossed wood. "Do you know how anti-venom is made?"

I could feel my eyebrows start to furrow in confusion before I answered. "You mean like for snakes?"

"Snakes, yes. But for any venomous thing."

I shook my head.

"It's made by capturing the venomous creature, taking that which makes it deadly, and creating a cure for its own toxins. We take what does the most harm and alter it to give everyone a chance at peace."

Holding my tongue was becoming more and more difficult. I knew what their "anti-venom" was.

They alter us to be the very thing that our families had most feared, only to wreak havoc on the families that followed. And all for what? The answer still wasn't clear to me. It could have been the resources at first, but what purpose would that serve now? The Rightleys had already perfected administering all of them.

"What is their goal? What reason do they have to continue to fight us if they know they have no chance of winning?"

He turned to the space behind his desk where a large picture was hung and waved his hand for me to join him.

"Can you find the Continent?" He stared at the picture on the wall.

I tried to hide the confusion I felt as I looked out of the window facing the ocean that flowed to the Continent.

He laughed. "Not there." He pointed at the picture. It was as tall as he was and just as wide. He placed a finger on a small abstract shape toward the top left. "Here."

My feet were sluggish as I moved in closer. Close enough to read the words Continent Alpha and Hartlem. The giant frame housed a map unlike anything I had ever seen. What had seemed to be an abstract painting swimming in cerulean swirls was a guide to the world around us. And there, in a small section of warm browns and mossy greens, was Coranta. A tiny speck compared to the other shapes.

"What is this?" My head felt heavy and unbalanced as I roamed my sight over the rest of the map. Beyond Hartlem there were three massive chunks of russet and moss colored splotches that could have held at least three or four of the Continent with in each of them.

He pointed to each in succession. "Here, Continent Bravo, is Artrian. Delta; Rainor. Gamma; Tranal."

My heart was pounding as I stared at the map. The skin on my arms felt uncomfortable and itchy as my body began to sweat. My hands were locked in place, though the urge to run my fingers over the paper was powerful. A year ago, I had thought the entire world was Coranta and the surrounding land. I had wished for a great wild world to explore like the adventurers in my stories.

And now, my mind was drowning in the knowledge of how incredibly small I was. How little I knew and how dangerous that ignorance of the world around me could be.

"These violent groups that surround us want to destroy Hartlem because they want what is ours. We provide important resources to the rest of this great world." His hands moved where mine had wanted to, tracing the outline of each new piece of land.

"Are the people there like us?" A sense of fear and wonder was weighing heavy on my chest as I spoke.

"No. They live in complete peace. Everything they know and love is protected; revered; safe. That's possible because of the things our research has accomplished. When Taliak was first discovered, we were in the midst of a great famine. We realized that the plants that grew here were special. Not only were they abundant, but they could be used to heal and cultivate the special abilities that you and the rest of the guard posses."

"And the people that were already there?"

"An amazing people. Kind and generous."

"So, what happened to them?"

"Nothing happened to them. They're still in Taliak. We do our best to protect them, but the rebels are fighting every day to destroy us and them. They believe that Taliak should be cut off from the rest of the world. They envy the peace we give the rest of our world."

"Our world? Isn't it theirs too?"

And there it was. If you want to know an enemy's true intentions, ask them what they are trying to protect. Nine times out of ten, that's exactly what they are trying to destroy.

He gave me a sad smile and went on, without answering my question. "But that's not the only reason I asked for you today. I wanted to give you an update and ask a favor of you. We have received word that the work on the barrier is running smoothly despite the rebels' attempt at blowing up our last shipment. We've just sent more supplies across the water."

Anger bubbled inside my chest, but I kept a stoic look on my face. The twitch in my jaw and the tension now racing through my entire body was making it hard not to sway.

The tremble I was sure would give me away stayed out of my voice as I spoke. "And the men and women in the pods? Have they been released yet?"

"Within the month, I should think."

The Director narrowed his eyes toward me. Despite not having any shifter powers, I worried about him finding me out more than anyone. With the extra boost of the serum completely gone, I had to be careful. Every conversation about the barrier went through my head. This entire time, even though I had had the means to rip him apart, he viewed me as some naïve child.

"That being said, it means that you will be going home soon." He gestured for me to take a seat at the front of his desk while he remained standing behind it, the colorful map making his dark suit stand out in stark contrast. "And after reviewing the reports made by your partner, I believe it would be best that you finish your time beforehand on Recreor Island."

Got him. "Reports, sir?"

"Yes. It seems that you have been failing in your duties to transport the civilians you find in your patrols to safety." He lowered his chin to stare directly at me. "It seems the serum, while giving you a formidable edge, may be affecting your ability to assess and properly care for the people of Hartlem."

I smiled internally as I thought of the three of us, huddled around an old table, writing those exact words down in Thakkar's final report. The Director couldn't even think of his own material.

He continued on, "While your abilities with or without the serum are useful, I believe we are in a place to do without them. Safety of our citizens is top priority." He smiled. Something about it left me uneasy. I risked pulling in the senses around me. It didn't surprise me to find that I couldn't sense him, probably the results of blocking serum. However, the floor above and below were missing a large amount of what I had come to expect of his own personal guards.

"Is that all, sir?" I was itching to get away from his pinning stare.

"Almost, just one more thing." He went back to his desk and busied himself with papers as he spoke. "We obtained the results from your blood work." He looked up at me and smiled. "Thank you for finally agreeing to submit a sample, by the way." He grabbed the small white box from his desk and handed it to me. "I want you to give this to Robinson on your way out. He is to deliver the results to our research facility on Recreor Island. The three of you will make sure it gets there safe. I need that delivered as soon as you arrive."

"The three of us, sir?"

"Oh yes. Your partner has served Hartlem well. It's time we rewarded his loyalty." He smiled. "Robinson has no doubt already informed him of his move."

Shit. This wasn't part of the plan. If Thakkar was going with me to Recreor, there was no way for me to get a message back to Adilah and the rebels. Thakkar part was to alert the rest of the Sense Guard once I was gone.

Without him here to guide them, I didn't know how Adilah would get close enough to convince them to fight with us.

I scrambled for a plan and let the first thing that came to mind escape. "Thakkar is a strong soldier and a very competent Sense Guard. Should he be relieved of his duties before finishing out his mission?"

"It would be best for him to accompany you to Recreor." His gaze narrowed, waiting for another rebuttal.

"Yes, sir." We would have to find another way to get a message to Adilah. I turned, doing everything in my power not to run to the door. I didn't fear the Director. But I feared what would happen if he found me out.

161

"Siana."

My ears pricked up as my feet slowed to a stop.

"Not that it means anything right now, but I think your family would be proud of the work you are doing for Hartlem and The Continent." He looked back at his papers. "Enjoy your rest."

I gave a single nod in his direction. My body relaxed as I made the last few steps to the exit. He was right. My family would be proud of what I was doing, but not the family he was thinking of. Nira, Josie, Henry and Rhett. They were the family that mattered and I would make sure that everything I did, from now on, would make them proud. Tears began to well as images of them came crashing in. The slow descent of the elevator brought me one step closer to them. To him. My heart sputtered as the first floor came into view. I couldn't let my mind wander. I had to make it to Recreor Island unscathed, which meant that was a thought that I had to tamp down. No matter how hard I tried, there was no thinking of them ,any of them, without giving myself away.

They would all be fine. I had to believe that with my whole heart if I was going to get through with Adilah's plan in one piece.

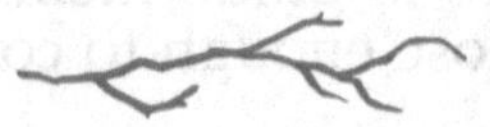

Robinson had pointed out the large rock island when I had first arrived in Hartlem. Through all our talks with Adilah, Thakkar had made Recreor sound like a dream. He said it was a space and community for those that the war had devastated. A place for them to go and work in peace without fear of the war reaching them. The way he spoke of it made it sound like some sort of paradise. But then again, the people of Hartlem claimed that Coranta had been a golden city of peace and purpose.

The stuff of dreams. I guess when you live in a war zone, anything sounds like paradise.

The waves became more and more turbulent as we approached the large rock. The dark gray stone stabbed up from waters surface as if it were trying to pierce the sky. How could anyone live on something so cold and unforgiving? Even the boat seemed to try to turn itself around as we approached. No horror story I had read in the past could encompass the feeling of impending doom that was creeping its way through my every nerve. Even my body seemed to think I shouldn't be here.

As the boat thrashed its way up to the dock, a large set of steps became visible as they wound their way up the steep rock wall. No wonder this place was safe from the fighting. Coming here without permission or help would be a death wish.

Flashbacks of another set of stairs popped into my head. The Courthouse that I had once feared seemed so welcoming now, despite the memories attached to it. There would be no one to catch me if I fell down these steps. Rhett's face loomed in the back of my mind. Would he look different now? How could he not? He was the new overseer of The Continent.

Would I find him in Rightley Manor when I returned? Would Nira and Josie be there too? Tears began to fog my vision as I thought of Henry. He deserved so much more. Would any of them be happy to see me after they learned everything I had put him through? I don't think I would be.

The wind raged at the air around us, making Thakkar's eyes red and watery as well. At least one aspect of this deadly terrain would help me. Robinson was already creating an imposing distance between us as he ascended the steps.

My breath came out in jagged puffs as I struggled to catch up. "This is your idea of paradise, huh?"

Thakkar didn't answer, instead he just shot me a worried stare. A deep coiling fear settled in my stomach as my chests and arms tensed. My feet were already sore by the time I caught up to Robinson.

"How long are you staying on the Island?"

He didn't turn to look at me as he continued up the steeply raked steps. "The Director needs me to evaluate a situation and deliver a very important package."

It surprised me Thakkar could hear past the rushing wind and distance down the steps. He was struggling even worse than I was to make it up the rocky rise.

"Hey Robinson. If this is how my retirement starts, I don't think I want it." He gave a short and breathy chuckle that our guide ignored. I couldn't help but smile down the few feet that stood between us. My heart ached for him. He had wanted this more than anything. He had earned it. Maybe I could come up with some way for him to stay. As soon as the thought popped up in my mind, I knew it wouldn't work. He wouldn't let me fight this battle alone. If I left Recreor, he would be coming with me.

A selfish part of me was relieved in the knowledge that I wouldn't be alone.

I couldn't help but think about how lucky his daughter would have been to have him. If she had been allowed to keep him. A sad stab of jealousy and sorrow stung my eyes. Fortunately, the ever battering wind could be blamed for any tears that fell while Robinson was around.

The stairs thankfully ended as we made our way through a dark passage on the side of the mountainous island. The small light that Robinson held showed walls that faintly glistened in what looked to be the same salty grime that was making my feet occasionally slide on the passage floor. An abrupt turn and a burst of light signaled the cave's end as we made our way outside again. If the outside of the island had been a horror story, this inland would have been a fairy tale. Beautiful houses peppered the inside of the craterous rock. Winding paths crisscrossed their way throughout the beautifully crafted scene. My feet cast several small stones bouncing forward, each landing with a soft tink tink on the descending path in front of us. Robinson's gruff voice was an unwelcome addition to the otherwise storybook scene. "Thakkar, stop gawking and move."

I hadn't noticed that Thakkar had planted his feet at the mouth of the cave behind us, staring out in complete wonder at the world below us.

"Naitee would have loved this."

He made it very difficult to stay cold. His face wasn't full of the sorrow that I had expected to see. My confusion rolled through me as I reached out to his senses. Wonder and awe. He was touching a memory of his daughter that wasn't tainted by sorrow. Staring out at a fairy tale world that she would never see didn't bring him to tears. Instead, it was spreading warmth out from him.

I let myself turn away and smile at the thought of him in another life. One where he got to be with her.

The warmth Thakkar had let escape him was still circling the air as we approached our mission. A large, red brick building seemed to have baked itself in the soft sunlight. If not for the smell of saltwater that hung in the air and the seagulls that squawked up above, it would be hard to tell that the town was sitting in the middle of the ocean.

The wooden door swung open as a man wearing an olive green uniform walked out to greet us. Sweat coated my palms at the sight of the man in what looked eerily similar to Med Burrow clothing. I pulled in the senses from the building, just in case. Most of them felt weak. My eyes darted around as I looked for signs of RightCorps' influence. Seeing none, I prodded again. This time, a gentle yellow haze began to ring my vision. The overall feeling of those inside was content. With a slow breath, I followed the rest of my small party inside.

"Siana. It's so nice to put a face to the stories." A strong feminine voice caught me off guard as we walked to the front desk. "Good to see you too, Robinson." The tall woman closed the distance between us, reaching out her hands to shake all of ours before her sight rested on Thakkar. "And you are?" She said it with a smile, holding out her hand for him to take. Her tall frame matched that of my male counterparts, and her confidence far exceeded even that. A broad smile curved up her face, making the lines at the corners of her eyes more pronounced, adding a warm glow to her already welcoming demeanor.

"Akshat." He held her hand in both of his as he shook. "Pleasure."

"Same."

"Your turn." I directed my question to our newest host as I stared at Thakkar, mentally urging him to keep it together.

He was far too giving with his emotions.

"Of course. I'm Dr. Heidi Pirth. Sorry about the forwardness. I've just heard so much about you that I feel like I know you."

Robinson brought the small white box out of his pack before handing it to Dr. Pirth. He pulled her just out of sight and spoke in hushed tones, making it hard to pick out what was being said.

"The Director wants you to work on this immediately. This is now your top priority."

That was the only phrase I could make out before they were completely out of hearing range.

"Thakkar what are we going to—"

"Not yet." He stared forward. The warm demeanor he had just worn was gone and in its place was a stern and worrying tension. "Wait." He whispered.

A deep red haze pulsed in the air around us while the taste of rust and metal clung to my tongue. Moments later, Dr. Pirth returned with Robinson and although her face and voice were bright, whatever they had spoken about had diminished her sunshine attitude but only momentarily. A smile widened across her face, softening the red in her cheeks as she approached me again, this time taking both of my hands in hers again, "You have no idea what you are being here is going to mean. I really do think it may be exactly what we need to break through." My left hand dropped to my side as she gripped on to my right and began to pull me away from ;my partner and the door.

"What is this place, exactly?" There were obvious signs of this being another research facility, but it held an odd warmth. As she pulled us forward, past the walls that closed in the entryway, the space opened up considerably into a large round room with several hallways leading off from it.

Well-worn chairs were pulled in a circle around what could have been some kind of waiting room. Shoes and coats of all sized were placed on racks, books rested on several cushions, and in the middle of the room was a large thread bare but cozy looking rug.

"This building has several purposes. The most important being that it houses those that come from Hartlem Proper until they are ready to assimilate into the community. It's also a gathering place for the people who live on the island," she gestured around the great open room before bending down to pick up several toys and books; placing them on the nearest side table with a chuckle, "but we also do a great deal of research here. You'll find that every space has a different purpose and all are open to you." She held out her hands to point out the colored stripes running down each hallway. "But we'll get to that another time. For now, there is someone who I would very much like for you to meet before we get you both settled in."

My mind wandered as she led us down a brightly lit gray hallway. A large green stripe painted along the floor guided our way as she prattled on. I struggled to focus on her words as we continued. Floor-length windows lined the wall to our left as we made our way through what had seemed like a medical building. I could see that it was much more than that. The windows looked out on a green covered courtyard filled with people of varying ages. All of which were smiling and basking in the warm sun. As I pulled at their senses, an array of smells and tastes made my head spin. The glow and warmth of each person was intoxicating. The sweet taste of vine ripened fruit mingled with a swirling fragrance of freshly crushed flower petals. Images of sunsets and soft waves rolled through the edge of my vision in bubbly yellows and bright purples as several of the people began to laugh. The sound of their happiness weaving together in a beautiful harmony that pulled at the corners of my mouth into a smile.

Pirth's voice flowed in and out as I gazed out on the residents, "…but that was before. Since he's been with us, everyone has hope and that's…" her voice trailed off again as I watched two little boys dancing around the grass, a young woman mouthing a song that I ached to join.

"…and now that you're here, maybe that will change."

A hand rested on my forearm as we rounded a corner. "Siana, are you alright?" Thakkar's voice was laced with worry.

I turned to look at him. "Of course." Worry snaked its way up my throat as I kept my hands from scraping against my pants, the blissful emotions I had just relished draining from my body in one fluid instant. Had I let too much show? Had Robinson seen it?

"Siana?" My entire body froze. I had heard that voice before. My name sounded well rehearsed from their mouth like they had said it so many times.

Dr. Pirth was standing next to the large wooden framed bed as I inched my way toward the familiar voice.

The matching dresser was piled high with books and so were the shelves that lined a far wall, creating a mini library. A heavy silver frame was the only other item that graced the shelves and the picture housed within it faded around the edges. My own eyes stared back at me from behind the clear glass casing. Beside me stood Nira, and a person I thought was long since gone. The same man that now sat in a corner chair; the lamp light beside him casting shadows from the well-worn book in his hands.

"Dad?"

Everything inside of me broke as I stared at him. If I had expected anything, it would have been a broken man. A man that had been trapped beneath the weight of age and ailment, but instead, he stood and crossed the space between the chair and door without hesitation.

"I'm so happy you could come see me." He spoke as if it had just been a short while since we had seen each other last instead of a lifetime. I couldn't move. Tears that Robinson and Thakkar could not see flowed down the front of my face as my father held me tight. But not tears of happiness. This man repulsed me. I wanted nothing more than to sense shift him into oblivion, but my emotions kept me trapped in his hug.

He grabbed my face in his hands.

"Siana, my baby, don't cry."

Horror raced down my spine as I could feel Robinson closing in.

"Let her cry. She's been holding it in long enough."

And there it was. The trap I had been waiting for was sprung. The only problem was, it had come from the wrong side.

"It will please the Director to know that he was correct." What I had expected to be a face pulled back in a smug smile was coated in indifference. If Robinson was feeling anything, I couldn't sense it. The thought sent a tiny panic shooting through me. "I'm curious to know how long it's been since the serum wore off?"

I looked around the room that he and Dr. Pirth had directed me to as he spoke. Similar to the one we had just left, this one had a bed and two empty bookshelves and only the one exit, which Robinson was blocking.

"The Director thinks it would be best for you to enjoy an extended stay on Recreor. Since you no longer have the ability to actually defend yourself, he believes the Continent would be far too dangerous for you." The joy Robinson was getting was evident in his tone.

I refused to look at him as he inched closer. The yellow wallpaper in front of me turning a deep shade of gold then black as his shadow loomed closer. He was too comfortable in my space.

I didn't turn as I spoke to him. "Do you know what the most dangerous animal is?"

His silence was my only answer. "It's the one you no longer fear. Remember that when you sleep tonight? When you no longer see me in your nightmares." I turned to face him. "That is when you should fear me the most."

The snarl on his face looked primal. It was the most emotion I had seen on him since we had set the barrier on the Continent. He kept every ounce of tension as he shouldered his way past Thakkar and out of the room.

"Laying it on pretty thick with that one." He fought to stifle the laugh that bubbled in his throat.

"Shut up." I let my body slump into a chair on the opposite side of the room as he shut the door.

"I don't think it's wise to make an enemy out of Robinson. I mean to say that he is an enemy, but it's best not to provoke him more than you have to." He moved to sit in the chair beside me.

"Stop giving me advise. Just because you're old, it doesn't make you wise."

He let out a genuine laugh at that, but only for a moment before a heavy silence coated the room.

"The Director knew the serum was wearing off." I thought back to the conversation we had in his tower office. "There's something that's really bothering me about all of this."

He worried at his beard as he spoke. "I'm listening."

"I read the letters from the Director to Ethan Rightley. They wanted me and Nira. So much so that they would close off access to everything to have us."

He nodded his head as he answered, "So why would he send you away now?" Thakkar leaned forward, an air of worry in his voice. "Maybe because you weren't loyal to him? Or because he realized that he wouldn't be able to control you?"

"Or because he found a new weapon." A puff of air left me as I sat on the hard bed.

"So, what do we do now?"

I shrugged.

Thakkar gave me a sad smile, that fatherly tone seeping in to his voice again, "Are you still planning on leaving? Knowing that your father is here in Recreor?"

"I can't sit back while everyone I care about suffers. We stick to the plan. Despite the…distraction, we push on."

"You would leave him?"

I shrugged my shoulders, as an invisible knife seemed to carve at my insides. "He left me."

A knock on the door proceeded Dr. Pirth's entrance. "I thought I would bring you some clothes since you will be staying with us a while. If there is anything that you need, please don't hesitate to ask."

"Thanks."

As she held out a green tunic and cinched black pants, another exchanged came to mind.

"What was in the package that Robinson gave you?"

She paused just before setting the pile of folded clothing on the bed. "Research."

Chapter Fifteen
SIANA

My bare feet were covered in splotches of mud as I kicked at the dirt patch I had created in the green space located at the center of the building. The bright morning sun fought to push back the chill that the night air had clung to as drops of dew rolled their way down, bowing leaves. Thakkar had been called to meet with Robinson what felt like hours before, and I had spent my time wandering and waiting for any news. I fixed my eyes on the large brown tree that guarded the space when he finally approached.

"What did you find out?"

A tendril of pain laced its way through the air to wrap itself around me, an acrid scent flowed with it. It was a fragrance that I hadn't known before. The feeling of it was clear to my memory, though. It was a mixture of guilt and shame. Failure coursed out from Thakkar in waves.

"They are going to keep you here. For now. Just until they can figure out what happened with your serum." He looked back toward the glass walls that split the space between inside and outside the facility. "I'm to continue guarding you and relaying any information to Robinson. As of right now, it doesn't seem like they have any inclining that I'm not with them however, they don't seem to have any intention of sending you home."

The cold wood and metal of a bench seeped past the thin material of my loose black pants and bit into my skin as I took a seat. The friction of my feet rubbing together sent bits of muck to the ground, but did little to stop the numb feeling webbing out from my toes. "Ok. Let's take this one step at a time." I took a breath. "We need to find a way to get a message to Adilah. She needs to know that we are both stuck here."

Another wave of guilt rolled through the air before Thakkar spoke, "And that they may have been successful in finding a way to help the rest of the Sense Guard be as strong as you."

My eyes went wide as my head snapped over to look him in the eye. He went on, his face stoic, although his emotions were battling below the surface. "It's my fault. The blood sample they were able to get because of me. Robinson said Dr. Pirth may be able to extract something to make the entire Guard as strong as you were." His eyes were glazed with tears as he refused to look at me. "They are remaking your father's serum and they are going to start more testing on you. I'm sorry. I'm so sorry."

A numbness sat heavy in my chest. "Would you want that? To be as strong as me? Could it help?" There was no more reason to cover the tears I had struggled to hold back before, but I held them all the same. Equal parts from habit and wanting to save him from more unearned guilt. We couldn't have known this is what would have happened. Getting me here had been our plan. We had done that together and we would figure this out together as well.

"I want an end to this fighting. To set foot back on the Continent and know that the ones that I care about don't need my protection because they can live out their lives in peace." My heart gave a sad lurch as he looked back at me with glistening eyes. "It's been long enough. And far too many have had to give far too much. It's time that everyone was able to rest, but not at your expense."

The lump in my throat burned as I swallowed back the emotions fighting to make their way out. I wanted to comfort my friend, who had been the closest thing to family I had here. "We'll get through this. We will get back to the Continent together and then it will be time for rest." My eyes shifted to the heavy footsteps that now approached the tree. I gave a quick glance back and forth to both men as another emotion pulled at me. Thakkar was trying to get a read on the man approaching.

"Siana. there you are. Would you like to get some breakfast with me? We can go over some tests that I would like to begin administering." He reached out a hand that I did not accept. A strange pull came over his face, but there was nothing else to read from him. He plodded back toward the inside of the building, clearly expecting me to follow. The tiny clumps of grass and ground that I had destroyed and kicked into a small mound flattened under my feet as I made my way to follow. My mind raced around the fact that Robinson and the Director now knew that I had nothing to barter with. They had been saving me to use as their big weapon, only to find that I no longer carried the ammo they would need to win.

The hallway that my father had gone down was painted with a red stripe, not unlike the green one we had seen while walking with Dr. Pirth the day before. I stared at him as he moved at a brisk pace toward a set of double doors. He looked normal. He did seem to move with subtle but strange stagnated movements and quick mutterings that you may see in someone that lived over the edge of paranoia.

His voice, however, was void of the same air of fear. If I had been able to read him, I would know for sure, but I was not at all surprised to find a block between his senses and mine. He didn't spare me a single glance as he went through the swinging doors and out of sight.

The doors were still brushing back and forth when an overwhelming sense of dread surrounded me. I glanced at the hallway behind me. A shiver raked its way down my body. A sensation like nothing I had ever felt before grasped at me, my heart palpitating in my chest as the red stripe on the floor began to convulse like a wounded snake writhing in pain. A veil seemed to have been pulled back while an invisible trail of eyes passed over me. I couldn't see or sense anyone else in any of the spaces around me.

My breathing began to swell and become heavy. A dizziness rolled through my head as I tried to pull in any other senses. There was no one. Not another living soul on this side of the building. I pushed further until I could sense others. Some just waking, bleary and dazed from a night's rest while others were already eating breakfast. The smell of breakfast meats, breads, and eggs soured on my tongue. Where ever we were headed, it wasn't toward a dining hall. My heart thrummed in my chest and sent an uneasy vibration through my veins. An alarm sounded in my brain. No, not in my brain. It was sounding in the hallway around me. Something wasn't right.

I turned back and was met by a wide smiling face; the teeth glaring as white as the rims around their enormous eyes. The chest of the person in front of me heaved in and out as it seemed to happily struggle for breath, its torso only inches from my own. A screaming in my ears was piercing. At first I would have thought it had been my own, but it was coming from behind the clenched teeth that were now making their way ever closer to my paralyzed face. I tried to open my own mouth to let out a scream of terror, but was met with resentful silence. I couldn't move.

This was more than fear. The thing in front of me had a hold of my body and was not about to let me go. I fought to let out any amount of shift that I could to protect myself. Nothing. I was truly frozen in fear.

I fought to shrink away from the grotesque teeth now so close that the hot air escaping with the never ending scream made my eyes water. Even my breath held in my chest, not being able to escape the terrifying stare. My eyes blurred and struggled to focus with it so close to me. I could only tell that its teeth had begun to part when the flow of the toxic scream carried a burst of air with it. An unearthly whisper scratched its way out of the thing's throat just before it abruptly halted. Its face fell and wide eyes softened.

Where what had looked so vile and evil before now stood a woman. Pale skin etched with a mapping of veins, but a human none the less. It was as if someone had flipped a switched. She turned slowly to look at the man behind her holding a small syringe.

"What was that?"

"Don't worry, sweetie. They can't really do much besides frighten you right now."

My fingers shook as I rubbed at the clammy skin around my eyes where the woman's breath had heated it. "Is she alright?"

"Oh, yes. She's actually progressing very well. I'm very excited to show your mother that. But for now," he patted her on the shoulder, "Genie, this is my daughter, Siana."

"It's so nice to meet you." Her hands were frigid, sending tiny shocks of ice as she took mine. Another ocean of icy shards ran through my blood. Did he just say my mother was here, too?

He patted the space where our hands met, "I think breakfast is still being served if you're hungry."

"Thank you, Dr. V. I'm starving." She gave me a warm smile, completely unlike the one she had given only moments before. My body was still sluggish as she made her way back down the hallway and toward the part of the building where so much life was held.

At that thought, panic took hold again. "You can't let her go that way! How can you keep her around here? There are children."

He linked his arm in mine before I tried to make a dash after the woman he had called Genie. He patted my hand tenderly, as if he were calming a small child. Perhaps he had done that when Nira and I were small. "She is not a threat to anyone here. Now, come. Genie isn't the only one starving. I can hear that belly of yours grumbling away."

A slight dizziness followed my head as I turned to look back the way the woman had gone while my feet traveled forward. My father pulled me all the way through the double doors. A cautious anticipation left my heart sputtering. and a site that I had never wished to see again hit me with the full force of the senses that would forever be linked to it. The gleaming metal counter covered in meticulously cleaned instrument was a carbon copy of the one in Hawthornes' lab at RightCorp.

My hand shook as I reached out to several syringes placed in a clean metal pan. They tinked around as the glass rolled. "Where's mom?"

His tall frame hunched as he shuffled around the space for a moment, gathering various items, seemingly unaware of the question I had just asked. A question that had pierced so many of my thoughts for years.

"Dr. Viteri?"

He didn't answer, but dropped a handful of different but familiar looking cylindrical containers onto the counter in front of me. My hand closed around an orange container, my fingers almost touching as they wrapped it. The words printed along the side of the canister were obviously from another era, but looked pristine. They had been stored and well taken care of. A strange feeling sunk in the pit of my stomach as I realized what I was holding. Dirations. I continued to spin the container in my hand to read the label.

New Breakfast Flavor.

"You want me to eat Dirations." I tossed it to the counter before taking a step away. "I just found you and you're already trying to poison me!"

"Siana, do not yell in the lab. You are going to disturb the others." He gently picked up the fallen cylinder and popped off the top, pulling a single foil wrapped circle and ripping it open. "And your mother gets so angry when you yell."

My eyes locked with his as he gave a sad smile and patted my shoulder. An intense urge to shake it off ran through me, but he pulled away before I had a chance to move.

"Dad." It felt strange to say it out loud. "Where is my mom?" I braced myself for his answer. The one I got, not what I was expecting.

"You're acting so strange today. She is probably on her way to the genome lab right now."

Nausea bubbled up in my chest as it became hard to breathe. She was here? How had Dr. Pirth not said something? Had Livia been wrong? Had my mother not died? Could she be here? The thoughts in my mind were coming as fast as by breathing as I tried to form a coherent question to ask him. I wished more than anything that Nira was with me.

"Can we go see her now?"

"Right now? Oh, no no no." He gave a soft chuckle. "She will be in the middle of sequencing with Nira right now."

"What? What are you talking about? Is Nira here, too?" Something clicked in a small corner of my mind, but I pushed it aside. "Where are mom and Nira?"

"They will be here soon." He tossed an unwrapped cake to me before taking a bite of his own. "She was able to get some big breakthroughs done yesterday with you. I know she will be excited to get started today."

"Yesterday? What are you talking about? Dr. Viteri?" I placed a hand on his shoulder. "Do you know where you are?"

He shook his head slightly before looking me in the eye. "You've gotten so big! How did you do that?" He started to wander around, picking up material from shelves and placing them all along the counter, along with our breakfast. His mutterings continued as he paced around the space. "How did you do that? How did she do that?" He continued before it became completely unintelligible.

"Dad?" I reached my hand out to him.

"I'm so glad you could come see me. Is your mother all finished with you for the day?" He smiled. A genuine emotion gleaming out from his eyes.

"What's happened to you?"

"We aren't completely sure." Dr. Pirth was standing in the doorway, her brows and mouth both pinched as she looked at the spread my father had going on the counter. I scanned his work. Everything was still there except for the Dirations he had just offered me moments before. "He's been like this since he came to Recreor Island. Apparently, long before that as well.

But his work is still intact. He's able to live a comfortable life here while keeping his work going."

"Is that safe for him?"

She pointed at the corner of the room where a small white device was affixed to the ceiling, a small green light flashing down at us.

"We keep a close watch. There's no reason for us to impede on his freedoms here. He may be sick, but he's still a human. He deserves to live on his own terms as much as he's able. Most of the time, he goes about his day to day with little to no interruption." She motioned for me to follow her back into the hallway and pointed to another camera at the far end of the hallway, pointing toward the door where we stood. "It seems this morning, however, was very eventful."

My hand went clammy as I rubbed my eyes again, the memory of Genie's teeth causing my blood to pump faster. "What was wrong with her? She was a monster."

"Monster? Genie is one of the sweetest people you could meet. She certainly wasn't doing anything that would warrant Dr. V jabbing her with..." she picked up the syringe lying on the counter, "this."

"Didn't you see her? She was awful. I don't think I've ever seen something so frightening before. And then out of nowhere, she just changed."

She peeked back in the room toward my father before rubbing my back softly. "Whatever you saw, I'm sure it did frighten you. You can be confident that nothing here will hurt you. I want to have a quick chat with Dr. V and then I will let you two finish catching up." She started through the double doors before turning back to me. "I think it's good that you're here. I believe that it will be good for both of you." She smiled again before making her turn to leave.

"Dr. Pirth..."

"Heidi."

"Heidi. Um, he said that my mom..."

"She's not. I'm sorry, Siana. Sometimes he still thinks he's in his old lab." She grabbed my hand and warmth spread out from her. It felt like I could trust her. "I don't know how much you know, and I would rather not be the one to tell you."

"I already knew she died. It's not a surprise."

"I figured that much. I just don't think that I'm the best person to..."

"Please, Dr. Pir—Heidi. We should be leaving soon. I may not have the time to get anything from him."

Her lips puckered as she gave a slow exhale toward the floor. "You know that your mother and father both worked at RightCorp labs, correct?" I nodded, although I don't think I was ever outright told my mom did anything for them. "Your mom was their top scientist, followed by your dad. Nobody knows for sure why, but on the day that your father kidnapped the three of you and ran, your mother tried to stop him. He killed her."

A strange sensation began scratching at my brain, almost as if a memory was trying to claw its way to the surface. "Are you sure. I mean, I've had so many people just appear out of nowhere. How can you be so sure that she's not hiding out there somewhere?" An awkward laugh escaped the side of my mouth.

"I was assigned to Willulf Fraction at the time. I was there when her body was shipped in for recycling a few weeks later. I'm sorry."

I stared at the door that separated us and him. "Why?'

"I don't know. He's never told me. I've tried so many times to get him to talk about it, but it's as if that day has been erased from his memory."

"And you feel like it's safe to have him around everyone else? After what he's done?" I couldn't peel my eyes from the door. Somehow, even as I said the words, I couldn't match the horrible act to the man that stood on the other side.

"Whatever happened on that day, it isn't who he is." She opened the door to look inside again. "This is who he is."

As I peered inside, I could see where he had taken everything that he had pulled out and separated it all into sections, each corresponding to a different experiment he was running.

"He's still a brilliant scientist. I wasn't exaggerating when I said that he is the reason for most of our medical advances here and in Hartlem. He's just…"

"Broken."

Her face became stern as she turned her attention from him to me. "Don't you call him that. No one here is broken. Broken implies that there is something to fix. We are all puzzles in different stages of completion. Your father has all of his pieces. He just hasn't figured out how to put them back together yet."

I liked the thought of that. "And me?" My fingernails scratched at the seam of my pants out of habit.

"You may still have a few pieces to find." And with that, she disappeared back into the lab as I made my way toward the other end of the building. The side that had people. The image of Genie would be scarred on my memory forever. Maybe Heidi had been right. Maybe she wasn't a monster now, but she had been. I was absolutely sure about it and I was going to keep an eye on her until I made sure she was safe.

After a handful of sharp turns, the long red stripe stopped abruptly at the end of a long corridor. I had traveled far enough to make my way back to the main entrance. The intersection of the hallway had several colored paths that I could take; the red behind me led back to the Doctors, and I was not looking to see them again for a bit.

The green path opposite me led back to sleeping quarters. I remembered that from yesterday. That left an orange path to my left and a green path to my right. My ears twitched as I tried to focus on listening for voices. Small conversations were trickling in from each hallway, but none clear enough to make any sense of what was being said. Orange or blue? The blue could almost have been the same shade as Henry's eyes. It was missing a depth to it though.

Poor Henry. What would happen to him if I remained trapped here on Recreor Island? The slow breath was hard to swallow as I forced myself to calm down. He would be fine. I turned and made my way down the orange hallway.

The lights that lined the ceiling of the hallway gave off a ghostly light. Not having electricity did make things a bit harder back in Coranta, but I really think I preferred it. Where the lamps and firelight gave a soft warm glow, the electricity here was harsh. The shadows where its light couldn't reach seemed almost colder and the hum of power set me on edge. Hurrying down the hallway, I passed several storage and records rooms but no dining hall. I continued ahead to a bend in the hallway before realizing there was nowhere else to go. Turning around, I found another smiling face. The initial shock of it causing a small scream to escape my lips. This smile, however, wasn't from some kind of monster. It was a little boy. He gave a glance side to side before looking back to me, his feet shuffling the entire time. He couldn't have been more than eight or nine years old.

"Hi. Are you lost?" I reached out my hand to show him some comfort in this creepy space.

He crossed his arms and stared me down with a smile still planted on his young face. "No. Are you?" The sass dripping from his words gave me a welcome chuckle.

"Yeah, actually, I am." I smiled as he gave a haughty shoulder shrug and pointed his thumb behind him.

"If you go back that way, you'll run back into the front desk. Red is med, Green is serene, blue to chew, and orange is storage."

"Orange is storage?" I smirked at his rhyme.

"Tell me one thing that rhymes with orange. Go ahead. I'll wait." And he did, as he crossed his arms and sat down on the tiled floor.

"Okay. You got me there. So, blue to chew, right? So the dining hall is that way?"

"Yup. So is the activities room and some other stuff like that, but I'm only worried about the food." He stood back up.

"So I guess I'm headed to blue then. It was nice to meet you…"

He reached out his hand to shake mine. "Weston."

"Weston. It was nice to meet you." I could feel his eyes following me as I made my way down the hallway. The only sound afterward was the gentle click of a door closing. I turned back to an empty hallway and smiled. What was he up to? A weight dropped in my stomach as I thought of little Weston coming face to face with Genie in one of these hallways or rooms.

I sped back down the hall to find him, checking each door where he disappeared before heading to the next. I pushed my senses out and met a strange smell I had never encountered before. It was sweet like fruit but had a smokey undertone. My mouth watered at the delicious smell. It was like nothing I had ever sensed before.

I continued until the smell was strongest outside a door just behind where I had been standing when Weston first appeared. I focused again. The faintest of sounds was coming from the door.

The echoing thud of my knocking seemed way too loud in the empty hallway. Shuffling paired with a chain of curse words made their way to me through the closed door.

"Come on, lady. I was nice enough to point you on your way. Can't you leave me in peace?"

"I'm just really not sure I can make it back without getting lost again. Could you take me to the dining hall, please?"

Silence accompanied my request, so I continued to knock on the door, this time a bit more forcefully.

"Okay. Okay. Just step away from the door for a minute, would you? The cameras are going to see you."

I stared around at the tiled ceiling for a moment before catching sight of a camera with the same green light as before.

"Go away for a minute and tell me when it turns red. Okay?"

"Okay." I paced around the hall for a minute, stealing glances up at the small green light. After a few minutes, the light when red and I rushed back to the door and began knocking again.

"What is your problem?" He said as he held the door ajar for me to squeeze through.

The room was obviously meant for storage. Boxes labeled with varies goods lined shelf upon shelf. Mostly medical supplies and some unknown chemicals could be made out. Weston had made his way back over to a cabinet sporting a keyhole for safety. Clearly, he had a key because he stood picking through its contents before pulling out several things and popping them into his mouth.

"Stop. What are you doing? Do you even know what it is that you're putting in your mouth?" I grabbed the green and purple plants from his hands. Turning them over in my palm. Each one looked like a smaller version of the oranges we had back in Coranta except theses faded from purple to green with a jagged end where it must have held on to a tree branch. Where Weston had taken a bite, juice had begun to seep out and pooled in a yellow liquid while dark seeds clung to each other in swirls within the middle of the fruit. "What is this?"

"It's better than the food we get here. That's what it is."

"Weston, there has to be a reason they store it here, in a locked cabinet, away from all the other food."

"Because they don't like to share?" Another sweet smile covered his face and hid the mischievous reality underneath.

I turned back to the door as footsteps started echoing a distance away. I could feel someone coming down the hall. They were searching for someone. "Weston, why did you tell me to wait for the red light?"

"The eyes only watch the hallways when it's green. The Red Hallway is always on, but everywhere else, it skips around." He closed his eyes and gave a slight tilt to his head, "I knew you were gonna get me caught." He grabbed another one of the strange fruits and quickly tore into it. My feet shuffled along the smooth floor. Not a trace of dust or cobweb covered the space. Which meant it was used very often. By the time I turned back to Weston, he had downed the fruit and hid. The only sign that he was there was a short trail of sticky juice spots that stood out on the white floor.

"Weston?" Before I got an answer, the door to the room swung open and a stocky man in his forties stood in front of me. His face was pulled into a look of exasperation for only a moment before he gave a stuttered apology.

"Oh, so sorry. I don't mean to be rude, but you aren't supposed to be back here, miss. Only the staff are really allowed to make use of this hallway." He shuffled into the room and headed straight for the cabinet, which was locked once again. Hands on hips, and a stern face on, he looked down at the drops of dark liquid. His eyes slowly trailed to mine before he closed them and let loose a troubled sigh. My gut clenched.

"Weston Thibault Anthony Rainer. You had better get out here right now and stop messing with this nice lady who most certainly has better things to do than to help you gorge yourself on the Dr. Heidi's fruit again."

A shuffling sounded under a pile of foil bags marked with several worrying warning symbols as the boy crawled out on his hands and knees. "Dad, I wasn't doing anything. I promise. I was just showing her around." His brown puppy dog eyes seemed to take up his entire face. "Right, miss?"

I couldn't help but be impressed with his initiative. My chest felt airy as I held in the laughter that was trying its best to bubble up and out. I gave myself a second before answering, "Right. I actually got lost and Weston here was helping show me around."

"Is that so?"

"Absolutely. He even taught me that fun little rhyme, so I don't get lost next time. Red is med. Green is serene. Blue is chew. Orange is storage."

His tight stance softened as he gave a loving glance down to the child. "I'm sorry, buddy. Thank you for being so helpful." He gave him a small tap on the chin before heading out of the door with his son in hand. "Why don't you show our new friend to the activity room to meet everyone?" He turned to me, "According to Dr. Heidi you will be with us for a while, is that right?"

My only response to his question was a tight-lipped nod before we made our way out of the storage room and down the hall toward the front desk.

"Weston, hold up." He made his way behind the desk to a door that stood ajar. As he pushed past it to grab a blanket from a small side table, I could make out several screens cycling between footage of hallways around the building. "Can you give this to your grandma when you head that way?" He handed a crocheted blanket in bright, prismatic colors to Weston.

"Ok, dad."

When we finally made our way down the blue-lined hall to the activities room, the smell of whatever had been served for breakfast was still faintly lingering from the dining hall. A gathering of people of all walks of life meandered about the space which connected to the outside garden at the center of the building. Thakkar was talking to a group of them when I entered and made my way over.

"I thought you were helping Dr. Viteri?"

"I was." I pulled in close so that only he could hear me. "Something isn't right here." I stared across the room where Genie was sitting with several children around her. She was moving her arms around theatrically while she told a story. The little ones around her laughing along with the tale. "I think they all need our help."

"So, we aren't trying to leave then?"

"Not yet." I leaned against the sun-warmed wall, trying to rid my body of the chill that had been planted there by the same smile that now focused on the group's children.

Chapter Sixteen

HENRY

The loud banging and hammering that usually came from the streets outside had stopped and been replaced by strange electrical surges. The lights in the small kitchen began to flicker again before coming back on. How many times was that now? It was happening more and more every day. It was getting difficult to keep track of how many times it happened.

The smell of noodles had just begun to flow through the room as the sounds of bubbling came from the stove; but with each flicker of the lights, it went cold again. I was going to run out of ingredients before Siana made her way home. A flash of light shone through the window above the old green couch, sweeping the kitchen in a bright glow before everything was plunged into darkness again. My heart went still as an earsplitting pop radiated through the darkness.

Panic encompassed me crushing chest wall into my chest as my hand brushed the door knob. The arc of electricity between my hand and the metal ball stung and caused my hand to throb. Whatever was happening outside, I doubted Siana was going to make it back anytime soon.

My hands felt raw as I rubbed them together. As I made my way back to the kitchen, my eyes fixed on the carpet where I had been pacing back and forth while the lights were on. You would think there would be a trail where my feet had worn into the dark brown fibers. Instead, it was as perfect as the day I had first moved in.

If nothing else, I could get tea ready, just in case.

A sporadic thump knocked at the roof. It had started not long after the banging outside had stopped. The echoing ting of rock on metal added to my thrumming headache as I pulled the kettle out and placed it on the stove. The two cups sitting on the counter were ready to fill. Siana's green mug shining on the counter, ready to welcome her home. A frightening flutter began to surge in my chest as I grasped at my heart. Focusing on my breathing was difficult as the pain that branched its way out from the palpitations became overpowering. Another flicker of lights came and went as my body lay on the cold floor and panic set it. A wave of terror coursed through me as I thought of her coming in and finding me here like this. The thought of her being completely alone here was all-consuming.

Darkness pulled at me again as everything flickered around me. A gentle voice called my name from a distance. "Henry!" My eyelashes felt glued together as I struggled to pull them apart. The image in front of me was blurry, but I could tell it was her, even in the low light.

"You have to be more careful with yourself, Henry."

"I was afraid you wouldn't make it."

"Where else would I be?" She smiled as she helped me up to lean against the counter. "No one deserves to live like this, Henry. Someone has to save them. I can save them, Henry."

"I know you can." My fingers brushed against the side of her cheek before hooking under her chin. I raised her lips to mine. My heart slammed in my chest as I took in her scent. Cotton Candy. I pulled her closer to me as another round of the sporadic thumping began again.

A deafening rumble crashed into the house and caught me off guard. I rushed to cover her and in doing so, knocked her green mug to the floor. Her head slowly tilted down. My eyes followed. Her green mug was shattered and sprawled out beneath us. A large chunk rested under her bare foot. Drops of blood had already made their way onto the surface and were mixing with the tea that had already gone cold. A tear streaked its way down her cheek.

"I can fix it. I can fix all of it." I bent down, picking up as many pieces as I could find. If I got them all, I could glue it back. She had given up much bigger things than a teacup, but I wanted to give it back to her, all the same. She deserved that.

"You can't fix it, Henry. It's already shattered."

The heavy concrete feeling of exhaustion I had become so accustomed to sank into every inch of my being. A flicker of dark gray walls encompassed my vision as her face vanished into darkness.

Chapter Seventeen
SIANA

"Recreor Island is for people that have done their part in the war. They come here to retire. The Director wouldn't risk hurting anyone here." Thakkar held himself rigid and still as the tension in his jaw gave a sharp angle to his often gentle face.

"Thakkar, I know you want to believe in Hartlem and that they're doing good work, but tell me, what have you actually seen that has been for the good of their people?"

"What you described doesn't happen. I mean, look at her." He gestured toward Genie, who was now helping several of the older residents in the garden. "Have you even spoken to her to see what actually happened?"

The last of the children that had been enraptured by her story telling were gone, leaving her alone. She was busy collecting the different materials they had left behind in a large wicker basket. "You're right." I peeled my body off of the wall and made a line for Genie. Thakkar grabbed at my arm before I could fully leave.

"Siana, please be kind. I agree we need to look into this, but we don't know what she has gone through or what she knows." His fatherly eyes rested on mine. "Don't make it hard on yourself by making enemies on day one."

"I'll try my best, Akshat." With a puff of air, he released my arms and followed me into the warm air outside. Even in the welcoming light, a chill flowed over me when thinking about the monster that lay, hopefully dormant under her unassuming mask. I put on a mask of my own before crossing the space, channeling every quirky heroine I had ever read about. "Hey, Genie, you got a minute?"

A small covering rested on her arm where just hours before, my father had injected her with something before she returned to the girl I was staring at now. "How are you feeling, Genie?" My hands closed around a small wooden tube with holes along the side that was lying on the ground several feet away from her.

Her brows scrunched in confusion, but she gave a nod as I dropped the toy in the basket. "I'm fine. How are you feeling?"

My gaze locked on her as she continued cleaning the children's mess. "You did give me a bit of a scare in the med hallway earlier, but I was just more worried about you. Do you help Dr. Viteri with experiments often?"

The basket she was holding gave a slight crunching sound as she pulled it to her chest. "I'm sorry. I'm not sure you have the right person. I don't believe that we have met before, but Heidi did say that we would have a new guest staying with us." She reached her hand out to shake as I reluctantly took hers.

I focused and pulled at her mind. Her eyes darted around in confusion as I stared down at her. I could feel apprehension coursing through her along with — pity. My face must have registered it was for me, because she pulled her hand away and immediately began apologizing. "I'm sorry. I don't mean to offend you or be
198

rude. I just, I think maybe you should see Dr. Heidi. I can help you find her, if you like." A sad smile rested on her youthful face.

"You really don't remember me, do you?"

"I've never seen you before in my life, miss." She patted my shoulder. "I'm glad you're here, though." She gave a small nod to Akshat before leaving us beside the towering bush of bright pink blooms. A sharp pain shot through my hand as I closed my finger around several flowers and ripped them from the plant.

My mind swirled in a ring of confusion. Had I really imagined it? No. Even if I had imagined the monstrous form she had taken, I had still met her in that hallway. She had been there. Small clumps of darkened pink began to fall to the ground as I rolled the now sticky petals between my fingers. Something about the interaction wasn't right. I believed she really didn't recognize me or even know where she was that morning, but could I have imagined the monster that I had seen? That smile. That evil, toxic grin would haunt my nightmares for years to come. How could that have possibly been my imagination? I always prided myself on having a vivid imagination, but even that was a bit much for me. A frigid lump stuck in my throat as my eyes locked on the dark splotches that stained my fingers.

"You need to get something to eat. Let's get you to your room. We can figure out a new plan there." He plucked one of the unharmed blossoms and tucked it into my hair. "I'm here. Whatever is going on, we will figure it out together."

"Thank you." With Genie completely out of sight, we began to make our way into the building. "Do you know where Robinson is right now?" More unfamiliar but content faces passed us as we made our way back toward the main entry way where all the halls converged.

"Last I saw him, he was leaving the building to go visit someone else on the island. He said he had some things to take care of while we were here and that if I need anything to talk to Dr. Pirth."

"You mean Heidi?" I smiled and gave him a light nudge, remembering the flirtatious conversation they had had just the day before. A slight blush bloomed on his cheeks as he smiled down at me.

"Okay, kid. Don't push your luck. I'm being nice, but it might not last forever."

I gave him another smile as I thought about how I could convince him of what I had seen. Hopefully, Dr. Pirth wasn't a part of whatever was happening. I could see the big lug being happy here after everything was said and done. I wanted that for him very much. Dr. Pirth. She had seen everything and even confirmed that Genie had been in that hallway, too. "I've got one stop to make before we head back."

He shook his head. "Of course you do."

"What do you say to a bit of TV television?"

The lines of his face formed deep trenches as he stared at me. "What are you up to?"

"It's a surprise." I linked my arm in his as we made our way to the front desk. I wasn't sure if I hoped that Weston's father would be there or not.

He was nice enough the last time I saw him, but who knows what his orders were as they pertain to the recordings? A gentle click click click came from behind the door hidden by the front desk. No one seems to be there as we made our way steadily forward. I looked around for any sign of life before pushing the already slightly open door all the way.

The light from the screens met us as we entered the

room, each one flashing a different scene from around the hospital. The only one without any type of static focused on the med hall. What I knew to be a bright red line was frozen in shades of gray.

"I'm not entirely sure we are supposed to be in here, Siana."

"I'm not entirely sure you are wrong, Akshat. Come on, we're gonna be here for a while. Might as well have some fun and relax while we can." I cast him my most devious smile, and although I knew with certainty that he saw through it, he went along with whatever I was doing. "Help me find, I don't know, maybe some tapes or some type of recording device or a rewind button."

"I take it we're not going to be watching cartoons, then?" Thakkar said, amusement painted on his face as he crossed his arms.

The screens cycled through static and black and white scenes. "I just wanted to get a quick peek of the med hall again. Maybe see some familiar faces."

"You want to spy on Genie again?"

"Hey, she said she wasn't there. She said everything was fine. If that's true, then she has nothing to worry about. I'm not spying on something that's not there, right?" I flashed him a closed mouth grin but my heart was racing at the thought of seeing it again. Even the thought of watching a recording of it had my stomach coiling into a painful knot.

"I guess that almost makes sense." He took a seat beside me. We spent the next little while sorting through endless minutes of silent footage.

My fingers nails tapped on the desk impatiently as we searched through watery eyes. My ears were starting to ring as I listen for anyone approaching the front desk door.

After what seemed like hours of searching, my eyes locked on the screen. Heart pitter-pattering in my chest, I stared at myself walking down the long, what I knew to be red, hallway with my father. I saw myself self turn, and look down the hallway where we had come from. And there, through a side hall, came Genie. She approached me slowly. My pulse raced and a bead of sweat traced the curve of my jaw. I knew how this movie ended, and yet I stared at myself, silently wanting to scream for past me to run.

Genie hunched down as if trying not to make a sound as she approached. When I turned, you could see the fear shaking through my body. You could see my planted, paralyzed feet, not daring to move an inch. You could even see the shiver that ran down my spine as she inched closer to me. What you could not see, however, was her distorted face. The stretched lips that encircled her face in a horrifying grin were absent. Instead, in front of me stood Genie. Smiling, yes, but a monster she was not. How could I have been so wrong? The image of that smile, so close to my eyes, still bounced around my head, hitting hidden corners of fear that I didn't even know I had. But staring at the screen, the only face looking at me, was her beautiful, serene, and youthful expression. The same one that she had greeted me with in the garden.

Was I losing my mind? Ever since the serum had worn off, I had felt strange. Weaker even. Is that what was happening to me? A panic flowed through my veins as I reached out to grab Thakkar's hand. "I could've sworn... I don't understand. She was a monster." I thought of my father, muttering away in his lab.

A sharp chill ran down my spine. "Is something wrong with me?"

Thakker took a moment and furrowed his brow before looking at me again. "If something was wrong with you, then she wouldn't have been there. If nothing else, she lied about not knowing you. She lied about where she was. That's enough for me. If you say you were scared and we know that she's there, then I believe you. And I believe that I'm going to do whatever I can to make sure you know what happened. We've got this, Siana." He stroked my hand as I tried to reconcile everything that had happened.

"What I don't understand is, I pulled at her senses in the garden. She believed what she said was true. She had never met me before. She wasn't lying. I sensed it. She truly believed she was meeting me for the first time." I picked at a thread that was coming loose from the cozy pants they had given me last night when I was taken to my room. It was an unsettling feeling to miss the familiarity of the Sense Guard clothes. It was never something that I wanted to find comfort in. I felt a gentle pull as Akshat patted small circles on my upper back.

"Let's get this figured out, and then we can get out of here."

I looked at him with hopeful caution. "I thought you were a big fan of Recreor?"

"This island is supposed to be a gift to those who have earned it. A place to find solace and relax. I could see the fear you held on that tape. Staying here would be no gift to you or to anyone. It would be a nightmare, and I will not leave you or them without a way to wake up from it."

My ears became painfully aware of a crunching sound coming from the doorway behind us.

There, moving his head around to see what we were looking at, was Weston; with a handful of hard bread sticks in his little hand. "My dad's gonna be back any minute now." He grinned and several small crumbs fell from his mouth to the front of his shirt. He made to wipe them away and ended up breaking the hard bread stick in his hand. He bent to pick it up from the ground and popped the broken pieces in his mouth. "Just in case you were looking for him."

He made the few steps from the door to a chair that had been moved toward the wall during our search. In one far from smooth move, he shoved his feet against the wall, the chair rolling over and nearly colliding into Akshat from the momentum of the push. Weston didn't seem to notice. Instead, he stared at the black-and-white screen.

The sly quirk that I had already come to associate with Weston had drained from him, along with whatever blood had pulsed through his face. His eyes were glued to the slightly flashing screen that had been paused and zoomed in on Genie's too wide, but still human smile. A small squeak escape him and the chair as he scooted ever so slightly away from the wall that held the screen.

"You don't look at a Wailer." His voice was quiet. So quiet that I barely caught anything that he said. "You're not supposed to let it get that close."

Akshat crossed the few steps to where the small child was sitting and knelt beside him. "What do you mean? What's a Wailer?"

"If you can see them. If you can hear them. You're too close." It sounded like he was parroting something he had been told many times. Almost like the hallway rhyme, but far more sinister.

The worn gray fabric of the chair scratched against my palm as I swiveled him away from the screen to face me instead. "Have you seen one of these Wailers before?"

He shrugged.

"Has Genie ever attacked anyone before?" Thakkar's voice seemed to stir him.

"We're safe." His demeanor changed. What had just moments before been a face of apprehension and fear became one of stoic bravery. "We don't hurt each other here. Recreor is a place to rest, not fight. We don't fight here." He was putting on a brave show. His words filled my head. He was here. What kind of horrors had his family faced to be allowed to live on the island? Did it have to do with what he called the Wailers? My chest tighten at the thought.

Voices started to echo down the hallway through the open door. That was our cue to leave.

My voice matched the urgency in my hands as I tried to cover up that we had been there the best that I could. "We should come up with an escape plan just in case we need to get out fast." Looking at my work, I was pretty sure I made more of a mess of things in my hurry.

Thakkar peeked around the door. "It won't be easy. In fact, getting off the island on our own is down right suicidal."

"Trust me, if you ever come face to face with one of those things, you're going to want a way out fast."

The voices approaching slowly warped from intelligible echoes to small snippets of a conversation.

I turned my attention back to Weston to find that he had already reset all the screens, and they were now doing their usual cycle between the hallways.

And there, on the far right screen, I could see Dr. Pirth approaching with Weston's dad.

"You better get outta here." Weston shrugged at my puzzled face before reaching into his pocket for more snacks. "You covered for me, so I covered for you. Were even now." Weston began spinning in his chair without another word.

"Heidi," Akshat moved quickly to head them off while I made my way toward the front door of the building, "I'm glad we found you. We were wondering if we could take a walk around the island today. Maybe take in some of the sights?"

"That's not something that you ever have to ask." She turned to me. "Siana, you are not a prisoner here. We thought that you might prefer your stay here as opposed to somewhere else on Recreor since your father is here, but, if you would like, I can talk to someone about having you set up in a cottage in town."

"That would be great. Thank you." Although I wasn't planning on staying long enough to need my place but it might be nice to talk without prying eyes or ears.

Chapter Eighteen
SIANA

An hour of walking around the island ended with a very sweet old woman leading us to a small cottage in the center of town. The chipping white paint of the wooden paneled living area was a stark contrast to the building we had come from. My nails were down to the quick from picking at them. We had been going round and round for hours and were no closer to an actual plan. "I still can't figure out a way to get a message back to Adilah. She has to be told what's going on here."

"Do you know if there was anyone else within the Sense Guard that she had made contact with? Anyone else that she trusted? Maybe we could somehow trick Robinson into taking something back to them." Thakkar's face fell as soon as he spoke the words. Even he knew that was a risky move.

"No. No one. Before me, she hadn't believed that they could save any of us. From what she told me, they were just a few weeks from taking all of you out."

As he spoke, Thakkar stood and peered out of the small window, studying the cobblestone path that connected each house. "And we are sure that we like her. Correct?"

"There's nothing to worry about anymore. She's on our side. Or, more appropriately, we are on hers." The small room had been filled with far too much furniture for its purpose. Almost all of which were shoved into a corner after I had taken the space over. Even with everything pushed out of the way, the small living area seemed minuscule with my pacing back and forth.

"Robinson will be leaving at the first of the month. That gives us over a week to figure out what is going on with the Wailers and figure out what your father has to do with it and get a boat off this island and back to Coranta. There has to be a way to get word back to her. The time line we discussed with her doesn't account for monster people or missing fathers." Akshat stared at his calloused hands as he thought.

My mind was struggling to focus as we tried to readjust our plan. We had gone over everything back at Adilah's base. We knew the Director would know about the serum once he got a hold of my blood and she had been right to assume he would send me to Recreor. The people of Hartlem love the Sense Guard and to see one be given grace to live out their life in peace must have been a PR dream come true. Turney was probably still basking in the glow of what was probably his grand idea. We were supposed to sail back to the Continent, take down the barrier, and let them know what was going on. Now that the dires were free, maybe they would fight for the freedom of others. Or at the very least, be open to offering a home to the people Hartlem thought to destroy. And for that, the barrier had to come down. But I couldn't make that decision for everyone.

It needed to be a choice. And so it was time to go home. Almost.

"There is a way to get a message to her." I bit the inside of my cheek as I spoke. I knew he wasn't going to like the answer but, "If you go back to Hartlem with Robinson."

"That is not happening, Siana." He crossed his arms over his puffed up chest. "First off, to deny the opportunity to live on Recreor is unheard of. It would be seen as an insult to the Director as well as highly suspicious. Secondly, you can't sail the boat by yourself all the way to the Continent. You have no idea what you are doing! You'll capsize before you even leave sight of the shore."

"I have no idea how to use a boat. You are absolutely right about that. But," my finger traced over several small lines that had been notched out of one of the door frames, "someone here has to. I'll find a way home." The rough wood I had been staring at tracked its previous owner's growth. A glow built in my chest before being snuffed out again. Someday, I would have that. A home to put my mark on. Someone to share it with. The squeezing feeling in my gut and chest made it hard to breathe as I hugged my arms in to myself. I let my mind wander to images of what it would be like to stay. I could almost picture us happy here. His image flashed through my mind. His bright smile. I shook the thought away.

Thakkar pulled me in. "I know you will." He gave a small smile and knock to my chin before hugging me again. "Just try not to cause too much chaos in the process, alright?"

It was difficult to breathe as I pulled my sleeve across my wet face. A single sniff to clear my nose before giving him a short laugh. "You know, that's not something I can really agree to, old man." An idea bubbled at the edge of my mind. "Besides, chaos might be just the thing we need to get us both out of here."

"Well, if we're going to cause a little trouble, we need a place to start." We sat down at the small table, the chairs scratching at the hard floor underneath as we pulled them closer and came up with a plan.

The day wore on this was until the sky outside the small kitchen widow sparkled and reflected the stars above.

My father's lab was just as messy as the last time I saw it.

"Are you ready for more work?" He smiled at me and began to bustle around the lab, first grabbing another pack of the strange Dirations and tossing it in my direction. "Here, you missed breakfast." My hands fumbled for it. The crunch of the foil wrapper accented each ungraceful hit of my hand as I swatted it back and forth in the air before it finally dropped to the floor.

Something in his back made a popping sound as he bent to pick up them up and place them gently in my hand. "It's okay, sweetie. I'm sure they're still good." He pulled at the edges of the wrapper until a puff of dust escaped from inside. Several of the small cake like discs must have crumbled when they hit the ground. It made sense. They had to be almost a century old, despite how new the packaging may have looked. I held my breath. I didn't want to eat it those things much less breathe it in.

"I'm really not hungry. Thank you, though." I said as he popped a piece of the broken food in his mouth, stretched out his back and quickly began moving about the room again. All the while, a green light flashed at me from the eye in the corner of the room. "So, Dad, what can I help you with today?"

A bright, warm smile flashed across his aging face. He couldn't have been far over fifty, and yet the deep lines worn into the space around his eyes spoke of decades beyond his years. "We need to set up for your mom's experiments. She's wanting to try out the new serum she's been working on."

A look of worry passed over his face as he looked around the room. His eyes not landing on anything before a reassuring nod and smile took back over his jaw.

"What will it do?" The door on the far side of the lab was slightly ajar, and I made my was back to it. What looked to be a closet full of test tubes and other lab equipment greeted me. The little glass tubes clinked together as I moved and shuffled them around of their shelf.

"She thinks it will allow you to absorb strength from a charged vessel."

"Charged vessel?" The door gave a satisfying click as it shut behind me. I turned back to him, the green light still flashed in my peripheral. "What does that mean?"

His hands darted in and out of cabinets as he piled more items on a worktable. "I believe, for today, that would be your friend Rhett."

My stomach squeezed in on itself at the sound of his name. My mind went off on a flurry of tangents. Did Rhett know about what was happening before I came here to Recreor? Had he spoken with my father? And what would be the point of telling a broken man anything when he was set to repeat the same few days over and over again, unless — Hope bounced like a spring around my chest? My father could hold on to new information, after all. He knew about Rhett. Not only that, but Rhett was here.

The green light flashed again. Damn it, Thakkar. Hurry up.

"Alright, let's get you prepped. How about it?" His hand was warm but awkward in mine as he pulled me over to the small chair beside his work station. "Remember, you don't tell mommy about our brave potion. Alright." He looked around the room again before reaching for an empty vial.

"Dad, where is Rhett? Has he told you anything about the Continent?" A tingling sensation erupted from the base of my skull. Something in my head was fighting to be seen. A memory that was struggling to resurface from the dark depths of my mind. My father's eyes glazed over. I wouldn't be getting anything from him in this state. Whatever he was remembering, he was stuck in it, and I needed answers now. I stared at the empty vial in my hand before sending out a gentle line to the man in front of me. I hadn't risked a full sense shift in weeks, but I needed information. My head split as a flash of a memory jumped around. A strange mixture of reality and memory that I had never experienced before. My perspective jumped back and forth between my father's eyes and someone else's. My mind raced around how that could even be possible.

An eery cold settled over me as my father repeated words that I was sure he had spoken to me before. The lines on his face smoothed and cratered in jumpy succession as I looked down at my own hands. The vial that had been empty just seconds before was filled with an all too familiar black substance. "What's happening?"

The images of my father twitched as some sort of strange overlay between his memory and the present happened. This wasn't right. Something was wrong with my Sense Shift. Was he pulling from me at the same time? Did he have that ability?

"I know you want to go see Rhett, sweetie. Just a bit of brave potion for my little adventurer, alright."

"Yes, sir." My mouth had opened, but a voice much smaller than my own had escaped. "Will it hurt?" The words were forming on their own.

His form was solid in its young self as he hugged my shoulders. "Do you ever remember it hurting?"

"No."

"See. The brave potion works. Every time."

Tiny hands raised the vial to my mouth before a familiar taste coated my tongue.

My eyes began to fog as he turned to someone behind him. My father argued with a woman across the room as a smaller blur made its way to me. "It's alright, Sia." Hands only slightly bigger than my own, cupped over my ears. Voices raised in a bubble of sound that didn't quite reach me thanks to the boy standing in front of me. Dark hair fell down over his forehead as he gave me a gentle, reassuring nod.

"Rhett."

The world flashed back in an instant. The boy's hands were replaced by the weathered but smooth hands of my father.

"I'm sorry, sweetie. You can't play with him today." His voice was hushed, and the sting of fear was gripping the surrounding air.

"Where did he go?" My heart pounded in my chest. The memory had been my own. Whatever they had done when I was little, Rhett had been there, too. Did he remember? Or was his memory somehow gone like mine? "Where did she take Rhett?"

His eyes were coated in a heartbreaking sheen as he patted my hand. "Alright, looks like we get the day together." His demeanor changed as he made his way around the room. He stopped, turning just slightly to me, listening to words that I was no longer voicing. "No. But we can wait for her in the courtyard."

"What? Wait for who. Where did she take Rhett?" My questions hung in the air, unanswered.

"I know. She'll be alright though. Even without the brave potion. I'll make sure the bad thoughts don't stay with her, alright." He turned back to me. "Don't worry. Daddy won't let her remember the bad stuff." If it wasn't the black goop that he called 'brave potion' that made us forget, then what did?

He was stuck in a loop. Something that had happened long ago. My head felt foggy as I tried to piece together everything that had just happened. My hand closed around a crumbling diration cake that he must have placed there during the shift. He was trying to protect me. The serum that had made me a murderer. It was a way to help two little girls escape something horrible. To be brave and unfeeling enough to make it through. He didn't create it for RightCorp. He made it for his daughters. To protect them from whatever was being done to them in the name of war and science.

The light in the corner still flashed green. What the hell was taking Akshat so long? How hard could it be to bribe an eight-year-old to turn off a monitor?

"Eat. It'll help you find better memories to keep." He patted me on the shoulder and watched closely as I lifted the disk to my mouth, almost on instinct. A faint but familiar smell of bread and syrup tickled my nostrils before I placed it on my tongue. His smile was bright as he watched me chew and painfully swallow the dry cake. As soon as it was down, he grabbed two more from the opened foil bag, placing another in my palm before eating one himself.

"It's alright to forget some things. Sometimes it's better that way." A heavy feeling oozed its way over my body as a calm enveloped the room. The yawn that escaped me was long and drawn out. Had I even slept since I arrived?

"Siana."

A groan scratched out from between my lips as I struggled to lift my head. The cold table under my cheek felt wet and sticky.

"Siana." A sudden but gentle shake started to work its way through my body. Another groan before the shaking began to build, more urgent this time. A blur of movement peeked through the small openings under my lids. "We have to move. Now." The urgency in Akshat's voice struck a nerve in my sleepy brain. The hairs on my arms stood on end as a wave of panic flooded me and adrenaline shot through my veins. The fog of confusion that I was left with made the room spin.

"Where's my dad?"

"I saw him leave just after you ate that." He pointed to the dirations still on the table. "Are you trying to die today? Who knows what those things have turned in to. They have to be a century old. You could have died!" He tugged me in tight as we made our way to the exit, but not before I stuffed several rolls of the stuff into my pockets.

"I think these are the reason I couldn't remember anything. My dad was giving us these things to help us forget."

We stopped at the door, waiting for him to check the small window in the double doors for anyone in the hall. "Dirations kill people. Everyone knows that."

"But what if they didn't? What if they just made people forget what was being done to them? It would sure make it easier to control a population that had no memory of wrong doings?"

He stared at me for a beat before continuing toward the door. "You ate some. Do you feel forgetful?"

A foggy sensation circled my head along with a bone deep sense of exhaustion. Besides that, I remembered everything. The brave potion, the small voice…Rhett.

"You said it yourself. They are at least a century old. Who knows what all that time has done to them?"

He opened the door, both of us moving as quietly as possible through the hall. The green lights still flashing on the camera.

"The cameras are still on?"

He scrunched his face at me. "That's why we need to move fast." He pulled a disk from his pocket. "They aren't recording anything, but if anyone looks at them right now, they'll still see us." He shook the disk before putting it back in his pocket. "They just won't have proof after."

Instead of heading out of the red hallway, we turned down another one of its branches. The one that Genie had come from before. Another set of double doors blocked our way forward, but these were heavy steel.

"What are the chances it's locked?" My heart was hopefully cautious as I reached for the door.

"One hundred percent." Thakkar reached for the opposite handle. We were both met with resistance.

Footsteps tapped on the floor behind us. My ears pricked uncomfortably as my spine straightened. Genie's face flashed in my mind. If I turned and met her eye to eye again, I feared that my heart may give out. The fear ramped up in my chest as the tap tap tap of feet inched closer. I couldn't believe I had once been afraid of the Courthouse. What I wouldn't give to be wandering around those rooms in the dark. I would trade that for well lit hallways here any day.

My eyes felt like they were swimming in glue as I turned them toward Thakkar, who was already turned away from the door, a smile plastered on his own face. I closed my eyes tight, grabbing for his arm. My feet were ready to run with him in tow.

I took a deep breath that stung as it slid its way down into my lungs.

"Hello, Heidi." Thakkar's voice was void of any fear.

"Good afternoon, Akshat." I let out a breath and turned. "Siana. Have you seen your father yet today?"

"Hmm. What was that?" I inwardly cursed myself as soon as the question left my mouth.

Thakkar spoke up, "We were looking for him and thought if he wasn't in his lab, he might be in here." He smiled. "What's in here, anyway?"

Heidi narrowed her eyes at the two of us before swiping a card against the keypad just behind Thakkar. "Let me show you."The metal door gave a satisfying click just before she pushed it open for us to follow.

What looked more like a forest than a lab covered the long, open space in front of us. Though it gave off the same architectural layout as the glass rooms that had been housed in RightCorp building in Coranta, this space was warm and inviting. Plants of all different sizes, shapes, and colors were spreading their foliage throughout each room. The smell wrapped itself around me like a familiar blanket just pulled off a sun-baked line. We walked forward, in awe of the rooms until my eye caught a small brown tuft of hair moving around the branches of one of the more spacious rooms.

"What is that?" My eyes stayed fixed on the animal as I asked.

Heidi leaned in toward the glass and smiled. "That feisty little fuzz ball is Juniper. If you value your fingers, I would suggest you not eat around her."

I stared in awe at the small creature as it scurried around the open space. A space that was most likely still some kind of lab. My gut clenched. "Are they here for you to test on them?"

Heidi didn't stop as she continued down the hallway, "We study them. They're from the Gray Forest. Most of them were injured when we found them. Bringing them here meant that they could heal safely and we could study their regeneration as well as the effects of plants that they live in and consume." She opened another door at the end of the long hallway. The bright light that came through was blinding as I shielded my eyes and walked through. The space was a copy of the one joined to the blue line hall. If I had thought the rooms behind us had been a forest, this would have been an entire jungle. Bright blue blooms speckled the green branches and vines reminding me of a now familiar children's story.

"Have you heard the story of the little boy and the Taliak Tree?"

A smile stretched across her face. "Much of our research has taken its roots from those stories." Her fingers closed around one of the petals, giving it a gentle brush without breaking its hold on the branch.

My jaw went slack as a group of rabbits raced around a small pool of water that sparkled as the light from the open sky bounced off of it.

"How do you get them all back here?" Vines and trees spread their mossy arms out to embrace every inch their thick trunks would allow. All the while, several people dressed in medical clothing could be seen throughout, clipboards and other recording devices in hands.

"We have a few small cargo vessels that have been converted for our research." She followed my gaze with amusement. "You should see them in the wild. It's truly spectacular."

The shock of her statement seeped into my voice. "You've been to the Grey Forest? To Taliak?"

She nodded, holding back a larger smile. All of this meant one very important thing. Someone on her research team, maybe even her, could drive a boat.

"You don't keep them all in cages?" A warm tone laced Thakkar's question as he stared out, hands on hips, surveying the entire space.

"We let them play, and live out their days as normal as possible. Just because we need them for our research doesn't mean they have to be aware of it. They are happy enough just to know that they are cared for."

An unwelcome thought was struggling to burrow its way to the surface. The last thing I wanted was to see this place for what it really was, but the similarities couldn't be overlooked. This whole place was a testing ground and at the end of the blue line was just another group of test subjects to them.

"What do you hope to learn from all of this?" I asked.

"Dr. Pirth." A familiar voice came from behind her. "Alpha Lab is on the com and they—" Genie came into view just in time to catch the red that crept up her face when she realized we were there. "I'm sorry doctor, I hadn't realized you were with anyone. I can—"

"It's alright Genie. I will be right there. Please go wait for me."

"Yes, ma'am." Genie left quickly through a far door opposite the one we came through.

"Lead the way. We will be right behind you." I was eager to see the rest of the space, hidden so well from the rest of the facility.

"No. No." She waved a hand at someone behind us. "I'll have someone help you look for your father. I don't want to keep you from catching up as much as you can. You're free to have a look around. Nowhere here is off limits to you. In fact, I will make sure you have access cards made as soon as possible."

And with that, she left.

Chapter Nineteen
RHETT

The sounds of Kindolph's scream were still bounding through my mind as I struggled to sleep as little as possible. Whatever Eilith had done to my powers had left me too weak to try to escape. My stomach gave a painful lurch. I had no idea how long she had held me in this room, but I knew it had to have been more than a few days.

The only time I saw her was just before I would pass out from exhaustion. Her ghostly face would stare silently through the window before my eyes would eventually but reluctantly close.

A dark black void that would slowly build to a bright light replaced my usual nightmares. An energy would pool in my body until I would jolt awake. But as soon as I tried to use my shifts, I would feel a pull and my energy would be sapped all over again. The murky water sitting on the counter every morning would do little to quench the burning in my throat. She had to be sleeping when I did. The pool of energy was my power seeping out of her and finding its way back to me. Time moved strangely here. Everything I did was marked by sleep.

A glimmer of hope attached itself to the very, very stupid plan I had been building. I had unlocked the cuffs that they had attached to my wrists three sleeps ago and I sat waiting to see her stare in at me with those death filled eyes. As if on cue, her head slowly came into view, like a dark creature from the depths of a nightmarish ocean coming to the surface to pull down its prey. The pull under was strong. I needed her to believe I was asleep. I needed to flow just to the edge of that dark void before coming back up for air. I thought of the one thing that always kept me from drowning. Siana's last words to me echoed in my head. I had to get back. I had to keep them all safe.

For the first time in many sleeps, my thoughts traveled to a light space. A space where she was there with me. A scene of me finding her again. Her face as I made my way to Hartlem to bring her home. All of this before I remembered why I had come here. To find something that would bring her back. Not just from Hartlem, but from the serum.

I could see a small ball of light in the distance through my closed eyes and I used every ounce of determination I had to pull it to me and pull myself from sleep. A familiar panic seeped into my bones as my eyes flashed open. Long shaky breaths helped steady my footing as I dragged the cuffs off of my wrist. I wasn't sure how long I had slept, but the water wasn't on the counter yet.

A breath hitched in my lungs as I cautiously tried a pull. Another jab of worry wormed its way into my mind as I took another slow inhale. I could feel the weight of my power slowly coming back, but I didn't dare try to pull it all at once for fear Eilith would somehow sense it and wake up. If my guess was even right.

A sound came from outside the door and it was getting closer. There was no time to over think. If I was going to get out of this hellhole, it would have to be now.

I would have to find another way to bring Siana back. Right now, I needed to get back and protect everyone at the rehab facility.

The space behind the door was covered in grime and sticky cobwebs that clung to my damp clothing. My body was a spring. Bracing my foot against the wall for purchase, I was ready to pounce on whoever came through that door. And thankfully, I didn't have long to wait. As soon as they opened the door, I slammed myself into it. The glass shards from the drink spread out quickly as the water mixed with the grime coated floor. I didn't give a second glance as I quickly stepped over the body of whoever brought the drink.

The sound of my feet slamming against the hard tile ricocheted off the long white walls. My eyes searched the brightly lit space for any oncoming threat. The hallway Kindolph and I had been pulled down before loomed ahead of me and I didn't hesitate as I bolted as fast as my legs would allow.

The door to the records room had been blocked by the tables I had tried to hide under. My heart beat inside my chest as my feet came to a full stop in front of it. The answer to everything they did to us could be in that room. Just a few feet away could be the answer to give everyone their lives back. To get her back. The knot in my throat hurt as I forced it down. My fingers itched to throw the tables aside and rummage through the space, but I had made a promise — and I would keep it.

Leaving the room untouched, I raced toward the stairs and started my ascent back to the surface. The many levels above were much darker and void of any sound but the occasional knock of a pipe or settling of the building. Which meant fewer people would cross my path, but I would be forced to trade speed for silence.

The warmth of my power latching on tighter fueled my escape. Each floor building my confidence more and more as I climbed each set of stairs closer and closer to my freedom from this place. My power reached out to sense anyone waiting for me ahead as the door I had used to sneak in came into view.

A pull tugged at my spine as I made my way back up to the roof of the RightCorp lab. My pulse quickened as an earsplitting buzzing wedged in my ears. The dark sky, which should have provided cover and comfort, seemed to crash down on me. My fingernails cracked as they dug into the edge of the roof. Another pull, this time stronger, made my arms give out. A brief moment of weightlessness enveloped me just before a deafening crunch went out as my body hit one of the metal housings I had used to pull myself up and into the labs before. As I rolled to the side as carefully as I could, I was grateful to learn that it was the metal and not my body that had made the sound.

Whether it was the shock of pain or the distance it had given me from Eilith, I was unsure, but the pull of her draining my power again released with a snap. I didn't waste the opportunity. My body continued to gain some modicum of strength as I made my way through the sleeping city.

The night stretched on as my heart continued to shred its way through my chest. Each building passed was another marker on my path out of Coranta. My heart slammed against my chest at every sound. The thought of her closing in on me was looming as thick as the darkness in the sky.

I had no way to gauge how much time had passed, but the yelling that I had been waiting for was finally starting to catch up to me. The city began to flicker to life as small lights came into view behind me. And there, ahead of me, stood the gate. The words Sense Shifters Killed On Site a welcome sign of escape. It would take at least a day still to get back to the others in my current state.

As I slid my way through the gate, I rushed forward, wanting to get as much distance between myself and the city as possible.

The rocks along the road were loud and rolled under my clumsy feet as a natural weariness started to coat my muscles. I had to stop. The burning sensation in my lungs was sending a nauseous spike to my empty stomach.

The dark city was only a short distance behind me before my legs finally gave out. The heavy breaths that escaped my lungs betrayed me as an unseen body came out of the trees. It wasn't until she was standing in front of me that I realized I wasn't alone.

The urge to swing out was squashed by the ache in my bones.

"What the hell happened to you?" Darkness engulfed her silhouette, but I knew that voice anywhere.

"Prue." I let my body go slack as several arms helped lift me.

"We've got a small camp. They haven't made us yet. Rhett, we were so worried." Her voice held notes of anger as she helped pull me toward the cover of the dense trees. "Get the med kit. We need to get these wounds dressed and taken care of immediately. Clear a spot for him to rest."

Everything slammed back into me at the thought of rest. We didn't have time for rest and I couldn't be selfish enough to take it. I grabbed Prue's hand. "We have to get back now. We don't have time to wait."

"Rhett, you're not going to make it back like—"

"They are coming to kill everyone. We have to go. Now."

Without another word, we turned, gathered supplies, and headed East to home.

Chapter Twenty
SIANA

The week had inched by without any kind of hint or explanation of the Wailers. Something was happening on Recreor, unfortunately, we had run out of time. The only thing we could do know, was use the information we had and make our way back when all was said and done.

Robinson's departure was still a few days away, but with any hope, he and Akshat would head back to the Director as soon as he realized I was gone. Which meant I needed to make a big exit.

Just as we had suspected, several boats bobbed up and down with the waves on the outskirts at the southwestern side of the island. It had only taken a small amount of exploring to find another tunnel at the top of the mountainous wall that enclosed the town below.

As I stood at the opening of the tunnel, staring down at the far calmer waters, I couldn't help but think that the ocean was welcoming me. Offering me safe passage back to where it all started. My whole body ached to take up the invitation. There was only one more problem left to solve before I could. Which unsuspecting researcher would be my ticket out of here? After all, someone had to sail the boat that would take me home.

"How is this port so much calmer than where we came in?" Akshat had been at the other end of the tunnel on lookout before making his way over the slick, uneven ground that led to me. Although, in our time here, it truly did seem as though we were allowed to go where ever we pleased. Doors were unlocked, nothing was barred. Dr. Pirth had even let us sit in on some of her experiments. It was starting to seem more and more like the horror I saw in Genie was nothing more than a trick of my mind. More havoc being wreaked by the serum my father had created. My brave potion leaving even more pieces broken inside of me.

"Are you in there?" He didn't realize how deep that question ran as he asked it.

"I hope so." I gave a soft chuckle before turning back toward the water. "I'm not sure what makes this side more calm but I'm thankful for it." I thought of the giant map that had been hanging in the Director's office. Over the vast waters straight ahead of us were the Continent and Coranta. And somewhere far off to the left, Harlem hooked around until it became something else. That way led to the unknown, the Grey Forest, and Taliak. Someday I would explore it all.

A new fire was lit in me as I we walked back toward the town below. I couldn't wait any longer. We hadn't found out any new information, and it was time to make my move. "I'm leaving tonight."

Thakkar cleared his throat before resting a large, calloused hand on my shoulder. "Let's get you a ride home."

The walk back was painfully silent as the tendrils of Thakkar's anxiety branched out by the minute. He was scared of what might happen, and I wouldn't lie and say that I wasn't scared as well. So instead, I said nothing, but continued to walk past the little cottage I had been given, past the pavilion that would have been great for reading a fantasy book in, past the store where so many of the residence grew or crafted goods to sell, until finally, we stood in front of the medical center.

Before we opened the doors, he asked the one question that I didn't want to answer. "Are you going to say goodbye to your father?"

My head felt far too heavy as I shook it in response, as if even my body rebelled against my answer. "He wouldn't understand." My eyes didn't wander to him. I knew if I saw the pity that I could feel rolling off of him, I would break. "Nira and I will come back for him." Even as I spoke the words, I wondered if he wasn't better off in his loop than facing the truth of what he had done and what his work had caused. Whatever that truth may have been.

The lab was almost empty at this time of day. Most of the researchers were mingling with the rest of the residents that lived in the medical center or heading to their own homes on the island.

The card that Heidi had given me made a satisfying swish as I swiped it to access the lab. There was a strange twisting in my chest as the metallic click of the lock sounded before we made our way inside. The hairs on my arms and neck stood as goosebumps spread out over my arms. An electricity permeated the air inside the lab.

What usually smelled of vegetation and wildlife now took on a sharp bitterness. Something was very wrong.

The decades of training and service kicked in immediately as Akshat took point. Whatever was happening, he could sense it too. No longer the pseudo father figure, now he pushed forward with the stealth of a soldier and I followed close behind.

As we approached the end of the hall that led out to the open courtyard, a realization dawned on me. The lab, which was usually filled with the sound of wildlife, was deathly silent. Not even the birds dared to make a sound. I wondered if they could sense it, too.

We continued out through the door, still looking for the unknown source of fear. We didn't have long to look. There, across the courtyard forest, were Dr. Pirth, Robinson, and Genie.

The darkness that had descended over the island hid our approach as we lurked behind various shrubs and vines, making our way within listening distance.

"We're done here." Robinson took a small brown package from Genie's hands.

"No. You can't do that. We've been working nonstop on this. The research — it's too valuable to give up now." Heidi's voice held a tremor to it as she grabbed for the box in Robinson's grasp. His other hand went out lightning fast as the sound of flesh hitting flesh pierced through the air. The doctor was on the ground, holding the spot where Robinson had just hit her.

My eyes darted to Akshat, who was strangling a vine in his right hand. I placed mine over his and squeezed before focusing back on the trio. Heidi was on her feet again, this time the fear that had coated her words was gone. A calm resilience took its place, "Alpha lab has reached out. They are willing to help. No one here needs to die."

A small bit of blood dripped from her mouth while she stared him down. "Let me continue my work."

"The Director is no longer interested." Robinson turned the package over in his hands several times, inspecting every inch of it as if he could see through to its contents. "This is what will change the course of this war."

He tucked the package in his pocket before a quick burst of movement came from all three of them. We darted forward, skidding to a stop just in time to see Genie lunge, taking both the doctor and Robinson to the ground.

The air shifted as we closed the distance between us, and so too did Genie. The beautifully youthful face distorted again to one of horrifying malice. The too wide grin peeling her lips outward and revealing all of her perfect white teeth.

Her head snapped up as we pulled Heidi from beneath her cage like arms, the air pressing down all around her. Robinson lay frozen, shaking, eyes wide as she lowered herself to be nearly flush with his face.

"What do we do?" My voice cracked as we scrambled to get further away from her. With each successful step backwards, the Wailer's features began to smooth and were replaced with Genie's. "What the fuck?" Was I imagining things? I didn't have time to process everything as Robinson stopped moving all together and Genie had set her sights on the three of us.

"Don't let her get too close to you. In this state, she releases a neurotoxin into the air that over stimulates the Amygdala.

"Meaning?" It felt like my feet were dragging through thick mud as she crawled toward us. Each step I took was excruciatingly slow, but my pulsed raced through my body like lightning trapped in a bottle.

The Doctor moved behind me as she spoke, "For a normal person, she could do irreparable damage to the brain."

Akshat was doing his best to move us all back, but even his movements were beginning to slow. "And what about Sense Shifters? What can she do to…"

"She'll kill you. She'll override your already sensitive senses and fear receptors until your heart stops."

I glanced back at Robinson. His chest was still as he lay flat on the moss covered ground. My heart hammered in my tightening chest as the Wailer paused to stand upright. The sirens had begun to build in my head again as I slammed my hands over my ears. She was too close.

My feet stopped. Fear and the toxins planted to the ground as solid as the trees that surrounded me. And if I glanced my eyes to the right, I could just make out the frozen form of Akshat. Shuffling sounded behind us and a pained moan came from behind the monster. Its fully distorted face was gruesome. The nightmares I had had about this thing had not done it justice.

It stalked toward me, inching ever closer to my face as my world began to topple and spin. In a flash, I saw movement behind the creature. Another moan while the teeth, dripping wet with saliva, closed the distance between our faces. It gaped its mouth open slowly, white teeth blocking out everything else in view. And with unearthly speed, she lunged.

My head bounced off the hard packed earth, panic continuing to rise as her body collided with mine. I could no longer see those viscous teeth through my clenched eyes. My lungs burned, spots of light exploded behind my eyelids, and my fingers tingled. Fear radiated through me like nothing I had ever felt before. Just before a dark nothingness set in behind my eyes, there were flashes of everyone I loved and would never get to say goodbye to. Why did it have to be me? Why? When I knew all along, it would end like this. It would end with me dying trying to save them. They deserved so much more.

Movement was coming back as her body slid awkwardly off of mine and thudded on the dirt beside me.

Warm hands latched on to mine just as I opened my eyes for a moment to see Genie laying beside me, eyes wide and unmoving just before a darkness took me under.

My eyes itched as I struggled to pull my lids open. Everything blurred into a dizzying mix of cerulean and smoky gray. My body warred within itself as a rocking motion made my bones ache and my head scream.

"Take it slow." Heidi's voice rang in my ears as I bolted upright. My head splitting as my body slid against a cold, wet surface. Hands came down on my shoulders, "Siana. You have to go slow. I don't think you were subjected to the wailers toxins for long enough to cause irreparable damage but you still need to take care."

Colors began to snap back into solid shapes as I pulled my body up. Cerulean turned to sky as smoky gray became the hull of a boat. "Thakkar?" My eyes darted around the vessel. The boat, worn but big enough to carry at least a dozen people, carried only two. "Where's Akshat?"

"He helped me get you on the boat. He explained everything as quickly as he could before we set out."

"You left him there?" The tightening in my throat felt like knives. "You just left him with Robinson and that thing!"

Her eyes narrowed on me. "Genie was not a thing." She turned and took her place behind the wheel. Her back was stiff as she continued, yelling over the sound of the ocean around us, "Akshat chose to stay behind. He's going to tell Robinson that he came in to find him almost dead and you trying to escape."

"And you?" I tried to inch my way closer, but the boat had other plans. It lurched to the side, and a large wooden box went with it, crashing into my hip.

"You really need to sit down. If you go overboard, I don't think I can get you back."

A long white chest sat bolted to the back of the boat. I made slowly made my way to it and sat, gripping on to the latched edge. The distance between us doubled, and I struggled to yell over the crashing waves. "And what is he telling them about you?"

She turned her head slightly, just enough to make throwing her voice back to me a bit easier. I could hear the slightest smile in her voice as she did, "Isn't it obvious? I'm your hostage. Now, hold on tight. I would rather be in smoother waters before night falls." She pulled a lever at her side and the boat picked up speed.

The sloshing of the waves made my stomach turn again as I tried to focus on the now disappearing island in the distance. It tore me up inside to leave Akshat and my father behind. I had found family again, just to have to leave them behind. But if everything went according to plan, he would be fine. Everyone would be fine.

Hours passed before another large wave hit the side of the boat, soaking my clothes and sending another roll of nausea through me. This time, I couldn't hold back as I leaned my body over the railing and purged my stomach into the choppy waters.

Dr. Pirth's voice was almost drowned out by the sounds of the ocean as she called to me, "It looks like it clears out just up ahead. Hold on a little longer and we should be free of these waves."

She was right. Eventually, the waves smoothed along with my stomach and frayed nerves. "Are you okay?"

My sleeve scratched at my face as I tried to wipe any lingering sickness from my mouth. "Um huh."

I needed another minute before I let any words out for fear of what else might go with them. She nodded and patted my upper back with a sad smile. As she moved beside me, something hard hit my side. Glancing over, I could see a small brown package sticking out from the satchel still swung around her shoulder.

"You took Robinson's package."

Her fingers closed around the box one by one, as if she were pondering whether to show it to me, until finally she pulled it from the satchel. "It wasn't his." She handed the small box to me. "I guess, if you think about it, it really belongs to you."

My brow furrowed as I unwrapped the book size package. Inside was a small metal case. Undoing the simple latch, it opened to reveal two vials. A yellow and orange liquid swirled around one of the tiny containers. An almost mesmerizing effect as the colors sloshed back and forth but never mixed. I placed it back down in the foam slot before picking up the other. This one I recognized all too well. My eyes locked on the thick, inky black goo. "How did you get this? I thought my dad didn't remember how…"

"He didn't. This is what we analyzed from your blood." She walked back to the wheel and stared forward. The only thing in the distance now, was more endless water. "That's what the Director wanted to give to the rest of the Sense Guard."

"But this is all of it? He can't make anymore can he?"

She stared ahead. "I'm sorry, Siana. He sent me a small sample of your blood, but there's no telling what they have done with the rest. What I was able to create hasn't even been tested yet. There's no telling whether or not it would have the same effects as before," She gave me a side glance before going on, "but it could be very helpful if the situation calls for it."

The box felt strangely heavy as I raised it, ready to see

it sink into the unfathomable depths that swirled beneath the boat.

"Stop." She grabbed at my arm before I even realized she had moved. "I can't speak for everyone, but if it was solely up to me, I wouldn't throw away what might be an advantage, especially if the Director bears down on us." A panic set in her face. "Don't you think Nira should have a say as well?"

I nodded. Anger bubbled inside of me again as I struggled to tamp it down. There was nothing I could do right now. Another problem to face when we got back to Hartlem. I stowed the box in my bag, as the doctor went back to her spot at the wheel.

"What happened to Genie?" My eyes locked with hers. "Why did you lie to me about her?" I was trying to avoid this conversation until we got to the Continent. She was driving the boat, and I didn't want to think of the outcome for me if things went wrong. Still, I didn't want to wait any longer to know who I was stuck with.

"I truly had no idea." As I pulled at her, she seemed genuinely sorrowful. A deep blue haze saturated the air around us as a sweet syrupy smell gently clung to the air. "My poor Genie. She had begged me to let her join the research team." A sourness shifted the atmosphere around her as she went on. "I can only assume Robinson had your father turn her."

Something still wasn't adding up. "How did you know so much about her? What kind of damage the Wailers caused or how the toxins work?"

She inhaled slowly before staring ahead, not meeting my eyes that were boring into her. "The Wailers were an accident. An anomaly. The wrong mixture of chemicals derived from the plants on Taliak." She finally looked at me. "I thought the files on Wailers had been buried along with your mother."

"What do you mean?"

"Your mother was the one who discovered the Wailers for RightCorp, but even they thought it pushed the boundaries too far."

"And she didn't?"

She looked back out at the water flowing endlessly out ahead of us. "She was a brilliant woman." A strange taste filled the air. It mingled too deeply with the salty waves to decipher it. The doctor went on, "The brilliant are not always burdened by the morals of mankind."

The conversation ended there, as if that would answer everything.

The sun rose and fell in the sky and eventually, far off in the distance, the shore of the Continent beckoned me home.

Electricity buzzed around Port Hartlem as we pulled our drenched bodies from the dark water. This was not the same pace I had left. The once weather worn town had been demolished and in its place was erected what seemed to be a full military facility. Our boat was still floating off in the distance as a raft with a blinding search light barreled toward it.

My blood boiled as I looked around me. The Director had had no intention of leaving the Continent. My hands raked down my sea drenched sleeves, ringing out any water that I could before moving forward.

"Come on. We need to get out of sight as quick as possible." I didn't check to see if she was following me as I swerved in and out of the dark gray buildings. The shuffling of feet seemed to be around every corner as we did our best to stay out of sight. The anger I felt continued to bubble and rise as a large chain fence with sharp barbs lining the top loomed up before us.

"How do we get around it?" Her voice was barely audible as she quickly glanced around for anyone too close to us in the small corner of darkness we were trying to compress our bodies in to.

My eyes floated around the darkness as I pulled on every cord I could sense, each one pulling taught as I let my anger flow through them. My heart thundered in my chest as a dark malice flowed from me and oozed its way down each connection.

I could feel each heartbeat race as I locked images of the Wailer in their minds. Heidi's face was one of untethered fear as her chest rose and fell rapidly. I hadn't noticed she had been grabbing my hand until I opened my eyes.

The sounds of screaming pierced through the air as she stared at me in horrified awe.

"Come on." My head was already beginning to split, and my vision blurred from the pain. "We need to move now before I have to drop the shift."

She didn't hesitate as we dashed toward the open section of the gate. "How far can we get before they start coming to?"

"Not far." My body slumped against the chain gate as she bit at her nail. A frantic energy poured off of her. A panicked whine left her throat before she took off running toward the sounds of screaming.

Several of the tethers snapped, my fear starting to build when the sound of an engine roared up beside me. The creak of a heavy door sounded as I lost hold of several more.

"Up we go." Heidi's voice whispered in my ear as the pain in my head crescendoed to a peak before I lost everything.

The heavy door slammed before she jumped in the opposite side and slammed on the petal, wheels spitting out rocks that collided with the metal fence and buildings before gaining traction and speeding away in the darkness. With any hope, they would be too worried about what had just happened to notice we were ever there.

Heidi kept her foot slammed to the floor as we sped down the uneven road. My head began to clear as another obstacle jutted out at intervals across the road ahead of us. The vehicle slowed for the first time in hours until it finally rolled to a stop.

My heart lurched in my chest as the things jutting out in the distance became clear. I stared at the pods that stretched out across the land in front of us.

What had once been smooth metal that reflected the sun in blinding rays, were now coated in rust and dirt. Each left out and battered by the elements and each with a life trapped inside.

Dr. Pirth's voice barely registered in my ear, "How close can we get?"

A lump formed in my throat. What kind of horrors were they living out trapped in those metal cages? Whatever they were, every bit of their pain and suffering was my fault.

"Siana?" The Doctor was louder this time but gentle took my arm. "Do you know how close we can get?"

"Um, yea." I straightened myself. Falling apart now was not an option. I looked at the road behind us and the distance from us to the pods. We were already closer that we should have been able to get. "No. I mean, the connection must have already deteriorated a great deal for us to be this close."

She puffed out a large sigh before kicking several rocks from the road. My skin itched where my still slightly damp clothes clung to me. Beside me, the Doctor let out a curse.

A large chunk of the road had broken off where erosion from the elements had worn it and sent her sliding down.

As I pulled her up, several more rocks slid down into the ditch. They felt rough in my hands as I picked them up, staring at the pod in the distance. I threw one as hard as I could. A sharp ping sounded as the rock bounced off of the ground in the distance and hit the hard metal casing. I stared between the vehicle and the road in front of us.

"It won't work, Siana." She was still trying to brush off the dirt that had begun to melt into her damp clothing as her eyes followed mine. "As soon as we hit the shift, that's it. It's lights out until we get pulled out, or worse."

"It's not that far. If I can reach it from here by throwing a rock, then at the most it might be forty, maybe fifty feet ahead of us."

"And double that for however far it stretches out on the other side. There is no way it will work."

The sizeable chunk of broken asphalt dug into my skin as I hoisted it up in my arms. I dropped it back down to the ground, barely moving my feet before it slammed down. A hopeful shrug was all I gave her as Heidi's hands racked against the sides of her head and into her clump of matted hair. She stared out at the open space.

"Shit. Shit. Shit." She pulled her hair up into a bun atop her head before turning back to me. "Let's do this before I talk myself out of it."

Both of us stood frozen as we started out at the pods and road in front of us.

"It's just a straight shot and we should be able to snap out of it as soon as we are out of reach." I hoped more than anything that what I was saying was actually true. "It might help if we back up and pick up speed first."

She didn't say a word as she walked to the vehicle and drove it in reverse another forty feet and put it in park.

Our feet shuffled under us as we both lugged the large gray chunk onto the driver's side floor. The engine roared in response as it pinned the gas petal down. We both climbed back in.

I reached out my hand across the seat, and she took it. A sharp inhale escaped us both as she reached up and released the parking brake. We were launched forward building speed as our fingers tightened on each other.

A large crack in the pavement sent us slightly off course as she grabbed the wheel with both hands and jerked it back into alignment with the jagged road. Only seconds had passed before the excruciating pain it. A scream ripped from Heidi's throat before she slumped against the wheel. Raging rivers of electricity were shooting their way through my body as I tried to push back against the barrier that I had created.

My teeth clenched together as another shock of pain stuck through me. My vision blurred as I struggled to look out through watery eyes. We had to be close. Only a few second more and we would be out of range.

Both me and Heidi were launched into the roof as the wheels hit another patch of uneven ground. Another scream raged through the space, this time from my own lips as Heidi's body landed back on the wheel, throwing us off the road and running in a line with the barrier. We now were rushing toward a line of trees. If we hit something, that would be it. There would be no coming out of the barrier and my hold on consciousness was starting to wane.

"NO!" The single word escaping through clenched teeth as I pushed back against the shift. The car continued to fly and collide over the rough ground, speeding closer to the trees as another pod flew by in a flash now to my right.

A primal shout left me as I struggled to pull myself closer to the wheel, the weight of Heidi's unconscious body making it difficult to turn as the scream that had been building continued to fill the cab.

I had made this torturous thing and now it had caught up with me. This was my punishment for making something so cruel. The memory of Hawthorn's lab surrounded me. The smell of cleaner and burnt hair. The fear that had consumed me as I pictured his face, smiling right next to mine.

No. Hawthorne was dead. I had ended him and I would put an end to all of this.

The scream I continued to let out built into a primal call. Something that rang out somewhere deep inside of me until an earth shattering snap replaced it. Doctor Pirth's body relaxed as I finally pushed her off of the wheel, the electrifying charge leaving my body.

My adrenaline was still building to an unbearable height as she began to stir, fear pulsing out in sickening shocks as she grabbed for the wheel and jerked it away from the tree line, narrowly missing the enormous trunk that had been looming just feet ahead.

"Get the rock off the fucking petal!" She didn't peel her eyes from the dirt covered window as she barked the order at me and I did my best to squeeze myself under her as she raised her feet. The jagged asphalt tore at my nails as I pulled against it with every ounce of strength I had left. Pain shot through my hand as my grip gave out and it was wedged between the rock and the floor. I grit my teeth past the pain and held it in place there, giving her room to slam on the brake.

Dust and smoke rolled out around us as we came to an abrupt stop. My hand pulsed painfully as she helped pull me out of the driver's side door and we both stood, staring off toward the way we had just tore through. Our eyes slowly made our way back together as a dizzying sense of delirium set in.

The laughter that escaped us was punctuated by hiccuping sobs as we clung to each other in celebration.

Somehow, we had made it through the barrier. We made it out alive.

The engine roared again as we started back toward the road, nothing else standing in the way between me and the people I had left behind.

Chapter Twenty-One
HENRY

An earsplitting snap rung out as pain rushed against every nerve in my body. My eyes stung as my lashes stuck together. Darkness surrounded me as I struggled to pull my arms up to rub my face, but found my arms pinned to my sides by an unseen cage. No sound came out as I tried to force a call for help past the razor sharp pain in my throat.

A single click of compressed air released into the small area around me, followed by a loud whining creak. A blinding light flooded into the small metal space accompanied by a wave of frigid but fresh air that stung as it hit my face.

My eyes adjusted as whatever was holding my body up fell. The hard ground was unforgiving as my body toppled forward. Rocks sliced their way into my arms that I had just barely had time to hold out in front of me.

I stared out into the distance, the blinding light coming from the full moon hanging in the sky. My body ached as my grip on the metal casing tightened and I pulled myself to stand. The world stretched out in front of me and there, in the distance, was the road that led back to Coranta.

RHETT

"I'm fine. Stop fussing over me, Josie." Another plate of food sat on the small table in the corner of my room and was quickly growing cold. Just like the one before. "A day of rest was just what I needed. I'm feeling better."

She picked up the untouched tray from dinner the night before and carried it to the wide-open door. "What's it like in the city?" She didn't look at me while waiting for my answer. Instead, her hands curled up and around the tray that rested over her arms, pulling it closer to her body. An empty cup toppled sideways, but she made no move to right it.

"We'll make it right." Was all the comfort I could give her. My heart ached to give everyone's home back to them. The road would be long, but we would make it.

"Nira's waiting for you." And with that, she took the tray and left.

With my strength fully returned, if not for a few bumps and bruises, I was ready to plan our counter attack. Sheridan had sent a group back to watch for any movement from the city. If they made to attack, we would be alerted. My nerves tingled, my mind on the razor's edge, waiting for the signal that they were coming.

Maps were already laid out along the long wooden table of the planning room as I crossed the threshold. "What are we looking at?"

Nira popped her head up with a tight smile. "Hey, you. Glad to see you up and walking around." That was as far as the pleasantries went before she and Sheridan started on their plans for defending our home.

An hour or so into arguing about defenses, whether we should attack or fall back before they arrived, a shift went out. Both mine and Nira's eyes met in apprehension as a steadily growing throng of voices made their way down each hallway.

"That's not the signal." Sheridan said as we moved down the long hallway that led to the entrance of the building. The shouts and cries turned to cheers of celebration and were becoming more pronounced with each quickened step. My powers still felt unsure from Eilith's assault back at RightCorp Labs. Nira let out a breathy sob before racing forward, leaving us both behind. "Nira?"

She didn't stop as she disappeared into the crowd that had gathered outside of the building. My heart raced, propelling my body forward before my brain could over think. Hope soared through my body as a faint but familiar feeling made it to my senses. It was small, but unmistakable.

The crowd parted as my heart took one final, earth shattering pulse before stopping in my chest. There, kneeling on the ground, holding on to Nira so tight, they might both have stopped breathing, was Siana.

She found her own way back home.

Chapter Twenty-Three

SIANA

The earth was shattering beneath me again. I started to wonder if I would ever piece it together. My knees gave out and planted themselves on the hard ground. Nira dropped in front of me and I took a long moment to breathe while she wrapped her warm arms around me. The comforting embrace wasn't the same as it had been before. How could it have been after everything that had happened? As soon as she moved to pull away, I let everything out without losing my grip on her.

"You fucking asshole! How could you make me think…" I couldn't say it. I couldn't force those words out of me again, even if I knew they weren't true. I wouldn't speak them into existence and chance fate. So instead, I buried my head deeper into her shoulder and continued my rant. "Stupid, selfish jerk! Did you ever stop for one second and ask yourself if I could do this on my own?"

A hand came down to rest softly on my shoulder as waves of concern and warmth flooded through me. I whipped my head around to glare daggers at the hand attached to Rhett Willulf.

"Uh uh! Don't you think for one second that you are off of the hook for this! In fact, if you ever touch me again, I will break that pretty jaw of yours."

A pang of disappointment mixed with the bitter taste of longing stabbed at my senses before it was abruptly cut off. He retracted his hand slowly and turned away.

My sister's soft voice swept through my rage. "Siana, you don't understand."

"You're right, Nira, I don't fucking understand. But neither do you." I gripped on to her shoulder, too scared to let her out of my sight. "I thought you were gone."

She didn't say anything, instead she sat with me. The only sounds were gentle sniffs and quiet sobs from tears that we could finally share.

"I'm sorry, Sia." Her hands were tender as she ran them through my hair. A gentle hum that Aunt Jerry used to sing trapped behind her lips.

Another stream of tears ran down my face. "Aunt Jerry."

"Deanna. I know." A breath puffed out of me as she pulled me in closer. "Rhett told me. We've been looking for her in the city." She didn't pull away as she continued, "We can worry about that later. All I care about right now is that are you are alright? What happened in Hartlem?" She finally pulled away, just far enough to look into my eyes. "What kind of chaos did you spread on our neighbors' shores?" My chest tightened and a hard chuckle escaped me.

"Not nearly enough." Wet trails streaked down my face again.

"I missed you so much, asshole." The fabric of my sleeve scratched at the skin under my nose as I used it as a makeshift tissue. "Uh!"

"You are so strong." Her face looked older than I remembered. Whatever she had been going through, it had taken a toll on her. She'd been so close to death twice. "You never should have had to be. Everything that you've done, I am so proud to be your sister."

I finally took a moment to look at the many faces that were closing in around us. Far more than I had ever imagined being in the Sector. "I hadn't expected anyone to be here. Why are you here instead of in the city?"

She stood, taking my hands and pulling me with her. "Rhett, would you mind making sure that Josie knows Siana is back?"

I turned to him, his eyes burned into mine while a vise tighten on my stomach. "Thank you for keeping your promise this time." His head titled in a slight nod followed be a relieved smile. Flashes of the shift in my father's lab made my head spin. Did he remember the lab as well? Another pang of bitterness stung my senses before he turned and left.

The hallways of their headquarters were warm despite the fallen look of them from the outside. I let my senses trickle out. Room upon room we passed held warmth and some hope. Pain hung in the air, in swirls of deep dark blue that just skimmed my vision. The only break in its weight were small sparks of bright white hope where ever we passed.

"What happened, Nira?" The question stuck in my throat, but only for a moment. "What did I do?"

We finally made it to a small but welcoming room. The bright blooms and cheerful decorations perfectly representing my sister's light. Or what I remembered it being.

What felt like an eternity passed before everything changed. "I'm going to show you everything that I can. But you have to remember one thing: I'm here with you. And I'm not going anywhere this time. I promise." She gave me another squeeze before the strings of her memory snapped into place in my mind. My eyes opened long enough to feel the smoke pouring into my lungs like liquid fire. She had taken me to the night I had lost her.

The room I was staying in was small, but warm. I stared out of the dirty and smudged window that face toward Hartlem. My only hope now was that Thakkar was able to get to Adilah before the Director or Robinson figured out what was happening. Heidi had been keeping herself busy in the short amount of time that we had been here. It had thrilled Nira to have someone else that shared her love of plants and the effects they could have. I was more than happy not to interrupt that, so when Nira asked if I wanted to join them, I politely declined. It felt selfish, but after everything, I had decided to spend the day alone. However, the knocking at my door made me think that my wish might not come true.

I opened the door to a worried-looking Rhett. The tray that he held was jostled a bit from the slight jump he gave. Was he not expecting me to open the door? I stared at him through the steam rising from the cups on the tray.

"I thought you could use… would like some tea. Or coffee. I brought that too, but I don't remember you drinking that while we were at the manor." He was still going on when I took the tray from him and moved toward the small table pushed up against the wall beneath the window. The steam rising from the cups formed a gentle coat of fog against the glass.

He stood at the doorway. "Can I stay?"

My eyes closed as I thought of all the moments we had shared before. Nira had shown me bits of everything last night, including the night I lost her, her meetings with Rhett, time with Ethan and Melissa. Melissa. I had thought the worst of her. Repulsion flowed through me as I thought of what I might have done to her if I hadn't been focused on Ethan. The damage I had done would have been unimaginable if it weren't for her and Nira.

I could feel him turning to leave. "Rhett. I'm sorry about Melissa." He stopped as I took several steps toward him. "I wish I had known her."

He nodded his head and started down the hall.

"Stay." He turned, only a slight hesitation in his step as I continued. "I'm not going to drink all of this myself. No reason for it to go to waste."

As he closed the distance between us, the memory of the woods flooded my mind as my heart began to pound. I remembered the fear that had consumed me as I ran straight through the trees, their razor like limbs cutting into my skin as I thought of the only person that had made me feel safe. I remembered his face and how it looked when he saw me, his arms outstretched and ready to pull me in to him.

"What are you thinking about?" A smug grin rested on his face as he stared into the small room.

"That we should take this to go." I put up a finger for him to wait as I put a sugar in my tea, leaving his coffee black. The cup was still burning hot as I took it by the handle and passed it to Rhett, a devilish look in his eyes as he took the hot cup in hand. "How about a tour? I'm dying to get some fresh air."

The rehabilitation center that the Sector had been using for a base was far more welcoming that the view from the outside suggested. The fence was dilapidated and rusting away into jagged spears. Whether intentional or not, it served multiple purposes. The unkempt wall gave a horror like feel while also providing an added level or protection in the form of sharp points that could easily pierce skin. The path up to the building would thankfully keep us far away from that portion of the facility's outer yard.

After hours of walking around inside and meeting more people than I could possibly remember the names of, outside was a welcome change. Rhett had taken every chance he could get to stand close to me, sometimes even brushing up against my fingers with his own. The shift that Nira had given me just after I arrived had explained almost everything. I knew he was at the lab. I also knew that he willingly kept that secret from me. "Let's play a game, Rhett."

His face was bright as he move in close, a cautious tilt to his head. "What did you have in mind?" He leaned in closer. "Hide and seek?"

My face pulled into a sly grin. "No. I was thinking more like Four Quest."

He took a step back, most likely sensing I was trying to catch him in something but not wanting to back down from a challenge. "How do you play?"

We crossed a grassy area to a log that was resting beneath a tree with long branches. The bright green leaves a flutter of waving fans. I folded a leg beneath me as I rested my weight on the fallen mossy seat and explained the game. "We both ask each other a serious of questions. We each get four turns. I'll ask you a question and you can choose to answer it or pass it back to me. If you pass it back, I have to answer, but it counts as one of your four."

"Is this really what you want to do?" His cocky aura had shifted. A look of genuine concern looked down at me. "You know I can tell if you want to lie to me."

"Same here. High stakes are always more fun." I pushed myself just out of arm's reach as he sat on the ground and leaned against the log. "And I'll even let you go first."

He let out a breath as he plucked several blades of grass; the wind carrying them away as he opened his palm. After a few moments of silence, he asked his first question, "What's your favorite color?"

"What?" My head swung back and forth, looking for any signs of someone looking in on our game. Any reason he would throw a question away. There was only us in this part of the yard. "That's really what you want to know?" I could feel an eagerness radiating off of him.

"I just learned to play, so correct me if I'm wrong, but I don't think it's your turn to ask the questions. Unless, of course, you're wanting to know what my favorite color is." He tossed up another handful of grass before shifting his body to face mine. A smug look plastered to his face.

"Green."

"Just green? Is it more of a green like the grass or more of a sea foam?"

"You've already asked your question. It's my turn." He chuckled at my abruptness but let me continue uninterrupted. "Did you know who I was when I first saw you in the Courthouse?"

He bit his lip and nodded slowly. "I kind of thought you would skirt the big questions for at least a few turns, but alright.

He took a breath.

"Somewhat. I knew you were Nira's sister. I didn't realize yet that you were a Viteri, but I knew that you were important. Question two; do you always take one sugar in your tea?"

My brows felt tight as they furrowed together. Why was he wasting this? "It depends on the tea. My turn. After everything that happened in RightCorp, why did you choose to go back?"

He was an open book as I read every sense that flowed from him. "It started out as a kind of revenge. After a while, I just wanted to help the people they had hurt." His eyes bore into mine. "After I found out who you were, I wanted to help you."

My frustration inexplicably built with every honest answer he gave.

"What's your favorite book?" He leaned back, arms crossed over his chest.

"I don't have a favorite book, but I do have a favorite genre of book. Why did you let me believe my sister was dead?"

He didn't hesitate. "We didn't know what kind of tests Ethan and Dr. Hawthorne were planning on running on you. And as much as it hurt to continue to lie to you, we couldn't let them know Nira was still alive."

It was his turn again. He stood, brushing off the bits of earth that had stuck to his pants. A few steps toward the edge of the tree, where the branches came close to touching the ground, was where he stopped to look at me. My stomach dropped. I could feel his electrified nerves as he refused to pull his gaze to mine until the question finally left his lips. "The night that we found each other in the woods. If I had asked, would you have run with me?"

"Melissa was there. And Ethan. Even if I hadn't felt completely betrayed in that moment, there would have been no way out."

"That's not an answer."

"That's not a question."

"It's not a question, or it's not one you want to answer?"

"This is stupid." My feet slipped slightly on the damp grass before I righted myself.

"It's not my game."

"Fine. You answer it then." A long pause held in the air as I thought about what my answer would be to the question.

Rhett began to cross into my space as he spoke, never once breaking his eyes from mine. "I would have followed you. If you asked me to run, I wouldn't have stopped until my feet bled. If you asked me to hide, I would have covered you until you were no longer scared. If you asked me to fight, I would have torn through anyone that stood in your way." He was only a breath away. I could feel both of our hearts as they pounded in unison.

"And what if I didn't want you to fight for me?"

"I will never stop fighting for you. But if you want to be the one to run into battle, I will hand you your sword."

Rhett was leaning ever closer as an excited laughter bounced through the leaves around us. My cheeks flushed with heat. Reality came crashing back as I realized how many people were wandering around the sizable garden. Several children were playing in the space around the several familiar looking raised beds.

He smiled, nodded his head, and took several steps back, making to part the long wisps of branches that blocked the view of the garden.

My fingers moved deftly through my hair as I twisted it into a long side braid. The heat of the morning sun was making me feel sticky as I moved away from the shade of the tree that had been shrouding us in privacy. "What's planted in the raised beds?"

259

Rhett followed, brushing the leaves back with the side of his hand. "I'm pretty sure I still have a turn left."

"Sure. How about a rain check?" I didn't wait for his answer, but I knew he wouldn't let it go forever. My strategy had worked against me. My heart was still racing as he came up close behind me and pointed out several areas of the garden.

"Nira has been a big part of helping the Sector grow the resources that we need. Especially now, since lines from Coranta have been cut off." Row upon row of vegetables lined the large boxes.

As we moved along the outside space, Sheridan joined us. "I wanted to catch you before we headed out. Josie and I are going to do another check of the barrier. We're hoping if Siana and Dr. Pirth got through, maybe we can get close enough to get a better idea of how to shut it off."

A spike of guilt shot through my skull. I had been selfishly enjoying my tour with Rhett. I had almost let myself kiss him. All the while, Henry rotted away in that pod.

Rhett could read me. His mood fell into a stoic line. "Thanks, Prue. Good luck."

"You too, boss." She gave him a small hit on the shoulder. "Enjoy your checkup." I leaned into the warmth of her side hug before she pulled away and left.

"Check up?"

"Nira and your Dr. Pirth want to try some new plants."

"Nira runs experiments on you?" The vision of the little boy from my father's vision flashed in my mind.

He reached for my hand, fingers falling through my own as I pulled my arms to my chest. "This is different." His voice was low. "Would you like to see?"

"No. Thank you."

He pulled his lip in, his hands delving into his deep pockets. "I'll be back soon. I promise."

I looked away from his retreat to find another set of eyes following me from across one of the garden beds. A little boy with bright eyes had picked a handful of greenery and was pulling a woman along with him toward me. The woman, though seemingly amused by the boy's excitement, walked with a very pronounced limp. My heart lurched inside my chest as I realized why a feeling of familiarity crept into my head.

I knew that face, those eyes, and the reason for that limp. The last time I had seen this woman, I was staring at her hollow eyes through the glass of a RightCorp lab room. I didn't have to see her leg to know what it must look like. My body was moving before I knew it as I crossed the distance to them. It wasn't until I was hugging her close before I realized how many boundaries I was crossing. I didn't actually know this woman, but the pain that they had subjected her to, a part of that, was because of me. To my surprise, she was hugging me back.

"I didn't think you would even recognize us, but my son and I wanted to thank you for what you did in Coranta. I know you couldn't have stopped it, but you stood up when no one else would. I think that's what kept me going."

"I'm so sorry." Tears were filling both of our eyes. "You must hate me for leaving you there, but if I could have taken you from that lab, I swear, I would have." My heart broke all over again at the thought of her being aware of what she had gone through.

"Oh no, no. The lab wasn't…" She was cut off as a little hand shot in front of her.

"These are for you." The green plants he held bent from his tiny fist, gripping them. A swirl of laughter caught in my chest as I smiled down at him. A small pout left him. "I couldn't find any flowers."

"Thank you. You know, I think these are beautiful, but my sister Nira would probably be fine with you picking flowers from her garden if you would like." I pointed toward a small section of fencing that Rhett had pointed out to be before. Colorful blooms sprouted pops of color from between the opening in the slats.

The little boy grinned up at his mom, who gave him a gentle nod. We all chuckled as he raced towards the closed gate..

"He seems so happy." I let the smile seep into my voice.

"He is. I just wish his dad could be here to see him."

"Where is his dad?"

"Still in Coranta somewhere. Before the Shift, he owned a bakery." She tossed me a sad smile.

How had I missed this when I saw her in that lab? It was the same woman that I had seen carted away from her child that day. A deep sadness crept into my veins as the reason for them being there was made clear.

"You were there to get your husband out."

"And he called the police on us. It wasn't his fault and he couldn't know. Everyone works, everyone strives, everyone gives, so the many survive."

My body recoiled at the words that had doomed so many. "How did you get out? Before that happened, I mean."

I got really sick when I was pregnant with Joey. I couldn't keep anything down at all. Anything that went down came right back up, including…"

"Your Soterapine."

She nodded her head and continued, "After a few days, it became unbearable to function. I was at the Med Burrow for help when they decided it would be best if they sent me to a rehab facility. The Willulfs saved me and my son. It was a hard road, and it took a while, but I finally got to where I didn't always feel awful. My goal was to move us to Fuller when we were ready. I should have just taken Joey and went. But the thought of leaving Luke in Coranta was unbearable. We went back to get him out and got caught up all over again. Getting sent to the lab could have been the end of me. It should have been. The second they split us up, I knew what was happening. It hadn't even crossed my mind before that they wouldn't just send us both right back to the Sector." She stared across the garden. "Everyone here took such great care of him while I was there." A deep sadness rested on her shoulders.

My voice seemed so small as I spoke. "Do you know where he is now?"

She looked over toward Joey, his head just barely bobbing above the tops of colorful waves. "He's right there. He lives in my little boy. At least until it's safe to look again."

"Will you stay here?"

"No. This place is for those who fight now. Joey and I are headed to Renbrough tonight." A beautiful smile graced her bright face as she went on, "We are ready to start a new life away from all of this."

"Renbrough?"

She linked my arm in hers as Joey bounded back toward us, an armful of bright yellow and orange blooms cascading over his arms. "It's where most everyone else has gone. They do runs once a month to move whoever is ready. Tomorrow will be the last move for most of us."

The conversation was still playing on a morose loop as I laid my head down on my bed, hoping to close my eyes and wait for Josie to come back with news of Henry.

Chapter Twenty-Four

SIANA

A pull tugged at my chest as the foggy haze covered my eyes. A black sky had plunged the room into darkness. The blanket that had covered me made a light thump as I jolted awake. I waited for the pull again as my eyes adjusted to the darkness. I only had to wait a moment before it came again.

My feet were still aching from my escape from Recreor, but my body refused to slow as I ran down the unfamiliar halls. He was calling to me. Something was dangerously wrong. I sent out a pull in return and was met with a block that left the feeling of ice on my tongue.

I had no idea where I was being pulled, but I needed to get there faster. Shouting came from ahead of me as a slice of light swung out from under a closed door at the end of another mostly darkened hall.

"Are you sure you measured it correctly?" The closed door slightly muffled Dr. Pirth's voice as my feet skidded to a stop in front of it. "I've never worked with these before, but this shouldn't be what happens."

"I'm sure of it but I've never worked with it before. I don't understand why his body reacted like it did." I charged forward at the sound of Nira's voice.

Tables full of experiments and various stages of fresh and dried plants were strewn around what looked to have once been a holding room. The dark metal of the bars stood out against the white of walls as the light from several candles and an overhead light bounced off of them. A gentle buzzing sound was circling the well sized space. Nira must have had a generator somewhere nearby to run her work.

Both Nira and Dr. Pirth were standing over an old Med Burrow style bed, a low and painfully slow beeping coming from an all too familiar white box. Several chords hung from its face and ran, in long red and blue lines, toward the floor and back up to the body on the bed. This was where the pull had come from. There on the table, unmoving, was Rhett.

"What have you done to him?"

Both women, at last realizing I was there, turned to me. Nira's eyes held a sadness as deep as the ocean I had crossed to get to here. Tears that had not been there when I came in were now falling as she grabbed on to my arms. "We were trying to find a way to amplify the shifts again."

I pushed her out to arm's length but didn't let go. A weight fell through my insides as my thoughts went back to everything that I had done. "You can't."

"We don't have a choice. Eilith is coming. Whatever they did to her, she is strong and we have no way of protecting anyone from her." Nira moved just out of my way so that I could fully see Rhett.

His shirt had been unbuttoned and peeled back, exposing his bare chest. Attached all over his skin were the red and blue wires that fed his vitals to the beeping machine. The pull I had felt before was still, but his chest still rose and fell. He was breathing, but the sound of the beeps was still getting farther and farther apart.

"Who protects him?" I couldn't look at either of them. My eyes were solely fixed on where he lay.

Dr. Pirth answered first. "When I suggested we use the serum, he volunteered."

"Nira. You saw what I did at the Courthouse. What I did to Coranta. How could you put every single person in this facility in that kind of danger?" Rhett's fingers had grown colder. As the machine continued to beep, I wrapped my hands around his. "It only took one drop for me to nearly kill him the first time." The first time he had stopped me. There in the Ethan Rightleys library, he had saved both of our lives with that yellow vial. The antidote. "Where is the other vial?"

Dr. Pirth. "We tried it. That's what did this." The fist she had clenched to her chest didn't budge as she moved back and forth around the room with worried steps.

Both women continued talking, devising plans with different plants that could help wake him. None of it could be made before that horrible beeping stopped. Something in his body was broken, shutting down, and fast.

"I just found you again, asshole. You're not going anywhere." His ear was cold as well as I leaned in close, hoping he could still hear me. I caught the few tears that streaked down my face with the back of my hand before straightening myself.

Deadly as it was, the serum my father created did miracles. It unlocked some part of the brain that could control almost everything within the body.

I thought of Nira, bleeding out on the floor of the Courthouse. The serum in my veins had healed her, and it could do the same for Rhett.

"You need to give him more."

Both of their hands stilled as they stared at me. Nira was the first to speak again. "No."

"Give him just enough to counteract what was in the antidote, and he should be able to heal himself."

"No, Siana. We barely gave him a fraction of a dose before, and he was nearly uncontrollable. If Dr. Pirth hadn't moved quickly... we can't give him that antidote again."

"I took an entire vial and here I am. It took time, but it burned off. More so when I shifted." I stared down at the lashes that feathered across his cheek. Those eyes had to open again, and it needed to be now. I pulled my gaze back over to the metal bars. "You need to help me get him in the cell and leave."

"You've got something wrong with you if you think I'm going to leave you in here with him." She gave a sideways glance at Pirth before shifting closer to me. "As soon as he took the serum, he started calling for you. But it wasn't him, Siana. Even his voice changed. Whatever he wanted from you, it wasn't good, and it scared me." That had been the pull that I felt before.

"Trust me. I'll be fine. But you have to get out."

"I don't think so." Dr. Pirth grabbed at her shoulders and she started for me. No doubt to pull me from Rhett's side. As if he could already hurt me. "There is no way I'm leaving you in this room with him alone."

"We put him in the cell first. I'll give him a tiny amount of the serum and close the door." I was trying to piece it all together as I went, but the beeping had begun to skip whole beats between. "He'll have to use some of it to heal himself first and the rest he'll burn through in a big enough shift." He wouldn't kill me. I knew he wouldn't. I didn't kill Nira. I didn't kill Henry. I didn't kill him. He wouldn't kill me. But that didn't mean that whatever happened wouldn't hurt. I took a deep breath before pulling the chords from his chest in one swift movement. "Now, help me get him in."

Even with all three of us working together, it was a struggle to get him into the cell. The dried flowers and herbs that hung from the ceiling in the cell left tiny flecks floating through the air as we knocked into them. Dr. Pirth was the one to hand me the vial. I pinned her with an unforgiving stare. She had given this back to me once before, and it should have stayed that way. "Now leave."

Nira gave my hand a squeeze before placing the key to the cell there. "If you're going to do this, make it count. Go for whatever activated his shifts."

I waited a split second after both had left the room before starting. Wasting time wasn't an option as I my fingers closed around a bundle of tea roses that had fallen to the floor. The thorns stuck my fingers as I carved a small line in the palm of his hand. My hand was steady as I took a single drop of the inky black serum and placed it on his hand. His blood mixed in dark swirls with the poison. I rested his hand back down and stood, walking to the other side of the bars and closing the cage behind me.

My head swirled as a shuttering breath left my lungs and fell to the floor. My feet moved sluggishly as I fought to pull my body further away from his.

A clicking sound started behind me. My chest rose and fell rapidly as I turned to see Rhett, running his fingers over the metal as he stalked my movement from behind the bars.

Something was very wrong. The visions Nira had showed me, what I had been like that day, this wasn't it. Where I had seemed cold and shut off, Rhett's face seemed to be enjoying whatever he was feeling. Reveling in it.

"Took you long enough to get here." Nira hadn't been wrong. His voice wasn't right. The warm depth of it had been replaced by something that sounded much more sinister as a serious of coughs ripped from his chest. The air seemed to vibrate as he rolled his neck, his broad shoulders stretching back as he sucked in a stream of air with a pained hiss. He was healing himself. Step one complete. He opened his eyes, already fixed on me. His face, full of anger before changing and shifting again.

My heart fluttered, and my stomach turned. A vicious smile was plastered on his face. A chill ran down my spine as the image of the Wailer had my heart pounding even harder.

The sound of snapping cracked like a whip around the room. He turned toward me. The gentle pull that always accompanied his sense shift was now a frantic tugging at my brain. His eyes narrowed slightly while taking in the reactions of my body. Blood surged through my veins and my pupils dilated. A warm sensation fluttered around my stomach as the sound became louder.

"If I didn't know any better, I would assume that you were having some very inappropriate thoughts about me right now." I leaned back against the far wall. He would need time after healing before he would be able to actually hurt me with his senses.

However, I was smart enough to know he would throw something if he could.

"I can assure you that they are perfectly appropriate." The pages of a book flashed in my mind about a little girl who fell into a rabbit hole. I imagined Rhett as the cat that had toyed with her. Right on cue, he flashed me a wide and wicked smile.

"Do I want to know what the sound was?"

He bit his lip. "Probably not, love."

"Don't call me that. Not like this."

"Like this? Oh, so now you want to pretend you have some kind of feelings for me?"

"Rhett, I can help you. Let me help you. We could—"

"What? Live happily ever after when all this is over? Ride off into the sunset like one of your little books? Oh, that's right. You hate me. You can't stand to be in the same building as me, let alone the same room. And yet, here you are. Despite everything you say, you are the only one here with me."

My fingers hurt where I held my fists tight to my sides, nails digging into the palms of my hands. "I'm the only one here because no one else can handle your shifts."

"Wrong!" He slammed the table against the far wall with a deafening crash and stalked his way back to the bars that separated me from his rage. "You are here because you're afraid I might have the guts to do what you couldn't."

A sharp ball caught in my throat as I made my way closer to his cage. "And what is that?"

"Come closer and I'll tell you."

I could still feel the pull as my fingers curled around the small metal key resting in my pocket. I would do whatever it took to get him back. He wouldn't kill me. He wouldn't kill me. He wouldn't kill me. The phrase turned over and over in my mind as I closed the distance. The lock gave a satisfying click as I opened it and made my way inside, locking it again behind me and tossing the key toward the doorway.

"I'm closer." I swallowed the lump that was stuck in my throat. It went down like knives as he stared at me. Stalked toward me. My heart slammed in my chest again as I felt a shift settle over my body. He was so close now, I could feel his breath on my face. The cold that I had become so accustomed to from him was leaching its way through my body.

I pushed back with my own senses but his were stronger. Whatever memory he was pulling from, it was strong. But deep down I knew, in this moment, I was stronger. I had to be.

My teeth chattered between words, "You're not going to hurt me, Rhett."

"I'm pretty certain freezing to death would hurt." He ran the back of his hand over my shaking arm as he traced his finger up and around my collarbone.

He was toying with me, and I didn't like it. This wasn't him.

"Real impressive." The disgust I tried to coat on my voice was overshadowed by the click of my teeth. I needed to push him. Whatever activated him, I knew it had to do with the cold. As much as I hated it, I needed him to go there again.

"What kind of pathetic little boy is scared of the cold?" I hated every ounce of myself for what I was trying to surface, but we needed him back. I needed him back. "Nira made it out of a fire. Whatever happened to you, it was nothing compared to that."

His smile deepened. "You know what, love? You may have a point there."

"Do not call me love."

He ignored my protest and inched as close as he could without touching me. "You want me to show you everything? Alright. I'll take you down with me."

The world shifted again. The room I had been standing in just moments before changed and darkness settled with a snap.

Wet trails ran down my face as I tried to call out. My throat felt tight, aching from yelling. Sharp pain ran up from my frozen knuckles. My palms came away sticky when I tried to rub them together for warmth. I had been slamming on the door for what felt like hours until I finally realized he wouldn't be coming back. The pain in my throat and hands had replaced the overwhelming fear, but now it slowly clawed its way back into every nerve in my body. The room still lay pitch black. It was better that way. If it was dark, I couldn't see what else was there. If it stayed dark, maybe I could pretend that I wasn't in the one place that I feared the most in all of Willulf Fraction.

I shuffled my way around the large metal table that I knew was bolted to the floor of the room, making sure not to touch anywhere near the top of it. The temperature in the room was still dropping as I made my way around, knowing full well what I had to do for him to let me out. My breath came out shaky as I readied myself for what would come next. I would need light to do it. I had a sinking feeling in the pit of my frozen stomach at the thought of where I could find it.

My heart slammed in my chest as icy cold sweat ran down my neck, causing more shivers to race through my body. The handle to the first freezer was only an arm's length away.

All I had to do was pull and I could find my way out of this room. I knew what he wanted. If I just did as he asked, he would let me out.

My breath caught again as my left hand gripped the handle and with a sharp inhale, I pulled. My hand stung as I wretched it from the metal bar. Frozen layers of my blood and skin stayed behind as an eery blue light cast the room in a deathly somber glow. The shadows fought to pull the room back into its death shroud as I peered through my aching fingers from my spot curled against the wall again.

Another sob made its way up. No. I had to keep it down. He was no doubt watching me. I forced quick breaths in and out as I built my nerve to stand and face my task. 'How can you run this fraction if you are scared of death? No son of mine will be this weak.' His words, like ice picks, piercing my chest. Sharp, but not as sharp as the instruments that glowed with a ghostly sheen around the room. My eyes trailed back to the freezer and the sheet that covered a mound of flesh beneath it. That wasn't what he wanted me to see, though. What he was waiting for me to uncover laid on the metal table in front of me. I stood, my feet felt heavy as I moved closer. Everything began to blur as my breathing became erratic.

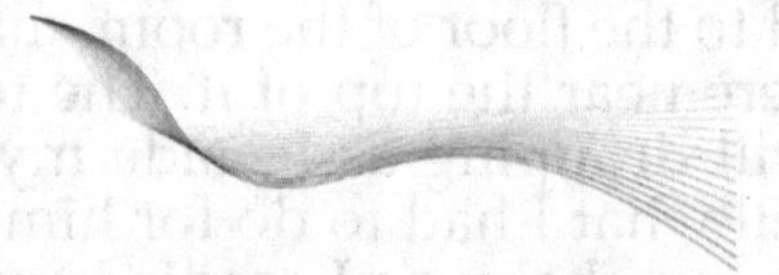

A pin point of heat started in my chest and began to radiate out as I fought back against the Sense Shift Rhett had pulled me into.

My eyes flew open to see Rhett clutching his chest. His eyes were large and bloodshot as he looked at me with panic. His breath was ragged as he fought for air, and my panic began to soar. I pulled him into my arms while screaming as loud as my voice would allow.

"Nira, Heidi, hurry! I think he's going into shock!" He stilled under my hands as they both raced Heidi raced her way into the room picking up the key as she did. "He's not breathing!"

The door to the cell opened painfully slowly as she made her way to where Rhett and I were. "I need you to hold him, just in case."

"Just in case what?" She pulled a small green shot from her shirt pocket and jammed it into his side. Almost immediately, he took a deep rattling breath before throwing me off of him. He charged at the Heidi but was caught off guard when I swung myself in front of her. My own breath slammed out of my body and spots popped in my vision as he crushed me into the spot where she was only a second before.

"Rhett! Come back!" I placed my hands on each side of his face while he stared at me. The horror of the shift combined with what he had just done began to rush into his expression. "Come back to me."

"Siana." He traced his hand over my face. "Did I—"

"No. I'm fine. Dr. Pirth is fine too." As he let out a pained breath, I could feel the fear leave with it.

He pulled himself away as my thoughts dizzied themselves with the realization that I could have just lost him. The scene from his Sense Shift would be singed on my mind forever. I never wanted him to feel that frozen fear again. I let my own emotions overpower me his body began to pull away from mine. It was too much to stand. My hands gripped onto the front of his worn black shirt as I pulled him back to me. His mouth collided with mine.

Sounds of a commotion flowed in from the hall but I barely moved. The warmth radiating out from him as he smiled against my lips made my stomach flip-flop.

"Please don't leave me again." I whispered into his chest.

"Same goes for you." He rested his forehead on mine as we breathed together.

"Siana?" My name sounded like a plea in his breathy voice. I opened my eyes, but Rhett wasn't looking back at me. I turned my head to where his eyes had landed.

A man stood only a few feet from the bars, skin pale and clothes hanging loose on his frame. "Henry!" A pang of fear and shame dropped into my stomach.

Before I could say another word, Henry had launched himself at Rhett. The sound of fist pummeling flesh was torturous in the small space.

"Henry! Stop!" Rhett was doing his best to block Henry's onslaught before he struck a blow to his gut. A rush of people forced themselves into the small space to pull the two apart.

When the waves of voices finally made their way back out, I was left with only a whirl of gut wrenching confusion and Josie.

"You were the first person he asked for." She didn't wait for a response. Only turned and left me to myself.

Chapter Twenty-Five

HENRY

It seemed like another lifetime ago since I sat at this same table. The carving of the tree was still here, but others had added to it. Several small birds had been etched out of the soft wooden top; encircling what would have been the sky. At the base, someone else had panted permanent blooms, stretching out toward the bark.

It was beautiful in its simplicity. And it was permanent. Even if someone patched the table; somewhere under the surface, this would still be here. Only flame or time could erase it from memory. Both were equally cruel.

"How are you feeling?" Josie slid a plate full of greens toward me along with a few boiled eggs. "We should be getting a truck soon, so if you hate this, you only have to endure it for a few days and then I can make you something else." Her worn apron had several holes and burns peppered throughout its front. And her usually bouncy hair was piled in a messy bun on top of her head.

She leaned into my side as she took her place on the bench beside me. "Or," she gave me a gentle nudge, "you could help me figure out something new to fix. Livia told me that you were quite the cook while you were here."

I took a bite of the egg and froze mid chew. My throat clenched tight, not wanting to accept the gooey whites or cold yolk that streamed down my chin as well. "Where is Livia?" A lively group was making a ruckus on the other side of the room. The distraction gave me just enough time to chug down a generous gulp of the water she had sat on the table in front of her.

She looked back at me with a weary smile. "You don't have to eat that." She took the egg that I had started to lift to my mouth again. The thought of making my partner feel bad made my stomach turn. Was she still my partner? Was I still a cop? I wasn't sure what my role in this new world would be.

"What am I supposed to do here?"

"Well, the vegetables are actually not bad and I've got some bread that I thankfully did not make, hidden away for times like this." The table shook slightly as she pushed herself up. "I'll go grab it."

"I mean here, Josie. What am I supposed to do with the Sector? How do I help?"

A red flush coated her face and neck as she sat back down and leaned in toward me. "You have already done enough. They shouldn't ask anything of you and you don't have to agree to anything. You have more than earned the right to walk away if that is what you choose. Renbrough is only a few days away and Fuller is even farther from this place. As soon as you decide where you want to go, we'll go."

"No, I don't want to go anywhere. Josie. What happened to you? Why are you—"

"Angry?" Her voice was loud as it cut through the laughter that spilled over the far table. She looked down at her hands as she rubbed at some invisible stain there. "I tried to get you out. I saw what that man did to you and how she just stood there. Watching. Siana let him hurt you and then throw your body into one of those horrible metal boxes."

The tears that rolled down her face settled in the cracks of the wooden table. I clenched in my chest and broke for her as she went on.

"I had the chance to run. I was in the car, trying to break a window, when the doors unlocked." She moved her eyes from her hands to focus on the far side of the table. "By the time I got close enough to see what was happening, they were hurting you, and I couldn't—"

"It's alright. I'm fine."

"No! It's not alright. I should have run to help you. I should have stopped her. There was so much time between when they put you in that pod and when she activated the barrier. I had time, Henry." She still didn't look at me, though I doubted she could have seen anything through the tears flooding her eyes. "I had time to help you and I couldn't move. Not until the shift hit me." A shake went through her body as she remembered. "The shock racked through me so hard.

I was right on the edge of the barriers' reach because suddenly, the immense pain that I felt stopped." Her brows pinched together. "Rhett pulled me out."

I rested my hand on hers, and she didn't pull away. "You can't blame yourself for any of that." I took her other hand and couldn't help but think of how many times she had said in front of me in the police station, upset about a case, and I hadn't thought to hold her hand. To help try to ease her pain.

A rush of adrenaline shot up through my stomach to my chest. "There is blame, but it's not yours." I moved my head lower to the line of her gaze and smiled.

She let out a laugh with a puff of air. "I went back so many times and watched from what I thought was the barrier. It started shrinking after a few weeks."

"How could you know it was shrinking unless you—"

"After the first time I got too close, I started tracking it." She wouldn't meet my eye again. "Eventually it stopped moving and held. Just a few yards away, the pods." She looked up at me again, her lips tugged at the corners. "I started throwing rocks at you. Just to see if I could wake you up."

"You threw rocks at me?"

"I did. Sorry, I was desperate." The smile that held in her voice brought a genuine one to mine. There she was. Until her face fell again. "I'm sorry I couldn't get to you before they started building."

"Building what? Who's building?"

"Hartlem. We thought it was another wall at first, but Rhett and Sheridan think it looks more like barracks of some kind. There's metal fencing and sharp wire all along the top of it. They suspected there was some type of military facility going in.

Until Siana came back, they had no idea the extent of what they were building."

"Siana." I hadn't meant to say her name out loud as I began to add to the carving on the table.

"She's fine. She's her again, although maybe not the same 'her' as we knew."

"Was she hurt? What did they do to her in Hartlem?" My ears burned as the thought of her being alone there flooded my mind.

"Henry, you were the one trapped in that electric hell. I don't know how you survived it, much less worry about anyone else's pain."

"But I wasn't in pain, Joe. Not until that POD opened, and I made it back here and saw—" the vision of Rhett kissing her brought another flood of heat up my throat that I struggled to swallow back down.

Her brows pulled together as she placed a hand on my cheek. "Henry, what happened in that Shift? Where were you?"

"With her. It felt so real. I thought. I thought I was helping her. That I had saved her. Every word. Every touch. Every kiss." My head fell back as I took as deep a breath as the sharp pain cutting through my throat would allow. My voice came out in a pained whisper. "I would give anything to be like that with her again." I raked my hands through my hair. "And it wasn't even real."

Josie threw her arms around me and I breathed her in as she spoke. "I'm sorry."

"Can I join?" Her voice was deeper than it had been in my Shift but it was still, unmistakably Siana. My gut tightened as Josie squeezed me just a bit tighter before patting my shoulder and letting me go.

Her hair pulled back into a mess of waves on top of her head. The way she held herself was even different from when she left. But the smile she gave me. The smile was the same. The laughter that masked the tears she was so clearly trying to hold back.

My body moved with a familiarity toward her that I knew now was just a dream. But, for a moment, I couldn't make myself care about that. Her weight crushed against me as we pulled each other in. The world swirled around me. The warmth that radiated from her melted away every doubt I had felt. She was real, and she was here.

"I'm so sorry. For everything, Henry. I shouldn't have left you." She pulled back and, wiping the tears from her face, continued, "After Robinson hurt you, I had this flash of something."

"Stop. We're all here." I threw my hand back toward Josie and pulled her in as well. The three of us stood there, the distance between us finally gone.

As both of them pulled away in different directions, ready to do what was needed of them to help the Sector, I slowly lowered my body back down onto the wooden bench and stared at the table. My hand dusted over the small flakes of wood that I had carved into it. There at the base of the tree was a small mug, steam curling up and a book laying open beside its unbroken shell.

A shadow fell over my carving as Rhett's voice broke my peace. "Nira wants you to join us in the meeting room."

It wasn't his fault. I had to keep repeating it to myself. She was never really mine.

"I'll fill you in on anything you missed on the way. Prue will fill you in on anything else when we get there."

I didn't spare him a glance as I made my way to the meeting room, but his feet echoed behind me all the way there.

Chapter Twenty-Six
SIANA

The ease with which everyone gathered around the table left me feeling like an outsider again. Even Henry seemed to fall in to a familiar seat next to Nira. My gut twisted again. He had lived in some sort of hell, so terrible he had yet to talk about it. And I had put him there. I had no right to be jealous of his comfort.

'They are getting whatever army they have ready. We had a tough time getting back just before they realized the barrier was down." Sheridan dismissed the food that Josie offered her before continuing on. "They are bound to have that area locked down as well by now."

"What do they want, Rhett? When you talked about Eilith, it seemed as though she knew everything. Kindolph would only have been able to tell her so much. Most of our knowledge about the RightCorp research, he wouldn't have known. What could he possibly have told her that would make her want us here? There have to be more resources in Willulf, so why isn't she focusing her sights there?"

"Not to mention the tactical advantage of being on the Southern front of the Continent. There is only one way in. If they held that and Coranta, no one could touch them."

"So holding power isn't her end game." I didn't move from my spot on the door frame. It still felt like an intrusion to join them at what was clearly their table. "She said she wants people."

"Right. But an army of dires who know what being controlled feels like? The people we got out would never join with her willingly, and she would have to kill them, anyway. As far as we know, there is no more Soterapine, so she couldn't control them."

The blood leached from my face. "Wailers."

Heidi's expression seemed to take on what mine had lost. "She has no way of knowing about them here. They were an accident that RightCorp had your mother bury. The chemicals, the experiments; there is no way they could have gotten them, much less figured out how to recreate it."

"It was my mother's research. It probably never left RightCorp labs."

"Wailers?" Nira's brows pulled in from confusion. "What does mom have to do with this? She didn't do anything for RightCorp."

"She did everything for RightCorp, Nira."

Nira cleared her throat. "We can talk about who is to blame later. For now, tell me about these Wailers and why Eilith wants them."

Heidi didn't even take a breath before she dove in with her knowledge of them. As she went on, the air around the table changed. Everyone leaned in as the doctor explained every minute detail of their existence and deadliness.

She had the full attention of every mind in the room — except for two. As I struggled to keep the memory of the fear I felt wrapped around me when I first met Genie, I met his eyes. For the first time since he came back, Henry was staring right at me.

Shouting came from the hallway as another Source member ran past me and into the room. "They aren't holding anymore. They're moving."

Nira was the first to stand. "Then so are we. We can figure out whatever reason she has after we take her down." She paused only a moment to squeeze my hand before following the man back out of the room, most following just behind her.

"It doesn't make sense." Josie stared after where everyone had just left. "This Eilith person doesn't want to hurt anyone, and yet she's charging in without any sort of negotiations."

Rhett was next. "I didn't get the feeling that she was much of a people person. Most of what she said was heavily coated with rage. She holds us responsible for what happened to her in the labs."

Josie did her best to calm. "You were children."

Henry said, "So was she. And when the time came to escape, you left her alone and unprotected."

"That's not what happened." Rhett held a growl in his tone as he spoke.

Henry's voice, though even, was laced with silent accusation. "It is to her."

"No matter what her reasoning, we can't just sit here and wonder. We need to get out there and help." Rhett was already moving before Josie finished her sentence.

My mind was reeling as the two of them glared daggers at each other, their silent argument turning quickly into a heated one. Josie was by my side, not bothering to get in the middle of them. "What is it?"

The panic began all over again, and sweat coated my palms. The image of Joey and his handful of weeds setting off alarms in my mind. "She's not coming for us. She's not even here."

The room went still again as the feeling came back in a rush. "She's made a distraction. So she can go after what she really wants. How long had it been since you've gotten any kind of word from Renbrough?"

A simple "no" escaped Josie's lips as she darted from the room, my feet slamming on the ground after her. Chairs sliding across the hard floor preceded the heavy thuds of Rhett and Henry's pursuit behind us.

"What's going on?" Rhett and Henry both shouted in unison.

"We have to tell Nira!" Henry almost slammed into me as I halted my run mid stride. "No. We don't have time for that." I screamed out ahead of me, "Josie!" Already a full hallway ahead. She paused only a moment. "Let them know we already left."

She nodded and disappeared around a corner that lead to the front of the building.

"Let's go." Rhett went to join, and my fingers barely grasped his shirt in his rush.

"No. We need to find a way to get out without them seeing us."

"Why?"

"Because you were right, Henry."

My heart tightened and a wave of horror washed over me. "We did leave her alone and unprotected. And she knew we would do it again." I looked to Rhett as a dark realization came over him.

"Fuck." Rhett brushed past me quickly. "This way."

Henry followed, but only physically. "I still don't understand. If she's not here, there then where? Where are we going?"

Tears stung the back of my throat as I fought to say the name out loud. "She's going to Renbrough."

Darkness had already started to spread across the land outside of base. "The barrier to our East is our best bet of getting out unseen."

"If time is running out here, don't you think we should be heading directly there?"

"I understand why you don't want to go that way. I can't imagine the pain you had to endure, but it's the best way."

"You don't know shit." Henry made his way to the front of our small group. "How are we going to catch up to her when she has cars at her disposal?"

"I don't think that she does. Who knows if it is actually true, but in the first reports Kindolph and the others gave, they had siphoned off all the fuel for the generators. If they are moving, they're doing it on foot."

"Why did she wait this long? She had to know we didn't have—"

"She never needed to get all the way to Renbrough. If she did, you would have known — been alerted. No. If she couldn't get there on her own, then she would cut them off. Put herself in a place to pull them in and then make a distraction so she could leave with her prize." That's when it hit me. It should have sent up a red flag back at Recreor, but I had been so eager to leave, I missed every sign. It had been so easy to find her.

Genie had attacked, but even Akshat couldn't have seen what sparked her to release the toxin. The research lab she had reached to continue her work. She had set a trap for me. And I brought her right to her work. I even let her get close enough to poison Rhett. "Dr. Pirth set up us."

"What happens if we don't get there first? Is this Wailer thing reversible? Like the Soterapine." A shadow crossed Henry's face before he continued, "Would you have to do what you did last time?"

For the first time since we left the rehab facility behind, they both seemed to be in silent agreement that that wasn't an option. There would be no more.

"So, we have no serum, no army, and no allies." Rhett spoke into the sky before turning to me. "Fire or freeze, I'm following you."

Henry's eyes brightened, a hope that he had been without since he made his way back shining through the blue. "Let's go."

We didn't stop. The tall grass that flowed in the night breeze wrapped us in shadows and helped us stay out of sight. The trek toward Coranta was exhausting. Adrenaline was the nemesis of stealth and it made the time draw out painfully slow. Several times either myself or Henry had gotten ahead of ourselves and nearly alerted the small camps of men and women surrounding the crowded landscape as we made our way to the city.

Coranta was not the home that I had left behind. It was the charred remains of a childhood that had never really been my own. Memories of the patchwork buildings scrolled through my head as we passed each. The smell of smoke settled over the notched and scarred bones that had once held up the city.

"What happened?" Henry's voice sounded another world away as my brain continued to struggle with the horrible sight.

"We weren't fast enough." There was a roughness to his voice. A deep sadness coated his words with a gravel that matched the jagged sidewalk that led us deeper into the ruined city. Silence followed. A phantom born from the pain and death that I had caused.

Everything that I had done had been for Coranta. Everything that I had given up and suffered through had been for the people that the Rightleys and Hartlem had held under their boot. And despite it all, I had murdered them just the same as I had snapped Ethan Rightley's neck. The memory of it tore at my insides as the sound filled the space around us and burrowed its death song into the crumbling buildings and piles of rubble that closed in around the city. I was death.

Rhett and I both tried to pull anything we could, but the streets of Coranta were void of life. "Was it like this when you escaped?" Henry scanned every corner and window we passed. "Was everyone gone?"

"Not like this." We continued to pass through more empty buildings.

Rhett's hand closed around mine. The warm pull from him taking the cold that I hadn't realized until then was seeping into my bones. "Breath." He demanded with a smirk.

"Fuck off." He squeezed my hands and let me go, but not before I gave him my own.

My body shivered as I shook off the dead cold that had been suffocating me. Thinking about what happened after what they were calling the Fall would do me no good now. I needed to move. We needed to get to the people still trapped.

As we pressed on, a glow burned at the top of the hill. Smoke billowed up to the sky in the distance. Rightley Manor stood in stark contrast to the blaze that was spreading somewhere behind it.

"I don't like this." Bumps covered my arms as both Henry and Rhett moved to my side in unison. A bitter green haze peeked around my vision just before they both stepped away.

"Me neither. We shouldn't have gotten this far without someone seeing us." Rhett rubbed at the stubble on his jaw. "Let's get a bit higher, see what's on fire, and go from there."

Without another word, we climbed.

The wind whipped through the branches in a sorrowful dance as we stared out over the broken city. There were no puzzle pieces to find here. Everything had been thoroughly destroyed. The only sign of life was the raging fire that was consuming the one place we all had reason to hate. At the bottom of the hill, far below the beautiful gardens and opulent fountains of Rightley Manor, was the RightCorp lab, burning so brightly it out-shown even the pristine marble arches that had guarded its dark secrets.

The smoke was building, and the wind was carrying it right to us. The warm leather of my coat felt sticky as I pulled the collar over my nose and mouth. "I don't understand. They should be here. But if the lab is burning…"

"Where are the people?"

A chill rushed down my spine, as a light in the mansion came on, casting a eerie beam slicing across the grass. A shadow moved across the lit window as each of us plunged ourselves into the overgrowth.

"Someone's there, but probably not the entire city." My mouth felt dry from the combination of the climb and billowing smoke.

"We were wrong then. So, what do we do? Is this Eilith still going to be making these Wailer things?"

Rhett answered, "I know she will if she hasn't already." His gaze was fixed on the house. "Siana, can you sense anything?"

I hadn't sensed a single person besides Rhett and Henry since we had entered the city. The house was no different. "No. Nothing."

"Exactly. Which means whoever is in there is blocking us."

"But the entire city was silent. Even if every single person could be hidden, there is no way they couldn't be sensed." Even as I spoke the words, my brain spun at the realization that anything could be true.

"Whatever the case, we don't have time to sit around and wait."

The statues that lined the long driveway cast frozen judgment as we stalked past. Patches of weeds and overgrown bushes fought to reclaim the path, providing much needed cover. The mansion felt like a hollow shell waiting to be filled in or torn down. I would take a hammer to it myself if given the chance. I would tear down every brick, every tapestry, every locked door. Everything but one garden and the library.

Rhett had already ventured inside before Henry and I could catch up.

My toe caught the edge of a marble step. Henry's hand rested on my elbow, keeping me from falling over my own feet. He leaned down to place a raspy whisper in my ear.

293

"So it's not just tables, then?"

I let out a small laugh as I remembered breaking into another, much less extravagant, home. Before I had a chance to reminisce, his smile fell and deep lines settling over his face.

"I wanna know what happened?"

"You don't know how to use your feet." His smile was wide, a gentle hint of surprise in his eyes. It was as if he was still getting used to his own jokes.

"That's not what I meant." I paused on the landing, the tall door lording over the entrance.

Henry's hands expanded and closed into fists as he gripped his bottom lip between his teeth. Whatever thoughts he had held on to were just on the edge of spilling over as his feet inched closer.

Rhett came back to the door, and Henry took a step back. A curious pain corkscrewed in my chest. "Follow me, but stay close. The foyer is clear and I can't see signs of anyone, but that doesn't mean it's not a trap."

My foot had just tapped on the dust covered marble floor of the foyer when an explosion boomed through the air somewhere across the city. It was followed by a deafening silence.

"Stay here with Rhett. I'm going to check it out and meet you back here."

"What? Why are we splitting up?" My voice was too loud across the open air, but Henry didn't stop. Before I could stop him, he had disappeared into the darkness that led back down the hill.

Inside the manor, the imposing steps sent an even stronger ripple down my spine than they had before. Eyes wandering to every corner of the room in front of me, left a terrifying hollowness in the pit of my stomach. Rightley Manor hadn't been touched. It had been left, frozen in time and waiting for its next heir. The only sign of life was a single trail through the layers of dust that led across the floor, up the banister, and through the open library door.

Chapter Twenty-Seven

Chapter Twenty-Seven
RHETT

Dust particles floated through the small shafts of moonlight as we moved forward. Siana stayed beside me as we ascended the stairs, her hand trailing the banister where someone else had already wiped the dust away.

The library doors stood open, but a quick glance revealed no one inside. A longing shadowed over Siana's face as we turned to leave. "When we rebuild, we'll move them to the Coranta Library." She nodded, but stayed silent.

Across the hall, Ethan's sick little museum remained intact as well. "But this we burn." Her voice was firm. It sent a welcome swell of pride and admiration radiating out through me.

"This we burn."

We continued through the house without another word until another explosion shook Coranta, this one much closer that the last. A cloud of unsettled dust hung in the air as we held on to each other, clinging to an open bedroom door frame.

"You two really are something. Even after all these years, you're still playing at being brave." Eilith's voice sent my head on a swivel as I frantically looked back and forth for its owner.

"Is that her?" Siana had already taken a step into the room.

"Is that her?" Eilith stalked forward from the shadows. Long white sheets covered tall blocks of furniture. They swayed as she moved past, solidifying her ghostly appearance. "You don't recognize your own sister? I'm hurt."

"You're not my sister."

"Ouch. That cuts deep." A smile that didn't touch her eyes spread across Eilith's face before she dropped it a second later. She did this several times before. "You're right. I never really liked you, anyway. Nira, on the other hand. Your mom and I really liked her." She tried on the smile this time. It felt genuine and horrible.

Siana moved to skirt a piece of the covered furniture. A rectangular lump that could have been a couch if not for the high edge of one of its sides.

"What are you doing with all the people you took?" Siana stayed fixed on her target as I slowly made my way around the edge of the room. The darkness here soaked through every inch of space. I couldn't think of a reason she hadn't stolen mine or Siana's powers yet. Or why she was here? Too many unanswered questions had fear bubbling in my gut. My foot connected with the base of a curved sheet. The thing beneath it let out a metallic buzz as I reached out my hand to brace myself.

"Your boyfriend is clumsy. And very loud. Rhett, would you care to stop playing over there and join us?" She turned her attention to Siana again, but I didn't move as she continued her strange conversation. "The harp is obviously not his instrument."

Siana had begun to slowly close the distance between the two of them. The memory of Kindolph's screams sent a spasm through my heart.

"Eilith. Where are all the people?"

Eilith peeled back her red lips into a vicious smile.

"You know, I was expecting to meet someone else here, but this little reunion has been a wonderful surprise." Her hands disappeared against a white covering as she ripped it from its place. Both of us took cover as Eilith tossed the sheet to the floor. The instrument was large, resting on a metal base. She ran her fingers over the strings.

My voice sounded loud in my ears. "Who were you expecting? Dr. Pirth?"

Her eyes didn't stray from Siana as she answered. My skin crawled as she refused to look anywhere else. "Heidi has been a great help, yes. It's been so nice to share with someone who understands." She moved to sit behind her prize, resting it on the floor between her knees, as if she were about to wrap herself around it. "Do you play anything, Siana? I know Rhett here probably couldn't even tell you what this was." She still didn't take her eyes from Siana, who was inching even closer still.

Another explosion went off in the distance as Siana pounced to close the one between her and Eilith. I moved and fast. Catching her just as she rounded another ghostly mound, this one toppling to the ground with a dissonant crescendo punctuated by Siana's guttural scream. Several long metal tubes rolled across the otherwise bare floor where Eilith sat.

Her face was painted with contempt as she finally broke her gaze from Siana to glare at the hollow tubes. "Warriors are silent. Warriors do not scream."

An itch crept up the base of my skull and out toward my ears as a deep, sorrowful melody began to work its way through the room. The sensation was not unknown to me but one that I disliked all the same.

"I'm embarrassed to admit that it took me more than a few tries to find this particular instrument's sound." She closed her eyes, reveling in the music for only a moment, before she set her sights on us again. "This was all I had, but I was content with that. Everything was perfect until your dad decided that, oh, you and his little Nira, his little warriors — you couldn't be touched. You had to be protected from mother."

The cello made a hollow thud as she shoved it away from her and to the floor, knocking aside several metal tubes and sending them rolling behind us. "But everything is fine now. You ran. You were cowards even before that. That's why she gave me power that you could have never wielded."

Eilith moved fast, darting behind another of the white sheets before either of us could reach her. My adrenaline slammed through me as we followed, pulling away the dusty covers and shrinking her places to hide. I spoke low to Siana as we moved past another large item that could only be a grand piano by its size. "We need to take her alive."

"No promises."

Laughter came from a space by the window. I rushed forward, not realizing until I got there, Siana was no longer behind me. The laughter continued. Sounds of children running around and playing only slightly muffled as if it were happening through a closed door or wall. The grounds below were empty.

A heavy crash pulled my attention back. Across the room, where the grand piano stood, was Siana, fighting against the wire that Eilith was holding around her throat.

"No!" I surged forward and Eilith's grip went tighter. My feet slipped out from under me as I forced my momentum to stop. Siana began gasping for breath as she gave her a small amount of room to breathe.

Eilith whispered into her ear. "You know, all I ever wanted was to join you. Just to be a small part of it. We were supposed to protect the Continent. Together." She ripped the wire off of Siana's neck, placing her foot in the small of her back and shoving her to the ground in the same quick movement. "But you ran. You left everyone behind because you knew you were nothing more that a selfish, spineless, waste of space."

I scrambled to my feet as she gripped the side of the piano for leverage before swinging her foot, full force, into Siana's side.

My powers surged and snapped out around Eilith, sending icy shards of pain toward her in torrents for a split second before a shock racked through my body, taking every bit of air with it. My knees collided with the floor as she stepped over Siana and placed her face just inches from my own. "Thank you, Rhett. I was starting to think you didn't want to share today. And we had so much fun last time."

Chapter Twenty-Eight

SIANA

Rhett groaned and seized through clenched teeth as my vision began to settle. "Stop." My voice scratched through my throat like shards of glass. I swallowed, the action causing the sensation of fiery claws raking down into my chest. "Please."

Tremors coursed through me as I tried to stand on unsure legs. The sound that she pulled from Rhett sent a wave of nausea rolling off of me as my knees gave again. "Shhhh." The sound sent the hairs on my neck on end. She was a snake tasting the pain she inflicted. I wanted to see her writhing on the ground before she died at my hands.

"Eilith, stop!" The shaking that had taken over my body just moments before had turned to a deadly stillness. The hatred that had coiled in my gut sprung toward her like a snake ready to strike and kill the object of its venom. "You will not touch him." The words ground out in a voice that even I didn't recognize.

"Little sister actually does have a spine. That's good to know. It will make killing you all the more satisfying." Her blood-red lips curled up in a wicked smile. "And trust me, it will be very satisfying."

A tendril of my senses snapped out toward her as I pushed out every fear, every feeling of excruciating pain, and every torturous thing I had ever known through her. She inhaled with a hiss as the smoke and glowing red light surrounded my vision, closed in. The lines of her face contorted into a mask of pain, her knees giving out under the weight of the monstrous shift. Her nails raked through her hair, clawing at the place where all the pain that RightCorp and Hartlem had inflicted now circled her mind like vultures. A guttural scream ripped through her body, carrying with it a violent tremor.

"Satisfied yet, bitch?"

The whites of Eilith's eyes were covered in a web of red veins as she slowly brought her gaze back to me. The pain still radiating off of her with every twitch and sickly whimper. Before I had a chance to revel in my victory, her arm shot out to the side and connected with Rhett's leg. The wails of pain that escaped his mouth matched the screams that had torn from Eilith. Now she sat, silent as death. Her smile a scythe that cut into my soul as she took the power that I had used to cage her and sent it charging through him. I tried to release the shift. She had taken it. She was using my power to hurt him, and I had let her do it. Walked right into her trap.

The weight caging my chest pulled me down to his side. A plea trapped in my lungs and burned. My eyes refused to look away as his head collided with the hard floor in spasms.

The sound of her shoes moving across the hard floor punctuated each of Rhett's moans. Each one a knife to my heart.

"Don't worry little, Sia. Your boyfriend will be fine. I have to say, I think you could do better." She slid her hand along the frame of the door, basking in whatever deadly thought that brought a giddy laugh from her as she turned through the doorway to leave.

"Don't do this." A whisper. A plea only for her ears. "Please. I will do whatever you want." Eilith didn't look at me. She stood there. A ghost paused in its haunting loop to stare at the living who dared cross it. She was waiting for me to offer up my soul to her. If my heart died here, I would have no use for it, anyway. "I swear. I won't fight you. We can go. You want a family and I can be it. Just let him and everyone else go."

She closed the distance between us, her breath leaving icy cold shards chasing down my skin where her face almost touched mine. She held out her hand. "Let's go."

The panic in my chest hurtled through my body as I took her hand. If Rhett would only wake up. She had a hold of my power, which meant he had his now. If he could only fight the shift long enough to use it.

Eilith didn't give me time to tell him goodbye before she began to pull me up from the cold floor. Every ounce of warmth seemed to seep from my body in her wake.

A metal thump and cry rang out from behind me as the hand Eilith had been holding dropped to my side. My hands flew out to cover Rhett from whatever new attack was being waged before my eyes snapped toward the sound. What I found there was the most beautiful sight I had ever witnessed. Nira, Josie, and Henry stood in front of me. In Nira's hands was a shiny metal tube and at her feet was an unconscious Eilith.

"Hands off my little sister, bitch." The tube reverberated on the floor as Nira tossed it down to pull me to her, stepping over Eilith's still body to do so. A pained sigh escaped her as she squeezed me tighter in her arms. "Are you alright?"

Before I could say a word, Rhett began to stir from where he was still laid out under us. Nira let go of her hold on me to help pull him to a sitting position.

Josie and Henry stayed by the door, looking out for any signs of someone coming to help our would be captor. When the coast was clear, they made their way over as well. Josie was the first to speak. "We are going to have a long talk about this martyr complex of yours."

"Agreed. But later." Nira hugged me to her before helping me take hold of Rhett. "Can you walk?"

He placed his hand on my shoulder and squeezed. "I never want to see this house again. Next time we do, you and I actually burn it down. Deal?"

"Deal." I gripped his arm as we made our way toward the door. "Henry, can you carry Eilith? Nira, don't use your shifts around her. She can drain and use them against us if you do."

A beat of silence hung in the air before Henry answered. "Where is she?"

Rhett pulled in a sharp gasp of air as both me and Nira whirled around. And there was the long metal tube and an empty space where her body had been.

"We don't have time to look for her. We have to get out of the city." Henry's voice was sharp.

"He's right." Josie moved to push us all forward and gestured to Nira. "One of the scouts saw the three of you make it to the city. We were just on the edge of the gates when those bangs started going off."

We hurried down the dark halls, eyes peeled for any more surprises as we went. "You were right about her building an army, Siana. As soon as they went off…it was awful." She looked to Nira for help.

"Everyone started pouring out into the streets. I hadn't sensed a single body up until then, but the streets were packed with people. At least, we thought they were people, until we got closer and they started to — warp."

She had done it. We were too late and she had turned the people we had fought to protect into her own weapons. The city was full of Wailers.

"It's the toxin. They release it in the air when they scream. You can't breathe it in. Especially you, Nira. If you, me, or Rhett inhale enough of it, were dead."

We left Rightley Manor behind, taking only a few tools from a garden shed to defend ourselves, and made our way back through the city. This time, it was far from silent. The sounds of fighting had begun to filter to us from somewhere in the distance.

The lights of Coranta gave off a glow that pulsed on the late night horizon. What was just a ghost town not hours before was now teeming with life. A rolling sea of gas and candle lit windows ringed with an unnatural red fog. And pooling out from every building around Coranta were the Wailers we had been so desperately trying to prevent.

We moved through the streets in a line. Both Rhett, myself, and Nira shifted as many as we could. We wouldn't kill unless we had to but Henry and Josie fought off anyone that got too close.

Whatever Eilith had been planning, it had to be big for her to do this to so many people. We pushed through the crowd of Coranta's fighters like the mirrored edge of an ax, slicing our way through both bodies and minds.

"Keep your nose and mouth covered! Whatever you do, do not breath the toxins in." The makeshift masks were tight around our faces. The Wailers around us shifted in and out as small amounts of the toxin still managed to enter our lungs.

Henry gave out a loud grunt as another attacker broke through my shift and flew at him. A split second of confusion on the towering mans part was all Henry needed as he used his momentum to slam him to the ground. He was out of eyesight by the time the loud crunch of the rake hitting the man's skull. Rhett stepped over several men and women that had fallen. Each laid still as we moved forward. Fallen soldiers of a war that should never have been theirs.

The crowd pulsed around us, paying no mind to the bodies they trampled over. Panic started to take the place of adrenaline as my legs began to shake in time with a loud banging noise just ahead. "What was that?"

"I don't know, but I think more are coming." The disbelief in Henry's voice seemed to echo off the bodies that were still fighting to push through my shift.

The smoke coming off of RightCorp was starting to carry down the street at our backs, making breathing even more of a struggle.

The crowd pulsed forward again as my hold of the shift wavered. Rhett's hand flew and connected with a shovel that had been launched like a javelin, and was flying straight for my head.

A spurt of blood splattered my face as he took the brunt of the makeshift weapon that had been meant for me. That second of shock was all they needed. Bodies lunged for all of us as I held on to Rhett's bleeding arm, Henry jumping to cover us both with his own body. The three of us tensed in unison, preparing ourselves for the onslaught of pain.

Time seemed to stop as we clung to each other. An unearthly calm washed over my mind as I thought of dying. I had never imagined it would be like this. Fighting alongside Rhett and Henry.

Someone whispered, "I love you." into the thick night air. I took another long breath as tears began to run down my face. "I love you too." And waited for the final blow.

A scream pierced through the night air. But nothing happened. My eyes felt sticky as I fought to open them through the smoke.

All around us, the people that had been raging to cut our hearts out with rakes were deadly still and silent. They stared at us with unwavering eyes. Henry's arms didn't move from his cage around me and Rhett as he straightened his spine. "What's going on?"

"Why aren't they trying to kill us?" The smoke billowed out from buildings toward the end of the street we had been fighting to exit.

A deep voice, warm but feathered with worry hung above us. "I told you not to make chaos, and here you are, buried up to your neck in it."

My heart sputtered as Thakkar rushed through the smoke, Adilah by his side.

The single laugh that followed was the stopper to the flood of tears that trailed through my soot coated face. "I'm just trying to help you even that beard out, old man."

He reached for me, and I took his hand. Blood smeared his palm. Rhett's blood. His arm was still producing a steady flow it where the shovel had connected. His face was beginning to pale as he gripped his arm tight to his chest. His eyes, though heavy with exhaustion, were still focused entirely on me.

"Adilah. I'm so glad Akshat found you."

"And we found the Sense Guard." As she spoke, the familiar black clad soldiers made a sweep of the street, taking the now very confused mob with them.

"How did you possibly convince them to help us?"

"You did most of that yourself, but we can talk about that later. For now, we have to figure out what Eilith was doing here." My eyebrows pinched together as I started to question her, but she continued. "We got to the center just after they had been attacked. One of your men filled me in on what was happening and where I could find you and…" She slowed, a look of deep concern painting her face, "my long-lost brother. Who you seem to be letting bleed out on the ground?"

Rhett gave a burrowing stare, while Henry's reaction was much more audible. "You're his sister?"

"Half, apparently." Adilah smiled.

Thakkar bent to help me carry Rhett. "We can have full introductions later. Right now, we need to find this Eilith."

"She's already gone." The pain in Rhett's voice stopped my heart. We had to get him help.

"Adilah, can you and the Sense Guard do a sweep of the city? See if she's maybe hiding somewhere? Rhett can't go anywhere like this. We have to stop the bleeding."

"Absolutely." Her footsteps were heavy as she took off further into the broken city.

"I'm coming with you!" Henry squeezed my hand just before kissing my forehead. "Please stay safe. I have to help find her." His steps were quick as he left to follow her.

"Henry!" I couldn't follow. I had to make sure Rhett would be alright.

"We'll fix this." A shred of pain coated his voice. Had he been hurt as well? Before I could call him back to ask, he was gone.

The first inhabitable house we found had been a trek to get to, even with Thakkar bearing most of the weight.

As soon as we got Rhett laid out, I rushed around the

space, finding whatever I thought might help fix him. Most of my knowledge being what I had read in adventure novels in the dark corners of the library. Thakkar took over, patching him up while I paced in front of the window. The darkness outside had made it a horrible mirror; the only scene plastered there was a reflection of Rhett's still body as he worked.

"He's going to be fine, but there's not a chance that he will be able to do anymore tonight. You need to stay here and keep your head down." He started collecting various items around the room before crossing toward the door. The long floorboards leaving a sharp creak in his wake. "Snuff out all the lights as soon as I leave. I'll do a sweep around the place before I make my way back to Adilah and the others."

There was no hesitation as I wrapped my arms around him, breathing him in as his arms tightened with our hug. "Please be safe."

He gave the top of my head a gentle kiss before leaving me with one more tight squeeze. "Don't you worry. I'm going to stick around long enough to see you in charge of this fight. In fact," He gave me a smile from the other side of the door, "I'm looking forward to it."

The darkness stretched its way around the house as I hastily snuffed out each light.

"Siana." Rhett's voice made me jump as I made my way back to him in the darkness.

"I'm here." My heart jumped at how weak he sounded.

"Could you help me sort out what happened and what's just delirium from the blood loss. And I need you to be honest, even if you think it's going to hurt."

"Technically, you only have one question left. But, hey, you took a shovel for me. I'll answer anything you want."

"Did Eilith get away?"

I sighed. Straight to the tough questions this go around. "I think she might have, yes. But everyone is out there looking for her."

"Alright. And those people that came? They are from Hartlem, correct?"

"Correct"

"And the Adilah one." He looked at me, "she thinks we're related somehow?"

"Siblings. Half-siblings, actually."

I could see him chewing on the inside of his cheek and he thought it over.

"Hm. Alright?" He stared at something across the room, eyes not focusing as he traced circles on my hand. Small shivers rattled up my arm as he went on. "So, none of that was blood loss. I heard all of that loud and clear." I could feel him trying to steady his breathing as mine became equally shaky.

"Yep. You heard all of that right."

"And when you said you loved me, too?" He looked at me, his eyes almost pleading while his fingers laid still in mine. "Did I hear that right?"

A puff of air left me with a small laugh. My eyes dropped to his mouth as I leaned down. He met me halfway. My stomach flip-flopped as he ran his hands through my hair, pulling me closer with his unhurt arm. A warmth spread out from my chest as he smiled against my lips. "As much as I enjoy kissing you, I'm really going to need to hear you say it. Just to confirm I wasn't hallucinating."

"I love you, Rhett Willulf." No matter who it had been for, it would have been true.

I curled up beside him as the others searched the city into the early morning light and the next day.

Eilith was nowhere to be found. Whatever they had used to make the Wailers, both from the city and those traveling to Renbrough, it hadn't been enough to hold. All it had taken was a large enough shift from the Sense Guard to bring them back. All, except for the ones that we had cut down. More innocent blood shed.

As Rhett slept his unhurt arm draped around me, I thought about everyone that I could still lose in this fight.

I needed it all to be over. I needed the world to make sense. I needed my family and friends to be safe. And I needed the chance to live, whatever that might look like.

A wave of determination flowed through me. This ended. No matter how. I would end all of it.

Rhett's hand was warm as he ran his fingers over my cheek. "You're awake."

"I don't think I could sleep if I tried."

A part of my heart soared as he slowly pulled me to him. A warm sensation pooled in my stomach as his lips brushed mine.

"Tomorrow we will fight again. Today, I need you to be here with me."

Even with him holding me, I couldn't shake the feeling that somewhere, out in the streets of Coranta, there was another heart, waiting to watch us burn.

A Message From The Author

Thank you for reading Dire Consequences, book 2 of
The Dire Series.

I'm constantly blown away by the love and support of
my family, friends, and readers.

The world of Coranta would not have been possible
without the compassion and wisdom of the many people
who helped me on my writing journey.

Everyone has a story in them and its never too late to
start writing it!

Keep an eye out for Sue James' other works in progress coming soon.

Dire Series Book 3

The final book tells the completed story of Siana, Rhett, and Henry. Projected release date is late 2024-early 2025.

Dead Listing

What happens when your dream home becomes the stuff of nightmares. After losing her husband in the house that they made, Paige struggles to cope with the difficulties of selling. It's hard to find a buyer when there are actual skeletons in the closet.

Projected release date is 2025.

These Dark Depths

"Death to the gods!" Probably not the best thing to say in a boat full of the superstitious believers. Tahlia realizes this a bit too late as she is plunged into the dark waters and face to face with the god of death.

Projected release date is 2025-2026.